TO SET THE RECORD STRAIGHT

"I wonder," the reporter said, "if I got my notebook could we sit out here and . . . talk?"

"You mean you want me to talk while you write, isn't that it?" Speaks asked.

"Well, that is why I came."

The reporter looked at Sam November.

"Don't look at me. I'll only say somethin' if I have to correct this old codger's faulty memory."

"I'll get my book," the young man said, and went back inside.

"What are you gonna tell 'im?" November asked.

"What do you think?"

"From the beginning?"

Speaks nodded.

"It's gonna hurt."

Speaks sighed and said, "The truth always does."

Legend

**ELMER KELTON
JUDY ALTER
LOREN D. ESTLEMAN
JAMES REASONER
JANE CANDIA COLEMAN
ED GORMAN
ROBERT J. RANDISI**

LEISURE BOOKS   NEW YORK CITY

A LEISURE BOOK®

March 1999

Published by

Dorchester Publishing Co., Inc.
276 Fifth Avenue
New York, NY 10001

ISBN 0-8439-4496-X

Legend

Introduction
by Robert J. Randisi

The concept of a collaborative novel is not new, but it has, in the past, yielded a product of dubious distinction. When I thought of the idea for *Legend* and invited authors to participate, I kept this in mind. Therefore, the six authors who have toiled on this project with me are total professionals as well as talented writers, and this comes out in the final product.

For the benefit of those readers who care about such things I will indicate who wrote what, although this is certainly, in every respect, a novel about the legend of one man. We all know that our lives are made up of incidents that shape our personalities, and this is what we have attempted to show about Lyle Speaks.

Elmer Kelton needs no introduction to anyone who has read westerns during the past forty years. His *The Good Old Boys* was made into a TNT movie starring Tommy Lee Jones, giving the viewing audience a chance to find out what his readers already know. No one writes about the West like Elmer Kelton. Elmer takes on the task of writing about young Lyle's quest to rescue his brother.

Judy Alter, author of several western novels depicting women's contribution to the West, writes about Lyle's first love. She is the author of *Mattie* and *A Ballad For Sallie*.

Loren D. Estleman is a multiple winner of the Western Writers of America Spur Award, for both short story and novel. He takes Lyle into the 1860s and acquaints him with buffalo hunting.

James Reasoner has only recently begun getting the recognition he deserves as a western writer. He depicts Lyle's brush with the Devereaux Gang in the 1870s section.

Jane Candia Coleman, author of the novel *Doc Holliday's Woman,* relates the story of how a woman finally captured the heart of Lyle Speaks.

Ed Gorman takes Lyle into the 1890s and brings him face-to-face with his darkest fears. He is the author of *Trouble Man* and *Ride Into Yesterday*.

Finally, all of the sections that are set in the 1900s were written by Robert J. Randisi. That means the opening, the bridges between sections, and the ending.

We feel we have succeeded in our task of pre-

senting an epic look at the life and times of Lyle
Speaks. We hope you, the reader, agree.

Robert J. Randisi,
St. Louis, Mo.
July 1998

Part One

Part One

Chapter One

Montana, 1901

Lyle Speaks was feeling suffocated by the onset of progress.

At seventy-four, Speaks was not ready to admit that the nineteenth century had come and gone, and with it everything he knew of life.

"That him?"

Speaks turned and watched as his wife of fifteen years, Clytie, came toward him carrying a tray with a pitcher of lemonade and two glasses on it. Clytie was fifty-four, twenty years his junior, and a handsome figure of a woman. She continued to wear her hair long, with a braid the size around of a man's wrist. Her yellow hair was streaked with gray now, but looked to him as soft and silky as ever.

"Must be," Speaks said. "What other damn fool would be makin' that walk?"

"I think it's mean of you to force him to do that, Lyle," Clytie said, setting the tray down next to her husband's chair.

"You know how I feel about those newfangled automobiles," Speaks said. "I don't want them on my land."

"You could have had a man with a horse waiting for him at the gate," she said. "This young fella has come all the way from New York to make you famous, and you treat him this way. Shame on you."

"Famous." Speaks spat the word out.

"That's what'll happen when he writes about you," Clytie said. " 'The Last of the Legends,' isn't that what he said he was going to call it?"

"I ain't no such thing," Speaks said. "If that's what he wants to do, why don't he go and find Wyatt Earp or Bat Masterson? They're still alive and kickin'."

"They're not as famous as you are."

Now Speaks laughed, and it came out as almost a cackle.

"That's a wife talkin', right there," he said. "Ain't no O.K. Corrals in my past, that's for damn sure."

"What about the Devereaux gang?"

"That story's exaggerated."

"And isn't that why you agreed to talk to him, after all?"

"You got that right," Speaks said. "Too much damned exaggeratin' goin' on about things. We're gonna set 'em straight, once and for all.

If there are gonna be stories writ about me, they're gonna be accurate!"

"Don't you go drinkin' all this lemonade before that fella gets here," Clytie scolded her husband. "He's going to need it a damn site more than you are."

"Don't curse, woman," Speaks said.

She laughed and said, "We're allowed to do that now, you old coot. It's the twentieth century."

"Don't go remindin' me about that!" he said as she went back into the house.

He poured himself a glass of lemonade as soon as she was gone, took a look around at his surroundings, taking stock as he always did when he sat here. He remembered when this was just a run-down shack with no glass windows, and a doorway that was missing a door. He and Clytie had built it up to what it was today, a two-story, nine-room house that had been their home, in one form or another, for fifteen years now. Of course, they could never have done it without the help of Sam November. Sam and he had started out as partners, but folks had taken to calling Sam a "sidekick" when they wrote about them. Didn't seem to bother Sam much, so Speaks didn't know why it should bother him. But that was something else he was going to straighten out when this writer fellow finally finished his trek from the gate to the house.

Which he was doing right at that moment.

Speaks watched the man put one foot on the

bottom step, set down a leather satchel, and then stop to take a deep breath.

"Mr. Speaks?" he said.

"That's right."

He started to say something else but had to stop to take another breath.

"That's . . . quite a walk," he finally said.

"State your name," Speaks said peevishly. He wasn't about to waste Clytie's lemonade on this fellow if he wasn't who he was supposed to be.

"Aubrey P. Fellows, sir, of the New York publishing firm of—"

"Don't care about your firm's name, son, just yours. Step up here and have a seat and I'll let you have some lemonade."

"Thank you, sir," Fellows said. "I can certainly use it."

He picked up his bag, climbed the remaining three steps to the porch, and made his way to the empty chair on the other side of the lemonade tray.

"Help yourself."

While the writer poured himself a drink, Speaks inspected him. Couldn't have been more than thirty, didn't look like he had to shave more than twice a week. He appeared intelligent, though, Speaks had to admit that. Looked like a writer. Pale, soft hands, just a bit on the pudgy side.

"Ah," Fellows said after he downed half a glass of the cold drink, "that's wonderful."

"My wife's recipe," Speaks said. "You'll be meetin' her a little later on. How was your trip?"

"Fine, fine," Fellows said, "right up until I got

to the front gate of your ranch, here, and then for some reason I was told I had to walk."

"I don't allow automobiles on my property."

"Why is that, sir?"

"Don't like 'em," he said. "They scare the horses."

"They're going to replace the horse very soon, sir," Fellows said.

"Don't like that idea, either," Speaks said. "That may be true back where you come from, but around here there are still plenty of places you can only get to on horseback. What's in the bag? Stuff to write with?"

"That, sir, and my clothing. I came right here from the train station. Ah, we did agree that I'd be staying here while I interviewed you, did we not?"

"We did," Speaks said, nodding. "Got a guest room fixed up for you. You probably want to rest up some, maybe change into some clothes that ain't so dusty?"

"I would indeed, sir," Fellows said. "Is there someone who can show me to my room?"

"If you mean a servant," Speaks said, "I don't hold with servants. My wife does all the cookin' and cleanin', so you'll have to carry your own bag up to your room."

"Ah, yes, sir, of course. If you'll direct me—" Fellows said, starting to rise.

"Sit back down, young feller," Speaks said. "Finish your lemonade. Clytie'll be out directly and then she'll show you to your room."

Fellows sat back in his chair and said, "Oh, uh, very well."

Speaks finished his lemonade and hurriedly poured himself a second glass before Clytie could catch him.

"Sir, I have to tell you how excited I am at the prospect of writing your story—I mean, the *real* story of Lyle Speaks, the legend—"

"Now, hold it right there," Speaks said.

"Sir?"

"That legend stuff," the older man said. "I don't want to hear that. Looked that word up once, do you know what it said?"

"No, sir, I don't."

"You're a writer," Speaks said. "You should know."

"Well, sir, I know what it means, but—"

"Tell me."

"Well . . . it has several meanings. First, it means a story or stories handed down for generations and generally believed to have a basis in fact."

"You sandbagged me, sonny," Speaks said. "You do know it."

Fellows smiled, taking this as praise, and went on.

"Secondly, it's used to describe the person . . . let me see . . . I have it, a 'notable' person about whom these exploits are told."

"Do you know what the word 'legend' means to me, young fella?"

"No, sir, I don't."

"A pack of lies!" Speaks said. "What I agreed to talk to you about is the truth."

"Well, sir, some legends are made up of the

18

truth, you know. We *would* like to use the word—"

"I tell you what," Speaks said, cutting the young man off again. "If you write down exactly what I tell you, in a truthful and honest fashion, telling people it's the truth, you can use that word."

"Legend?"

Speaks waved his hand and said, "That one, yeah."

"Well, sir, I think I can promise that."

"Then we're agreed."

"Yes, sir."

"Good."

At that moment Clytie came walking onto the porch. Aubrey P. Fellows bounded to his feet and removed his bowler hat.

"Aubrey P. Fellows, ma'am," he introduced himself. "I believe we exchanged telegrams?"

It was, indeed, Clytie who had gone to Brandenburg to send out the telegrams to publishers all over the country, offering the story of Lyle Speaks—the true story.

"How nice to meet you, Mr. Fellows. Has my husband given you some lemonade, or did he drink it all himself, again?"

"First glass," Speaks lied, holding his glass up and giving Fellows a look that said the young man had better back him up.

Rather than lie, Fellows said, "Yes, ma'am, he was kind enough to offer me some, and it was delicious. A special recipe, he tells me?"

"Special," Clytie said, "and secret, so you won't be writing about that."

Legend

Fellows laughed and said, "No, ma'am."

"Clytie," Speaks said, "would you show Mr. Fellows here to his room and let him get freshened up?"

"Of course." Clytie looked at Fellows. "We're very happy to have you staying with us. Have you eaten lunch?"

"Yes, ma'am, I had something in town."

"Well, I'll be serving dinner in a few hours, if you can wait that long?"

"That's fine, ma'am."

"Then I'll show you to your room."

Fellows picked up his bag, started to follow Clytie into the house, then turned back and asked Speaks, "Will Mr. November be joining us for dinner?"

"Always does," Speaks said.

"Excellent," the writer said, and hurried to catch up to Clytie Speaks.

Speaks settled back in his chair and looked out over his land—as much of it as he could see. The barn, the corral, several hands working the horses. He, Clytie, and Sam worked the place alone for a few years before they were able to hire a hand or two. Now he had nearly forty men working for him, and when it was roundup time that swelled to double the amount.

He watched as one of his men climbed aboard an unbroke colt while two others held its head. Once they let it loose the animal went crazy, trying to throw the man off its back. Speaks remembered the first time he tried to break a horse. He could still feel the shock in his tailbone when he hit the ground. Couldn't do that now, though. Hitting the ground like that would bust him up, or so Clytie kept telling him. All she wanted him to do now was paperwork, and sit on the porch drinking lemonade and dozing. Problem was when he dozed he dreamed, and when he dreamed it was always about the past. He didn't like the dreams, because he didn't always like the man he was back then—the man he was before he met Clytie. That's how he got the idea of telling his story, having it written down so maybe he'd stop dreaming about it.

He let his head drift back, canted a little to one side, thinking about the first story he'd tell the writer, going back to when it all started, before he was "Lyle Speaks," when he was just plain Lyle . . .

Chapter Two

The Brazos River, Texas, 1845

Lyle Speaks had taken on the twice-daily milking chore at age twelve, and at eighteen he was still stuck with it. On this cool May morning the foaming bucket was three-quarters full when he called it quits and arose from the three-legged stool. Two ragged-looking barn cats, whose job it was to help keep mice out of the feed, cried piteously for a taste of the steaming milk. Lyle poured a bit into a broken-edged saucer just inside the corner of the rough shed.

"Come and get it," he said, "before the mice do."

A three-hundred-pound bull calf, confined to a pen built of peeling logs, bawled for its turn at what milk remained. Lyle had left one teat for it. When the calf grew large enough, and before it lost its milk-fat bloom, the family would butcher it and share the beef with neighbors to the east. The neighbors would do likewise when they had a calf ready. But for much of the time the Speaks family and their friends had to rely on venison or on pork from the smokehouse, for no one had slaughtered lately. Beef was said to be plentiful down along the Mexican borderlands, but it remained something of a luxury for most Texans along the Brazos.

Lyle slid back two log bars to let the calf join its mother, which smelled it to be sure it was her own and not some orphaned dogie being foisted off on her. The calf eagerly tested the four teats and found the one Lyle had left. A rim of milk foam quickly formed around its mouth as it punched at the udder. The brindle cow was a picture of patience and contentment, chewing on bundle feed remaining from last year's crop. She had withheld milk for her offspring and was letting it down now. She probably thought she was fooling Lyle, but maternal instinct made most milk cows do the same thing.

Lyle saw Pa at the log barn, feeding two plow horses and his favorite mule, which he had ridden back to Georgia from Texas during the revolution against Mexico after the battle at San Jacinto nine years before. Not everybody could say that his father fought in the war against Mexico. True, Pa had taken a bullet in his leg, but his many exciting experiences had given him stirring stories to tell, whether or not they were gospel truth in every detail.

Lyle had no such stories to relate, no adventures to look back upon. Except for limited time spent in the settlement's school and a few visits as far downriver as San Felipe de Austin to get acquainted with kinfolk, he had not been away from this farm since the family had settled on it some seven years earlier.

If what folks were saying was true, he might soon have a chance to fight in his own war. There was a lot of talk about Texas joining the union, and speculation that Mexico would declare war against the United States if that happened. Lyle sort of looked forward to it, for he had not even been in an Indian fight.

Though an occasional Indian scare arose even yet, Lyle had never seen an Indian, unless he counted the occasional peaceful Tonkawas who came to trade or to beg. Pa had fought alongside them in a battle at Plum Creek five years before. He said they could be merciless against their Comanche enemies, but to Lyle they had always looked harmless, even pitiable in their poverty.

He wished he could see a few real Indians, like the fierce Comanches. That would be something worth talking about. Folks claimed their stronghold was far to the west, in rugged limestone hills beyond San Antonio and on open buffalo prairies beyond the hills. Badly bloodied at Plum Creek after a huge raid all the way down to the Gulf, they rarely penetrated this far into the settled lands anymore. However, farmers still made it a point to pen up their horses and mules each night in the fall of the year when the Comanche moon shone full and bright. The Indian horses would be at their peak of strength and endurance then after a summer of good grazing. The Comanches used to come looking for fresh ones to add to their caballadas and fresh scalps to tie to their lances.

This was only May, when spring rains had just recently turned the grass green. Horses had not had time to recover fully from the weight loss and general debilitation that came from a long winter.

It was generally agreed that the Comanches had not turned peaceable, but now that settlements had pushed farther west they did not have to come this far to do their raiding.

Lyle waited until the calf had gotten all the milk the udder would yield, then penned it again and turned the cow out to graze. Pa limped over to meet him so they could walk together back to the double log cabin that was home to the Speaks family. Sometimes Pa's leg wound bothered him and sometimes it didn't. When it did, he took it as a sign of imminent rain or, in wintertime, a cold norther.

The pain in Pa's face told Lyle it was hurting him now. Lyle said, "You better let me handle the plow today, Pa. Looks like your leg is due a rest."

The corn was up but in need of work, and the ground was warm enough for planting cotton. It seemed in springtime that a farmer never could catch up on anything, especially sleep.

Pa said, "I'm a long ways from crippled. Your mother was tellin' me we're about out of meat.

She'll be needin' you to take your rifle and go scare us up some venison."

That responsibility had gradually shifted to Lyle, for Pa's sight had begun weakening, a result of a Mexican rifle butt striking him just above his right eye at San Jacinto. Pa proudly claimed that Lyle was the best shot in the Speaks family since Grandpa Ethan back in Georgia, but Lyle remembered that Pa in his prime could take out a squirrel's eye at a hundred yards. Marksmanship ran in the family like the tall frame, the strong hands, and the stern blue eyes that marked all the Speaks men. Even sister Beth could handle a rifle. He had seen her knock off a prowling coyote long before it could reach the chicken pen. Lyle's two younger brothers were learning, though Jeffrey at five could hardly hold the rifle barrel steady without propping it on something solid.

Rex, the old red dog, came out to meet Lyle and Pa, wagging its tail vigorously. Lyle paused to scratch the floppy ears.

The cabin was of the traditional Texas frontier variety, two separate log sections under a single roof with an open dog run in the center to let the air circulate. Pa and Mama slept in one side, Beth in the kitchen side, Lyle and the boys in a loft over the dog run. A couple of hundred yards past the cabin, on a small oak-shaded knoll, was a modest rock-fenced family cemetery where Lyle's parents had buried some of their hopes.

Lyle glanced up at a meat hook secured to a rafter in the dog run. Little but bone was left to show for the last yearling doe he had brought home.

Mama bent toward the fireplace, where meat fried in a long-handled skillet. Like her menfolk, she was tall and skinny, for a pioneer woman's never-ending work left little opportunity for putting on weight. She glanced back as Pa and Lyle walked through the open door. Brushing away a lock of brown hair streaked with gray, she said, "I'm fryin' up the last of the venison."

Lyle nodded. "I saw."

"I wish you'd go out after breakfast and see about fetchin' us some fresh meat. The smokehouse ham has got to stretch 'til hog-killin' time."

"I will, but the deer ain't none too fat right now."

Mama smiled. "Neither are we."

Sister Beth, a red ribbon in her hair, used an iron hook to lift the lid from a Dutch oven sitting atop glowing coals on the hearth. The pleasing aroma of hot, fresh corn bread brought a grin to Lyle's face.

"That look good enough for you?" she asked.

"A king couldn't have no better."

Beth's smile mirrored Mama's. Beth was seventeen and had the attention of every unattached man and boy over the age of sixteen for miles around. Pa said she was ripe like a peach, ready for the right man to do the picking. But he kept close watch on them. Not just anybody would do for his daughter.

The two younger boys, Caleb and Jeffrey,

came in from the dog run, where they had splashed their hands and faces with water from a washpan Mama insisted they visit before every meal. They quarreled over which should fetch wood for the fireplace this morning. Mama squelched the argument by decreeing that Caleb should do the chopping and Jeffrey should bring in the wood. Because Lyle had taken on the milking chore, among others, he had been exempted from cutting firewood when Caleb had been judged old enough to handle an ax without slicing off his toes.

As soon as they learned that Lyle was going hunting, the two boys clamored to go with him. Pa said, "Now, Lyle wouldn't slip up on a blind ox if he had two loud and clumsy boys trailin' after him. You young'uns help your mother hoe the garden today. The weeds are threatenin' to take over after them last rains."

The boys groaned.

Pa said, "It's a choice between weeds and vittles. If you think you'd like to eat weeds . . ."

The boys reluctantly accepted the verdict, for Pa and Mama were law, judge, and jury. There was no appeal.

Had it not been for the fact that meat was so badly needed, Lyle would have been pleased to have the boys tag along. They might have scared off all the game within five miles, but they were eager learners, and Lyle enjoyed doing the teaching. He said, "This evenin' before dark we'll take Old Rex and see if we can scare us up some rabbits."

That pacified the two, and they lit into the

venison and brown gravy as if they had not eaten in a week. Beth broke off a piece of corn bread of her own making and smiled with pride in the flavor of it. A look of satisfaction passed between Pa and Mama. Lyle rarely saw them kiss each other, but they showed their affection with their eyes and with hands that often reached to touch, then fell away.

If Lyle Speaks could have had his family made to his own order, it would have looked just like this one. He knew that one day he would have to strike out and find his own way, but he was in no hurry to leave this happy place.

Carrying the rifle, he struck off toward the tree-lined river. Rex followed, and Lyle had to speak sharply. The dog tucked his tail and turned back disappointed, even a little hurt. Despite good intentions, Rex would probably succeed only in running off any game before Lyle could get a good shot. And deer were getting to be none too plentiful, because so much land was being settled up and so many families were looking for venison to augment their beef and pork. More and more they were having to settle for squirrel.

Two puddin'-footed plow horses looked up from their grazing. The mule had strayed off to himself a hundred yards away. Given time to ponder such matters, Lyle had sometimes wondered if the mule was too proud to associate with the horses or if it was the other way around.

Lyle knew this land . . . the forest, the open country. He had walked every foot of it many times. The republic of Texas had deeded Pa this parcel for his service in Sam Houston's army. Texas often paid its debts in scrip or in real estate. It had precious little cash money but lots of land, even though much remained firmly in the hands of Indians who recognized no courthouse deed.

The day warmed quickly, as it was prone to do in May, so he knew the hunting would not be easy. Deer would be taking their rest in the deep shade instead of moving about, browsing. But meat had to be hunted when it was needed and not just when it came handy. Lyle had ventured at least two miles from the cabin without seeing any sign of deer. He sensed that even starting back now he would be hard-pressed to make it home by noon. That was a minor inconvenience; he had missed many a meal in the quest for meat. But he wished he had brought along a piece of Beth's corn bread to stave off the hunger pangs.

He had spotted a couple of squirrels along the way and hoped he might find them again if he did not happen upon a deer. They would at least make stew for supper, and he could try hunting again tomorrow. Maybe he would have better luck starting before breakfast, in the cool of early daylight when the deer were up and filling their bellies.

He heard a couple of distant shots. He could not tell with certainty where they came from, for the heavy timber along the river muffled and distorted sound. Well, maybe somebody would have venison tonight, even if the Speaks family didn't. He started back on a different track than the way he had come, disappointed but still hopeful that a deer might yet jump up and make itself a target.

He was near the edge of the timber when birds flushed from the treetops ahead of him, their wings beating a staccato rhythm that startled him. He heard horses, their legs threshing through the tall grass, hooves treading softly in the sandy soil. The sound told him it was a sizable bunch, possibly headed for San Antonio.

They would play hell with his chances of finding a deer now. Their passage would send all the game into full flight.

He started toward the edge of the timber, thinking there was an off chance he might know some of the travelers and find out what was new in the settlements downriver.

Something stopped him just short of the timber's edge, a premonition, a vague sense that something was not right. He ducked behind a patch of undergrowth. Thirty or forty horses and mules passed in a stiff trot a hundred yards out in the open. A quick glimpse of the nearest rider told him the horsemen were Indians. He flattened himself on the ground, not even trying to look at the others or to count them. He feared that if he watched them they might spot him. He held his breath until his lungs burned. He did not even look up.

These were no Tonkawa beggars. One glance had told him these were the kind who would slit your throat and lift your scalp and dance around you while you died. Comanches, he felt with a cold certainty. The word *Comanche* could make even the bravest man reexamine his courage. A chill traveled up Lyle's back and down again.

Though he had looked for only a moment, that had been long enough to recognize Pa's two workhorses and the mule. He thought he knew now the reason for the shots he had heard. Pa, scrapper that he was, would not have let the Indians come close to the cabin, but he could not have prevented them from taking the stock.

Pa would be almighty put out about losing the animals. Lyle could picture him stomping the floor and raring to go in pursuit, on foot if need be. But Lyle had heard enough stories to know that a man afoot was no man at all when it came to trailing after horseback Indians.

He gave up all thought about deer or squirrels. To fire his rifle now might draw those horse-stealing rascals back. If any hair cutting was to be done, he preferred to let Mama do it for him, and not some Comanche. She always trimmed it when it got halfway down the back of his neck. She was particular about how her family looked. They might not have any money, but she was not going to let them go around looking like poor white trash. She had too much old-time Georgia pride for that.

Trudging in the direction of the cabin, he felt more and more depressed, mourning over the loss of the horses and the mule. He did not know how Pa would raise money enough to buy replacements to pull the plow and the wagon. Maybe he could borrow from somebody to get by for a spell. Most neighbors were glad to help one another, though the size of the horse and mule herd told Lyle that others had lost their stock too. It was going to be a tough year for some folks on the Brazos.

He saw smoke as he stepped out of the timber and into the open meadow beside the rustling green stalks of growing corn. He stopped abruptly, letting the stock of the long rifle strike the ground. He took a sharp breath and felt his pulse begin to race.

The cabin was burning.

Chapter Three

He saw no one fighting the fire. Hair bristled on the back of his neck.

"Mama! Pa!"

He set off running hard, stumbling, falling to his knees, pushing to his feet and running again, heeding not that he had let the butt of the rifle drag in the sand. Carelessness like that was a sin in Pa's eyes.

He shouted until his throat went raw. His voice fell to barely more than a whisper. No one stirred.

He came first to the dog. An arrow had been driven into Rex's side, blood just beginning to congeal. Rex had probably rushed out to challenge the horse thieves and had died for his brashness.

Lyle heard a crashing sound and turned to see

the blazing roof collapse on the bedroom side of the double cabin, pulling part of the burning wall down with it. The kitchen side was a roaring mass of flame. Shortly it fell too.

Briefly he sustained a hope that the family had escaped down to the river and had taken shelter in the timber. But as he moved closer to the fire, holding his arm in front of his face to shield his eyes from the blistering heat, hope collapsed like the cabin walls. He saw three forms lying on the ground . . . Pa, Mama, and Caleb.

Mama lay closest to the cabin. The heat had set her skirt to smoking. Lyle laid down the rifle, grabbed her thin arms, and dragged her farther away, hoping she might still cling to a shred of life. But she was limp. Life was gone.

He went next to Pa, then to Caleb, hoping, despairing. He found not a flicker of a heartbeat. Even had it been there, it could not have sustained itself long. Mama had two arrows in her body, Pa three, Caleb one. The scalps had been slashed away.

Lyle fell to his knees, grasping for breath. When he managed to push the grief aside long enough to think, he reasoned that the family had taken refuge in the cabin. The Indians had set it afire, then killed them as they rushed out to escape the flames.

He realized he had not accounted for Beth and Jeffrey. He trotted around the ruins of the cabin, calling his sister's name. All he heard was the crackle of burning wood and crunching sounds as pieces of the wall tumbled into the blazing coals. He made another circle, wider this time, but still he saw nothing of her except a strand of red ribbon tangled in the top of a tall weed crushed by horses in their passing. Lyle pulled it free and held it in his hands, then looked up in the direction the raiders had taken.

There could be no doubt. They had carried off Beth and Jeffrey. Lyle tried to call her name again, but his voice broke. He knew he had to follow after them. He had to rescue them somehow and bring them home. He stuck the ribbon in his pocket and returned to pick up the rifle. The steel burned his hand. He had left it lying too near the fire, but at least the powder had not exploded.

He set off in a trot in the northwesterly direction the Indians had taken, upriver. Weariness and grief rapidly overtook him. His legs became heavy. Soon he could hardly drag one foot after the other. He stopped, despairing. Afoot, he would never catch up to the kidnappers. They were moving much too rapidly.

"Beth! Jeffrey!" he cried. "What can I do?"

He swayed, tears burning his eyes, tickling his cheeks as they coursed down. His mind was in turmoil. It was unthinkable to give up and leave his sister and brother to whatever fate the kidnappers willed for them. Yet anything he tried to do would be futile unless he could get a horse.

The crossroads settlement would be the place. It was five miles down the river, but surely somebody there would lend him a mount. They might even ride along with him.

Every mile he walked or trotted downriver was a mile farther away from the Indians, from Beth and Jeffrey, compounded by the fact that they were moving at a strong clip in the opposite direction. But he saw no choice. He dragged a sleeve across his face to wipe the tears, and he struck a trot. He tried not to look as he passed the smoldering remains of the cabin, but he could not help himself. His gaze was drawn to Mama and Pa and Caleb, and he wiped his eyes without stopping.

Slowly the grief began giving way to a growing anger that in turn gave way to a burning rage. There had been no reason for the killings. The raiders could have taken the stock and gone on. Somehow Pa could have gotten more; the family would have survived. But no, they had done murder, most brutal murder, probably with no more compunction than Lyle would have felt about shooting a doe, had he found one. But at least when he killed it was for a purpose, not for pleasure.

He gave in to a fantasy of the darkest hue. He pictured himself catching up to the raiders and slitting their throats one at a time. He fancied that they would flop around in their death throes like a chicken when he wrung its neck, and he would glory in their dying. He recognized that the circuit-riding preacher who conducted services at the settlement would not approve, but the minister had not found his family slaughtered and mutilated. Anyway, the fantasy had its uses. It gave Lyle heart and put strength in his legs to keep him moving.

Legend

Halfway to the settlement he saw horsemen pushing hard toward him. His first thought was that they were more Indians, following the first bunch and looking for further mischief. Rage overwhelmed his sense of fear. He brought the rifle up and checked to be certain he had not lost the powder from the pan. He might get only one shot, and then they would swarm over him, but he would take one with him.

He lowered the rifle as the dozen or so horsemen approached. Their hats and caps, the first details he could make out, told him they were white men. He was almost disappointed; the prospect of vengeance had been sweet. He had not allowed himself to dwell upon the price.

He wanted to blurt out his troubles, but he choked, his throat so tight he could not speak at first. He judged by the rifles and shotguns that these men were in pursuit of the Indians. A blocky man of middle age rode half a length ahead of the rest, his black, piercing eyes a match for his fierce black beard speckled with gray. He had a booming voice. Authority clung to him like a tightly fitting cloak.

"Son, you're in danger out here afoot and by yourself. There are Indians about."

Lyle recognized him as a big landowner named Benson, from east of the settlement. Pa looked up to him as a community leader. Lyle struggled for words.

"They killed my folks."

An angry murmur arose among the men. The bearded one said, "You're the Speaks boy, ain't you? Name of Lyle?"

38

"Yes, sir." Lyle felt his eyes burning anew. "They've killed my pa and ma and one of the boys. They've carried off my sister and little brother Jeffrey."

"And how come they didn't get you?"

"I was up the river, huntin' for meat. Else I'd've been there. I could've helped Pa fight them off."

Benson's face pinched with the gravity of the message.

"Or, more likely, got yourself killed with the rest."

"I'd've given them a fight first." Lyle was surprised at the sudden angry strength in his voice.

A youth roughly Lyle's age rode forward, his eyes full of concern. "You say they carried Beth away?"

Lyle recognized him as Sam November, one of Beth's many suitors. Sam's folks had a farm much like that of the Speaks family, granted by the republic for his father's service. Of them all, Lyle had regarded Sam as being most likely to win Beth's favor when she was ready to bestow it. Pa's too. Sam had a reputation for being levelheaded and sober.

"I'm afraid it's so."

Sam's lightly stubbled face seemed drained of blood. He turned away for a moment so no one could see his eyes, then removed his left foot from the stirrup and leaned down, extending his arm. Painfully he said, "Swing up behind me. We'll take you home."

Lyle had no home to go back to, but he complied, careful not to strike man or horse with the long rifle barrel. He seated himself behind the cantle. Having no spurs, Sam thumped his black boots against his brown horse's ribs and put the animal into a long, jarring trot as the black-bearded Benson led out.

Sam asked, "You real sure they carried her off?"

"I looked all round. She wasn't there, or Jeffrey either." Lyle took the red ribbon from his pocket. "I found this a little ways past the cabin. It's hers." He swallowed hard. "What do you reckon they'll do to her?"

Saw was a long time in answering, and his voice was harsh. "You'd best not even think about it. If God has any mercy, she's already dead."

Lyle felt a cold, heavy lump like lead in his stomach. "I wish I'd been there and they'd killed me too."

A man on a bay horse rode up beside Lyle and Sam. Lyle recognized him as the circuit-riding minister, a lanky man who coughed a lot and looked older than his years. Folks whispered that he had contracted lung fever in the swamps of Louisiana. Texas had not been able to cure him.

"Never let the Lord hear you speak such words, my boy. It's for Him to call us when it's our time, and not before."

Lyle clenched his teeth.

"What did he call my folks for? They never done nobody any wrong."

"There are things past our knowin'."

Looking at the other riders, Lyle recognized

several of the determined faces. The men were acquaintances of Pa's, farmers mostly, and a storekeeper. They seemed out of their element here, all bunched up on horseback and armed as if for war.

Lyle said, "Looks like you-all figure on catchin' them Indians."

The minister coughed. "We'd like to. They've made a sweep downriver, gatherin' up horses and mules. They caught Old Man Arthur and his darky in the field. Killed the old man and wounded the darky most grievously. If he lives, it will be only through God's mercy."

Lyle gave in to bitterness.

"If God's so merciful, how come He lets such a thing happen? Why don't He strike them heathens down with a thunderbolt?"

"It is not given to us to know His reasons. He tests the strength of our faith."

"Mine don't amount to much right now. I don't think He's even lookin' in our direction."

"This is no time to give in to blasphemy."

Lyle's voice was heavy with irony. "You think He's fixin' to hit me with a thunderbolt?"

"I fear the Lord more than I fear the Indians." The minister gave in to a fit of coughing.

Holding on to Sam, Lyle sensed that the young man was sobbing quietly. He knew nothing to say to ease the grief, for he was having trouble enough containing his own.

Light smoke still rose from the ruins of the cabin, though little remained but gray ashes and smoldering logs lying in a heap like blackened bones, spots glowing red where fire still bore stubbornly into the heart of the wood. Lyle was gratified that scavengers had not yet found and molested the bodies. One rider fired at a buzzard circling overhead. The bird seemed not disturbed, but several horses danced in fright at the noise.

The black-bearded Benson dismounted and stared grimly down at a still figure. Lyle slid to the ground, tears starting afresh. Anger had dried them awhile.

The minister said, "Your father was a good and brave man. I am sure that to his last breath he fought to save his family."

Benson nodded agreement. "He killed his share of the enemy in the war. We'll not likely ever know how many redskins he took with him. They carry away their dead."

Lyle could not find his voice, but he hoped they were right. He wished Pa could have killed them all.

But since Pa couldn't, he would, given the chance. If Indians had a happy hunting ground, they might also have an unhappy one. That was where he would send them, and glory in the sweetness of revenge.

Benson said, "These folks need to be got underground before the wolves find them. Reverend, I wish you and Sam'd stay and help the boy bury his family. The rest of us will ride on."

Sam said grittily, "I'm goin'. I got to find Beth."

Lyle said, "I want to go with you-all."

Benson was firm. "You're too wrought up. No tellin' what kind of reckless sashay you'd be liable to pull if we catch up to them. Anyway, you're afoot. You've got a job to do right here."

He waved his arm, and the rest of the horsemen moved out with him. Lyle slid down over the horse's rump and landed on his feet. Sam November looked back at him, his face incredibly sad.

The minister said, "He's right, my boy. We owe your folks a decent buryin' and a bit of the Word." He leaned over Pa's body, and a tear rolled down his cheek, unwiped and unashamed. "Your Pa and me, we rode into more than one battle together. Rough-spoken he was at times, but he knew the Lord."

He looked toward the small log shed which for some reason the Indians had not chosen to burn. It had probably seemed too piddling a thing to bother with.

"Do you suppose you'd find a shovel in there?"

Lyle went to the shed, which faced out into a crude corral where the family had occasionally gathered their few cattle. He found the milk cow's calf dead, an arrow between its ribs. Its hind quarters and a strip along the back had been cut away. If the Indians had come across the cow, they had probably killed her too.

Several headless chickens lay scattered about. He could visualize the Indians chasing them, laughing as they wrung their necks.

Damn them, he thought, *they kill everything that breathes*.

He carried the pick and shovel out to the small prominence where Pa and Mama had buried two babies. A modest grove of trees shaded the graves much of the day.

Lyle did most of the digging, for the minister's health was frail. There was no wood from which to construct coffins, or even blankets in which to wrap the dead. Everything had gone up in smoke with the cabin. The minister spoke glowing words about Pa and Mama and Caleb and said a long prayer. When he was done he picked up the shovel.

"If you'd like to go back down the hill, I can take care of the rest."

Lyle said, "What I'd really like is the borry of that bay horse." He glanced in the direction the Indians and the volunteers had gone.

"They're hours ahead of you."

"They'll stop for the night. I won't. The trail they left, I can follow in the moonlight."

"The Lord may never forgive me for lettin' a lad so young ride into the unknown by himself. But if you're determined, take my horse and my blessings." He unstrapped a gun belt and holster. "Take my pistol too. You may have need of it."

Lyle saw nothing incongruous about a preacher packing firearms. Sometimes the word of God had to be backed up by fear of the devil. "I hate for you to have to walk all the way back to the settlement."

"I walked halfway across Texas. I can handle this." He coughed, then extended a rough hand. "The Lord ride with you."

Lyle swallowed hard, unable to express his gratitude as strongly as he felt it.

Chapter Four

As he had said, he was able to follow the trail in the moonlight, the grass beaten down by the horses and mules the Indians had taken and those of the men who pursued them. The last of his tears had dried. He nursed his grief in silence.

The minister was right, Lyle was young to be alone. But Pa had been no older when he had set out on his own back in Georgia. Lyle felt he was old enough and big enough to do whatever was necessary to survive. He wouldn't need somebody telling him what to do. Pa's and Mama's mature guidance had been burned into his soul as with a branding iron. He would never forget the many lessons they had taught him.

Fear fought to take over, but he forcibly put

it down, at least to a level he could control. Determination was stronger.

Night came, the moon still full. The trail remained visible, though Lyle had to slow to a walk and watch the ground carefully. The horse needed a rest, and so did he, but there would be time enough for rest when he found Beth and Jeffrey.

He had traveled far into the night before he saw the distant glow of a fire. That had to be the pursuers, halted for the night, he thought. He wondered at first at the foolishness of lighting a fire the Indians could see, then decided the raiders were still so far ahead that it was unlikely the light was visible to them.

He did not want someone to mistake him for a Comanche and shoot him. He shouted, "Hello the camp!"

A voice answered, "Who's out yonder?"

"It's me, Lyle Speaks."

The voice bade him to come on in. Lyle saw the broad-shouldered Benson standing beside the glowing remnant of campfire. Sam November came out to meet Lyle. Solemnly he shook Lyle's hand, but he did not speak. Probably he could not.

Lyle was hungry and thirsty. "I don't reckon you'd have any coffee?"

Benson said, "Sorry, but this is a hungry camp. We didn't have time to gather provisions. Oscar Petrie had the foresight to bring a bottle of whiskey, if you don't think you're too young for such."

"I could sure use a sip of it."

Men lay about on saddle blankets, their horses staked within quick reach in case the Indians doubled back to hit anyone who had the temerity to trail after them.

Lyle said, "You can still see the trail in the moonlight. How come you've stopped?"

"The Indians crossed the river here and went on. They've gained so much ground we can't hope to catch up. Men and horses are given out. I'm sorry, son, but come daylight we're startin' back."

Lyle flared. "I ain't! I'm goin' on after Beth and my little brother."

"It's useless. If the Comanches have not killed them already, they will."

"You ain't found them anywhere along the trail, have you?"

"No."

"Then they're alive. As long as they are, I'm goin' on." He tapped his heels against the horse's ribs.

Benson caught the reins to stop him. "You'll only forfeit your own life. You'll not save theirs."

Lyle slapped his hat against the horse's rump, and the animal broke free of the man's hold. "Boy," Benson shouted, "you come back here."

Sam November hollered, "Wait, Lyle."

The horse hesitated at the riverbank, and Lyle had to kick him smartly to force him into the water. On the other side he heard a horse swimming to catch up with him. He turned in the saddle and recognized Sam.

"You ain't stoppin' me."

"I'll not try. But I'll not see you go by yourself. I'm as anxious about Beth as you are."

Lyle watched for sign that anyone else was coming, but the others remained beyond the river.

He began watching clouds build and worried that they would curtain the moon. They did, in time, to a point that he could no longer see the trail. He held out until he lost the tracks. He doubled back, looking for them.

Sam rode out to the side, trying to help him.

"I'm afraid we've done all we can 'til daylight."

Heart sinking, Lyle held to hope as long as he could, but at last he had to concede.

"I reckon we have."

"The animals need rest, or we'll soon be afoot."

Lyle slept but little, for the images of Mama and Pa, Beth and his brothers were flashing in his mind. The nightmare kept coming back, whether he was asleep or awake. At the first faint light of dawn he was up. Sleeplessness and grief and desperation had his stomach agitated like milk in a churn. He checked on the two horses to be certain they had remained staked. He saddled the preacher's mount and began moving in a broad circle, looking for the tracks he had lost in the night. With the first bright peep of sunshine over the eastern horizon, he found them.

Sam was saddling his own horse when Lyle returned.

"I take it by the look on your face that you found the trail."

"I did." Lyle pointed. "They veered off yon-derway."

He leaned down to look at the tracks and some horse droppings. "Reckon how far ahead of us they are?"

"I'm no tracker, but I'd guess the sign to be several hours old. Probably from early last night."

Lyle choked down a momentary feeling of hopelessness that came over him unbidden.

"What chance you think we've got of catchin' them?"

"Not much. And if we did, what would we do, just the two of us?"

"You should've considered that before you came with me."

"I considered it. But I know I've got to find Beth, whatever it takes."

Lyle had been considering too. He had trusted from the first that he would somehow find a way when the time came, though he could not see ahead to a plan that held much hope for success.

"We could ride in on them and grab Beth and Jeffrey and light out before the Indians know what happened."

"They've got good horses. Chances are they'd run us down."

"Can you come up with a better idea?"

"I've been tryin'. I ain't thought of a thing."

They rode on through the morning. Lyle was keenly aware that he had eaten nothing since breakfast yesterday, and it was near noon. The breeze, out of the northwest, brought him a faint smell of woodsmoke. He sniffed, not sure he was right. He saw that Sam was aware of it, too.

Sam said, "They must finally have stopped to camp last night."

Lyle swallowed against a rising apprehension. "You think they might still be there?"

"Not likely, but we'd best proceed like they are. The most important thing to know about Indians is that we don't know a damned thing about them."

The tracks led toward a narrow creek fringed with oak and scrub timber. Assuming that the Comanches had camped at the water, Lyle saw no way to approach without being spotted if anyone was still there to see them. He straightened his shoulders, building his courage.

"I'll go first. She ain't your sister."

"I'm figurin' on her bein' my wife. We'll go together."

Lyle reasoned that if any Indians had remained there, they would probably have scattered their horses out to graze. He saw none. Nevertheless, he half expected to hear a war whoop and see Indians come boiling out of the timber. All he heard was a flutter of wings as birds flushed away from the horseman's approach.

Nearing the water, he heard Sam shout, "Lyle, stay back!"

Lyle hauled up short, listening but hearing nothing to indicate trouble.

Sam dismounted and knelt over something on the ground. Lyle caught a glimpse of gray clothing fluttering in the breeze. Sam stood up and strode toward him, his face dark and fearsome. He held up both hands as a signal for Lyle to stop.

"Don't come any closer. You'd best steel yourself."

Lyle knew before he was told, for he remembered that Beth had been wearing a gray dress.

"It's her?"

Tears flowed down Sam's cheeks. His voice was forced.

"I covered her with her dress the best I could. You'd better not look at her—not her face, anyway. You'll want to remember her the way she was."

Lyle dismounted and leaned against the horse, clenching his fists so hard they hurt. He thought he should be crying, for Sam was, but all Lyle's tears had been burned out of him. A shout rose in his throat, and he let it burst free.

The images of Mama and Pa and Caleb came rushing back with a vengeance. When he could control his voice he asked, "Did they scalp her like they done the others?"

Sam's answer was barely more than a whisper.

"They did. They usually do."

"And did they . . ." Lyle could not bring out the words.

"They usually do." Sam choked. Finally he said, "She'd want to be buried with her family. We'd best be takin' her home."

Lyle looked about desperately.

"Where's Jeffrey? Do you see him anywhere?"

51

Sam seemed to have forgotten about Lyle's younger brother in his distress over Beth.

"I'm sorry. I never thought to look."

Lyle made a quick search but found nothing of Jeffrey.

"They must still have him."

"If they haven't killed him already they may be thinkin' of takin' him into the tribe, of makin' an Indian out of him."

Lyle had heard they sometimes stole boys young enough that they could make them forget their former lives and train them in Comanche ways.

He said, "You take Beth home. Bury her where I buried Mama and Pa and Caleb."

Sam's jaw dropped. "You ain't figurin' on goin' on alone! They'd kill you in a minute."

"What difference would it make? Without Jeffrey I've got nobody left, nobody who cares whether I live or die."

"You've got friends, and there are people you don't even know yet who will be your friends. You'll marry someday and have a new family."

Lyle could not see that now. He could see only that the last close kin he had was out there somewhere, a captive, probably frightened half to death and wishing for someone to come and fetch him home. Except for Lyle, there was no one.

He tried to clear a blockage in his throat as he looked toward his sister's lifeless form, partly covered with what remained of her gray dress. Her legs were bare, almost white. He remembered how shy she had always been about showing them, even to family.

"You take Beth home. I'm goin' on. I'll get Jeffrey back, and I'll make them pay for what they've done."

"Vengeance can be a terrible burden."

"Don't you think I'm justified?"

"But it can make a man forget what he's about and turn him into somethin' he'd never want to be."

Lyle barely listened, for in his mind he was already in bloody confrontation with the Comanches, dropping them one by one like birds in a turkey shoot.

Chapter Five

He hardly knew what he was doing for the next few hours, riding awhile in a walk, then a trot, watching the trail. He felt weak from hunger, and he burned with thirst, for he had been so consumed by grief and a building anger that he rode across a creek and did not even stop for a drink of water.

He found himself toward nightfall in a land of tighter soil where the tracks were less obvious than before. He knew that at darkness he would have to stop, for he would no longer be able to make out the trail as he had done the previous night. The rising of the moon would not be enough help. He kept moving until he came upon another creek. There he stopped to water and stake the horse and make camp, such as it was.

He had no food. He had been afraid to shoot even a rabbit for fear the Indians might be close enough to hear. The sign seemed much fresher, indicating that he was traveling faster than they were. They probably felt confident now, for they had moved well beyond the more heavily settled region.

Now and again he would sleep restlessly, haunted by dreams or hallucinations; he did not know one from the other. He would awaken with a start, thinking he heard horses' hooves, but there would be nothing except the distant howling of coyotes or wolves. Again, he would think he heard men talking, but it would be only the calling of night birds.

He wondered if he might be going crazy. He reasoned, in rational moments, that his problem was hunger and fatigue, compounded by grief and the urgency of his mission.

He was riding again at first good light. After a couple of hours he came upon the spot where the raiding party had camped for the night. Their fires still smoldered. He made a quick search, fearing he might find Jeffrey's body as Sam had found Beth's, but he saw no signs of his brother. He did find, however, a half-eaten piece of burned meat, evidently from a slaughtered horse or mule. It did not matter. He fell upon it and wolfed it down ravenously, muscle, gristle, fat, and all, leaving nothing but a piece of bone. It was not enough, but it had to serve.

At the dregs of the camp he found the remains of a horse that had been butchered. The heavier-muscled portions had been carried away, but with a pocketknife he cut off a slab of what remained. Still hungry, he tried to eat it raw, but one bite made his stomach turn over. He would carry it along. Later, perhaps, he would have a chance to cut it into strips and wrap it around a stick so that he could cook it over an open fire.

He had never eaten horse before. It was not considered civilized, but Pa had been forced to it during a long, hungry scout in the Revolution. He had said it wasn't bad at all, once a body got past the idea that he was committing cannibalism.

Toward noon the horse gave Lyle warning, turning its head a little to the left and pointing its ears. Lyle was instantly alert. In the distance he briefly saw three figures. They could have been cattle or buffalo, but somehow he knew they were horses. He reined quickly toward a small brush thicket and hid himself. After a long wait another glimpse showed that his suspicions had been correct. These were Indians. He had heard it was a trick of theirs to circle back on their trail and overtake pursuers from the rear. They must have suspected they were being tracked. They rode somewhat west of the trail they had left in their first passage, probably with the intention of cutting back in and looking for sign of pursuit.

They disappeared after a while. Lyle itched to go on but knew it would be dangerous. There was no telling how far ahead the rest of the Indians might be. He would stand his ground until he knew the way was clear.

After an hour that seemed five times longer, he saw them coming back along the trail they and he had left. If they found his tracks—and he did not see how they could miss them—they would follow him straight into this thicket. He held his breath, hoping they would pass him by.

They went to the place where he had broken away from the trail, and they seemed to pay no notice. They were going to miss him.

He watched them, stripped down to little but breechclouts and moccasins, bows and quivers slung over their shoulders. One carried a rifle or a shotgun; Lyle could not tell which. Their bodies showed signs of old war paint, though they had not freshened it, so it looked ragged, half washed away.

He would have managed to hold his composure had he not seen the scalp tied to a warrior's rein. It could have been anyone's . . . a stranger's, easily as not. But the thought that it could have been Mama's or Pa's, Caleb's or Beth's brought all his anger, all his torment, boiling back. He imagined Beth at the height of the horror that had befallen her, and judgment deserted him.

"You son of a bitch!" he shouted, and aimed his sights at the warrior without yielding a moment's thought to the consequences. The boom of the rifle made his horse pull back, almost breaking away from him. The Indian at whom he had aimed jerked as if kicked by a horse. He nearly fell. One of his companions grabbed him and lifted him back up. The other quickly loosed an arrow in Lyle's direction. Lyle knew the cloud of powder smoke had given away his position, and he expected the Comanches to charge him. Frantically he set about reloading the rifle, pouring powder down the barrel and ramming a ball after it. He still had the minister's pistol, which would give him one shot if they came within its effective range.

Instead of rushing him they pulled away, one holding his wounded companion upright on the horse. They put their mounts into a run. By the time Lyle had the rifle reloaded, they were almost out of reach. Cursing aloud, he sent one bullet after them, but he knew it fell short.

He was tempted to jump into the saddle and go in pursuit, but he began to calm and to realize what a foolish mistake he had made. They had been about to pass him by, and he had let his sense of outrage get the best of him. He might even have signed Jeffrey's death warrant. It was well known that Indians under pursuit sometimes killed their captives rather than let them fall back into the hands of their own people.

"My God, Jeffrey, if they kill you now . . ."

It would not be altogether their fault. Some of the blame would be his.

Watching the Indians disappear beyond another line of trees, Lyle realized they would almost surely come back, with reinforcements. This thicket was not a place he would want to be when they did. To follow them carried risk, but not as much as remaining here where the only question was how long it would take them to come back and kill him.

He chose to follow, for if Jeffrey was still alive he would be with the main body of raiders. And without Jeffrey, Lyle did not see how he could bring himself to go back home.

When the Indians failed to find him in the thicket they would almost certainly try to track him. He decided the best idea was to fall into the trail the warriors themselves had made in their retreat. He could only hope they would not notice his horse's tracks imposed atop so many of their own.

He found blood where the injured man had lain on the ground and his companions had pressed handfuls of dry old-season grass against the wound until the blood congealed and the flow stopped. Several wads of crimson-soaked vegetation lay in evidence. He derived at least a little satisfaction from the fact that someone had paid. . . . Not enough by a long way, but it was a start.

His biggest risk was that he might run head-long into those who came back to get him. He hoped he would see them first, but he had to depend heavily on the horse. Pa had taught him long before to observe the way a horse pointed its ears. The minister's bay had already proven itself watchful.

This time Lyle's instinct warned him before the horse did. He felt a compulsion to leave the trail and veer off into the oak timber. He chose a stretch of hard ground where his tracks would be difficult to see.

Through the foliage he tried to count the Comanches as they passed by, most of a hundred yards away. He saw close to a dozen. Jeffrey was not with them. Neither was the warrior Lyle had wounded, as far as he could tell.

Fearfully, he considered the probabilities. Either they had killed his brother or they had left a few behind with him, along with the wounded man.

He had no plan, exactly, beyond simply taking advantage of whatever opportunity might present itself. He thought the last thing they would expect would be for him to show up suddenly among them. He checked the minister's pistol. The rifle was ready, for he had reloaded it immediately after taking the one forlorn long shot at the retreating warriors.

He waited for the Indians to pass out of sight, in case one might chance to look back over his shoulder, then set out on a trail easy to follow, in the direction from which the latest party had come.

His skin prickled from the back of his neck down to his legs, for no previous experience had prepared him for a situation like this. He tried to remember if Pa had ever told a story that would fit, but nothing came to mind. In the war, Pa seemed always to have had other men beside him. He had not, as far as Lyle could remember, ever had to face a number of the enemy alone.

Gradually the tingling sensation eased and his hands ceased their trembling. He knew he could not afford to let his mind wander to the many frightening possibilities. He had to concentrate on what was most likely and what he could do about it. He had to assume that Jeffrey was alive, and that somehow he would manage to get him away.

He almost rode up on the two waiting Indians before he saw them. He stopped in the timber for a quick survey. One Comanche knelt before a small fire, roasting meat on a stick. The other lay on a blanket. Lyle assumed that this was the wounded man. He might or might not be capable of putting up much fight. Three horses were tied to nearby bushes. There must have been a third Indian somewhere.

Lyle did not see Jeffrey at first and felt a growing fear that his brother had been killed. Then the boy came half running, half stumbling out of a stand of oak, carrying dead branches in his arms. A third warrior trailed close behind him, lashing him across the shoulders with a leather quirt. Lyle's fear turned quickly back to anger.

"That," he said under his breath, "is the first son of a bitch I'm goin' to shoot."

He did not wait for Jeffrey and the single warrior to reach the others. He gripped his rifle in his left hand, along with the leather reins, for he knew he could not aim the weapon accurately from the back of a moving horse. He checked the pistol again and put his mount into a run before he left the shelter of the timber.

"Jeffrey!" he shouted. "Get ready to swing up behind me!"

The startled Indian dropped the quirt. He had

a bow in his hand, but Lyle shot him point-blank before he could bring an arrow from its quiver. The warrior dropped like a stone and lay still. Jeffrey seemed to freeze for a moment, staring in disbelief, then heaved the dead wood away and came running. Lyle reached down to grab him and help him up behind him. He accidentally dropped the rifle.

There was no time to pick it up, for the second Indian came running, loosing two arrows before Lyle got Jeffrey firmly seated behind him.

The wounded man lying on the blanket tried to rise but could not. He crawled desperately toward a bow that lay far out of his reach. Lyle saw him as no immediate threat and concentrated on getting the Indian still afoot. He put his mount into a run again, toward the tied horses. They broke loose and began to shy away.

Lyle heard a thump as an arrow drove into his horse's chest. The animal screamed and plunged forward on its left shoulder, sending Lyle and Jeffrey rolling in the grass. Lyle lost the pistol as he had lost the rifle. He groped but could not lay his hands upon it.

Wielding a knife, the remaining Indian was upon him. Lyle stepped back as the blade slashed at him. It sliced across his arm, snagging in his sleeve. He felt a sharp sting, lost his footing, and almost went down. He managed to regain his balance and grab the warrior's wrist. Grunting, the veins standing out in his neck, the Comanche struggled to twist his arm free.

Lyle felt his opponent's breath hot on his face.

He saw death in the hating black eyes as the two men grappled, their faces inches apart. He saw sweat cutting trails through the dust on the other man's cheeks and felt his own sweat burning his eyes. He fought for breath.

Jeffrey shouted, "Look out, Lyle! The other one!"

The wounded man had reached the bow. Jeffrey picked up one of the fallen sticks and hurled it, striking the Indian hard. The man fumbled in his effort to fit an arrow to the string. Jeffrey went running with a heavier stick and smashed it across the warrior's head. He jerked the bow away from the Indian's weakened hands.

Lyle had but little chance to watch what his brother was doing. His opponent's strength and weight was a match for his own. They pushed and pulled, groaned and sweated, each trying to twist free of the other's grip.

The Indian's foot slipped, and the two fighters went down. Lyle landed on top and managed to knee the Indian in the groin. He felt the man's sweat-slick arm go slack for an instant and wrested the knife from him.

Screaming with rage, he drove the knife blade in almost to the hilt beneath the breastbone. The Comanche made a hoarse cry and went limp. Lyle jerked the knife, holding it in both hands, and plunged it down a second time, harder. All the fury, all the grief, all the despair he had harbored came storming to the surface. Crying out his bitterness, he stabbed the warrior again and again until at last the knife blade snapped. Lyle slumped, his emotion spent. He trembled, gasping for breath, His hands and sleeves were soaked with blood.

He heard Jeffrey mumble, "You've killed him enough."

The boy's face was ashen. His eyes reflected horror. Lyle gradually realized how far over the edge he had gone, how close he had come, for a few moments, to madness.

Pa's stories had not prepared him for this. There had been death in them at times, but somehow it had seemed clean and painless. There had not been all this blood, all this mutilated flesh.

He swept Jeffrey into his arms and hugged him so hard that he heard some of the boy's breath gush out of him.

Lyle tried to brush the blood from his sleeve, but it had soaked through. He looked down at the mangled body and felt as if he would throw up, except that he had little in his stomach to lose. He struggled to find his voice.

"The others'll be comin' back directly. We'd best be gettin' gone from here."

Jeffrey pointed to the wounded man he had struck with his stick. The Indian seemed dazed.

"What about him? You goin' to kill him, too?"

"He can't do anything to us. I've killed enough." He shuddered again. "More than enough."

All the way from home, he had wanted to kill. He had thought killing those who had killed his family would take away the pain of loss, lift the burden of grief. But he felt no better. Indeed, he felt much worse.

Blood washed nothing away. It added stain of its own.

Jeffrey said, "Your horse is dead."

"We'll take theirs."

The three animals had begun grazing nearby, quickly recovered from whatever fright they had taken at the surge of violence around them.

"Like as not they're stole. But if we don't find out who they belong to, I reckon they're ours." They would replace the ones the Indians had taken. "Find my rifle. The pistol, too."

It was a struggle, freeing the saddle from the dead horse, but he managed. He walked toward the nearest of the three, speaking softly and gently. The animal seemed about to shy away but nosed at Lyle's outstretched, cupped hand, as if used to being fed that way. Lyle caught and saddled it.

"Think you can ride bareback?" he asked Jeffrey.

"That's the way they brought me here."

He caught one of the horses and gave his brother a boost up onto its back. Mounting, he caught the third horse's rein. He paused, taking a final look at the man he had stabbed to death. He felt cold now, and trembly. It frightened him, realizing how far into savagery he could descend, given provocation.

Two mornings before he had still been a farm boy with no inkling of the fury that lay dormant in him. Today he was a man awed by the darkness that could rise from within.

"Let's go," he said, touching his heels to his horse and leading the other.

Jeffrey said, "We got no home to go to."

"They didn't burn the land. We can finish raisin' Pa's crops, and we can build another cabin."

"What'll we do without Pa and Mama and them?"

"The best we can. If what we've been through didn't kill us, what could?"

He quickly put the horses into a lope, due east away from the Indians.

Chapter Six

Montana, 1901

"Sawin' wood like an ol' man."

Speaks opened his eyes and looked up at Sam November, who was looming over him. Speaks wondered when his friend's face had gotten so lined and weathered. His eyes were still as clear as ever, though.

"Ain't sleepin," Speaks said, "I'm thinkin'."

" 'Bout what?"

"Stories."

"That writer feller show up?"

"He did."

November sat in the chair Aubrey P. Fellows had vacated, grabbed the third empty glass, and poured himself some lemonade.

"What have you been doin'?" Speaks asked.

"Checkin' fence over by that dry creek bed. Had to pound a couple of the posts in."

"You ain't supposed to be doin' that kind of work, Sam," Speaks said. "You're too old."

"Yeah," November said. "You got Clytie to make you think that, don't you be tryin' to make me think it. When I get too old to pound a fence post into the ground, why, just pound me into the dirt."

It was no secret November had never approved of Speaks's marriage to Clytie—and he spoke with more than just disapproval when mentioning the couple's three-day courtship.

Still, it was a testament to the long friendship of the two men that November's disapproval of Clytie had not ended it. The way Speaks saw it, November was entitled to his opinion, especially since he always treated Clytie with respect—even when she tried to tell him he was too old to do something.

"Fella wants to talk to you too."

"Me? What about? You're the legend."

"And you were just along for the ride?"

"Never wanted to have me no reputation."

"Well, want it or not, we both got it," Speaks said. "Speaks and November, of Texas."

November made a rude noise with his mouth, finished his lemonade, and stood up.

"Is he gonna let us enjoy dinner before he starts questionin' us?"

"Don't worry," Speaks said. "Once he tastes Clytie's cookin' he ain't gonna want to talk for eatin' it."

Speaks started to get up, and November said, "Need help, old man?"

"Memory serves me," Speaks said, standing, "you're a year or two older than me."

"But I look better."

Speaks started to protest, then just said, "Ah, you always did. We best go in and get cleaned up for dinner."

Speaks was right about Fellows and Clytie's cooking. The young man's appetite kept him busy all through the meal. After dessert he followed Speaks and November out to the porch for cigars.

"Clytie won't let me smoke the damned things in the house anymore."

November made another rude sound with his mouth. It was a habit he had acquired over the past fifteen years, watching his friend become domesticated. Of course, he didn't do it around Clytie.

Fellows accepted a cigar and the three lit up. Speaks expected the young man to choke, but he was pleasantly surprised when Fellows blew a string of perfect smoke rings.

"Smell that air?" Speaks said. "Makes a man want to be on horseback again."

"Do you ride much anymore?" Fellows asked.

"When I can."

"Not often enough," November said. "His wife is afraid he'll jog somethin' loose."

"I wonder," Fellows said, "if I got my notebook could we sit out here and . . . talk?"

"You mean you want me to talk while you write, isn't that it?" Speaks asked.

"Well, that is why I came."

Fellows looked at November.

"Don't look at me. I'll only say somethin' if I have to correct this old codger's faulty memory."

"I'll get my book," Fellows said, and started back inside.

"Leave that cigar out here!" Speaks snapped.

"Oh." Fellows set it down on the table that had held the lemonade that afternoon, then went inside.

"What are you gonna tell 'im?" November asked.

"What do you think?"

"From the beginning?"

Speaks nodded.

"It's gonna hurt."

Speaks sighed and said, "The truth always does." He tried to blow a smoke ring, but botched it.

November didn't correct Speaks, not once. And to his credit Speaks's voice did not crack once. The only outward sign of what he was feeling was in his eyes, and only November and Clytie knew him well enough to have noticed it.

Aubrey P. Fellows wrote frantically as Speaks talked, never once tried to halt the story so he could catch up. It was several moments, however, after he finished talking before Fellows looked up at both him and November.

"That's quite a story."

"It's not just a story," November said tightly.

"No, no," Fellows said, "of course not. Well . . ." He closed his book and stood up. "I, uh, have enough for a start, and I am rather tired from my trip. I think I will turn in, if you gentlemen will excuse me."

Fellows went inside while Speaks and November sat in silence for a while.

"I give you credit, Lyle," November finally said, standing up. "You don't pull no punches."

Clytie was asleep when Speaks finally came to bed. As he settled into the soft mattress he wondered how long it had been since he last told that story about losing his family to the Comanches. He'd thought about it for too many years, but somehow being with Clytie had softened the pain. He touched her cheek and hoped that he had done the same for her when it came to memories of the death of her first husband, Drew.

Telling it to Aubrey P. Fellows out loud, though, that had been something different. It had affected not only his own life but Sam November's, as well. November had expected to marry Speaks's sister, Beth. Even after all these years Speaks knew his friend still mourned Beth, the wife Sam November would never have. Speaks couldn't remember a time when November had even looked at a woman the way he himself looked at Clytie, and at Melanie before her.

Both men were quiet at breakfast, and Fellows was a smart enough young fellow to go along with the mood.

After breakfast, however, the questions resumed out on the porch.

"What about your brother, Jeffrey?" Fellows asked.

November looked away. Clytie came out at that point with a tray of coffee for them. If she had heard the question, she didn't react.

"I don't want to talk about my brother right now," Speaks said.

"All right, then what's next?"

"Lyle—" November said before his friend could answer.

Speaks looked at November, then in the direction his friend was looking. A lone rider was coming up to the house fast, kicking up clouds of dust.

"Who is it?" Speaks asked.

"Charlie Baffert, and he's in a real hurry."

"Ain't he supposed to be movin' the herd?" Speaks asked.

"Yep," November said, "him and four others. Rode out early this morning to relieve the night crew."

Speaks and November descended the porch steps. Fellows watched from his chair, sensing something was wrong. Clytie could feel it, too, and she hugged her arms, getting ready for the bad news.

Charlie Baffert was off his horse before it could stop, wading through a cloud of dust to where Speaks and November stood. The cloud settled into the lines on his face, rested on his eyebrows and eyelashes, making him look older than the fifty he was.

"We got trouble, boss."

Fellows didn't know if the man was talking to Speaks or November. He understood that November still held the position of foreman. It was something he wanted to ask November about, whether or not he resented being foreman when he'd started out being a partner. That was part of the "dirt" his publisher had told him to look for. "Those two have been friends for a long time. There's got to be some conflict somewhere. Find it!" This was not the time, though.

"What's wrong, Charlie?"

"We lost fifty head."

"Whataya mean, lost?" November asked.

"I mean they was took," Baffert said, "rustled."

"Damn!" November said.

"That ain't the worst of it," Charlie said. "The boys is dead—shot dead."

"How many?" November asked.

"Four of 'em," Charlie said. "We went out to relieve them. They was dead, and the horses gone."

"Who's dead?" Speaks asked.

Fellows saw the man's eyes go to Speaks. It was clear, then, that he had been talking to November up to that point.

"Mr. Speaks," Baffert said, "ol' Clay's dead, along with McCarthy, Stevens, and Mott."

"Clay?"

"Oh, Lyle," Clytie said, her voice breaking, "not Clay."

November put a hand on his old partner's shoulder. Clay Artax was the first hand he and

November and Clytie had hired, some fourteen years before.

"He shouldn'ta been out there," Speaks said. "The old fool."

Artax was sixty-five, still a working hand, and up to now Speaks had admired him for that.

"Can you still ride, Charlie?" November asked.

"Sure thing, boss."

"Go for the sheriff, then. He'll want to bring a posse."

"Yessir." Baffert looked at Speaks. "I'm real sorry about Clay, Mr. Speaks."

"Thanks, Charlie," Speaks said. "You better get going."

"Yessir."

"Charlie," November said as the man re-mounted, "who's out there?"

"Dave Lukas, Nat Baily and Chilito. Chilito's tryin' to pick up the trail, the others are bringin' the . . . the bodies back in."

"Can't be too hard to pick up the trail fifty head's leavin'," Speaks said as Charlie rode away.

"Sons of bitches," November shouted. "Must be the same gang got twenty head from the Bar X last month."

"What will you do?" Fellows asked from his chair on the porch.

"What can we do?" Clytie said. "We sent for the sheriff."

Speaks and November exchanged a look.

"There's nothing else we can do," Clytie said firmly. "Nothing."

Chapter Seven

"You're a crazy man!" Clytie said.

"It's taken you fifteen years to realize that?" Speaks asked calmly.

He'd been less than calm since the news about the death of Clay Artax and the other men. The loss of fifty head was incidental to the murders.

For hours he seethed inside, he and November both, avoiding each other, not wanting to see what they had each become.

Old men.

Age was what was keeping them from saddling horses, taking off after the murdering rustlers. Too many years held them back, forcing them into waiting hours for a sheriff and a posse, which would probably show up in automobiles. And you could bet those rustlers were not going to be found anyplace you could get to in one of those infernal contraptions.

Clytie knew what was going on. She knew why the two old men were wandering around, staying out of each other's sight, and she knew where it was all going to lead. She knew she'd argue, and she knew she'd lose, but it had to be played out.

"What's going on?" Fellows had asked her at one point.

"You came here looking for a story, Mr. Fellows?" she asked.

"That's right."

"Well," she said, "I'm afraid you're going to get more than you bargained for—but you may have to go the extra mile to get it."

"I don't understand."

She'd looked at him and said, "You will."

Finally, the two partners, the two lifelong friends, ended up in the same place at the same time, as they knew they would. It was in Speak's office, where he did his hated paperwork, but also where his gun rack hung, loaded with the guns he'd used over the years. Various Winchester and Henry rifles, handguns, shotguns, some belonging to Speaks, some to November, some neither man could remember owning.

"You got the key?" November asked.

"In my pocket," Speaks said.

November rubbed his jaw.

"It would be somethin' wouldn't it?"

"Somethin' to remember," Speaks said, "but

it would be somethin' we were doin' for Clay, and for the others, too."

"Who are we kiddin', Lyle?" November said. "It'd be somethin' for us."

Speaks reached out and touched the Winchester, the one he'd been carrying when he met Clytie, then touched the Colt, the one he'd used to save her from the wolves.

"Be better'n dozin' on the porch," he said.

November nodded, and Speaks used the key to unlock the gun rack.

Now he was packing his saddlebags, November was off doin' the same, and Clytie was telling him how many kinds of fools they were.

"You're seventy-four years old, Lyle Speaks," she said. "Your bones can't take all the riding you're gonna have to do."

"My bones will be fine," he said. "They'll be better than they are sitting in that chair on the porch, that's for sure."

"And what about Sam?" she asked. "He's older than you are."

"Sam's a bull," he said. "He always has been."

"Lyle," Clytie said, giving one last try. She grabbed him and turned him around for it. "You're not the man you used to be. You're not that Lyle Speaks anymore, you're *my* Lyle Speaks, and I want you alive."

He took hold of her arms and looked into her amber eyes.

"Clytie," he said, "I'll bring both Lyle Speakses back to you. I promise. Have I ever broken a promise to you?"

"No."

"And I won't start now," he said. "I *am* too old for that."

She hugged him then, tightly, and then said, "That fool writer wants to go with you. He wants to write it all down. The last chapter, he says."

"He's a big boy," Speaks said. "If he wants to come he's more than welcome, but he'll have to keep up."

"Tell him that," she said. "He's as big a fool as you two are, only younger." She pushed away from him. "I'll pack you some food. You'll probably have to run a cold camp or two."

"Sure you don't want to come along?" he asked her, remembering her creeping around down by the creek with her shotgun fifteen years before. Saved his bacon that day.

"Don't think I haven't thought about it," she said, "but no. You and Sam go ahead, run off and be fools. I'll be waiting here with liniment and bandages."

Liniment, he thought. Maybe he should pack some.

When he got to the porch Sam November was waiting with three horses saddled and ready. They were the best horses on the grounds: a roan for Speaks, a steeldust for November, and a bay mare for Aubrey P. Fellows.

The writer came out moments later, wearing trail clothes.

"Where'd you get the outfit?" Speaks asked.

"Your wife was kind enough to supply the

clothes," Fellows said, looking down at himself. He still had his eastern boots on. Clytie couldn't help him there. Speaks's boots were just too damned big.

"I thought they looked big on you." Speaks looked at November. "Sam, you want to tell this youngster what he's in for?"

"He just has to keep up," November said, "and duck his head down when the shooting starts."

"And I'll take it all down," Fellows said, his eyes shining, "as it happens. The two old legends on the trail of outlaws again."

They both stared at him.

"Sorry," he said, grimacing.

"We're old," Speaks said. "It's that other word I object to."

"Oh," Fellows said. "Legend."

"That's the one," Speaks said. "Mount up."

Being in the saddle, on the trail again, was exhilarating. Of course, Speaks was angry that his friend had been killed, his men also, and his animals stolen, but damn it felt good to be on a horse again.

Baily and Lukas had returned with the bodies of the dead men, but Charlie Baffert had not yet come back with the sheriff after some five hours.

Clytie walked out onto the porch and handed Speaks a burlap sack filled with provisions.

"You two old fools keep each other alive, you hear me? Sam November?"

"I hear you, Clytie," November said.

"And you, you young fool," she said to Fellows.

"Ma'am?"

"You write it all down and don't get your head shot off."

He swallowed and said, "Yes, ma'am."

Baily and Lukas came over to the porch.

"Want us to go with you, boss?" Lukas asked.

"No," November said, "Lyle and I will meet up with Chilito. You and the rest of the boys, you watch the herd, you hear? If we come back and find out you lost any more horses, you're all fired."

"You bet, boss," Baily said.

"You ready, Lyle?"

Speaks nodded, hugged Clytie one more time, and mounted up.

Right from the start it was a thrill.

Now they were tracking not only the herd, but Chilito, following in his footsteps, as it were.

"Chilito is a Mex we hired a few years ago," Speaks told Fellows. "He could track a sand flea across the desert."

"I've got to write that down," Fellows said.

In spite of himself Speaks was impressed with the way the writer was handling his horse. He was even able to write in his notebook as he rode.

"You ride pretty well."

"I've spent a lot of time riding in Central Park," he said.

"Well," November said, "this ain't no park out

here. This is rough country. The flats are hard, the mountains are harder."

"Where do you think they'll go?"

"Right now we're between the Powder and the Tongue Rivers," November said. "If they stay here we'll find 'em easy."

"And if they don't?"

November snorted and said, "We'll still find 'em, it'll just be harder."

"It's better'n a hundred miles to the Black Hills south of us," Speaks said, "and about the same to the Crow Reservation to the west."

"What about east?"

"The Powder River mountain range," Speaks said, "but they ain't headin' east, or north, from the looks of it. They're stayin' on this side of the Yellowstone."

"How do we find them?" Fellows asked.

"First we find Chilito," Speaks said.

By the time dark came they still hadn't caught up to Chilito.

"They must be travelin' at a good pace," November said, feeding more sticks to the fire. "That Mex is stayin' with them."

"Do you think we'll catch up to them tomorrow?" Fellows asked, trying not to rub his sore backside.

"Probably," Speaks said. "Here." He handed Fellows a cup of coffee. "Enjoy that, because by tomorrow night we'll probably be runnin' a cold camp."

"Why?"

"So nobody can find us by the fire," November said, "or the smell of coffee."

"I just thought of somethin'," Speaks said. "You got a gun, boy?"

"A gun? Me? No, sir."

"You got to have a gun," Speaks said. "Sam? You got an extra?"

"I got that old Colt I used to hunt buffalo that time, remember? Still shoots straight."

"Give it to the lad." He turned his attention back to Fellows. "Can you shoot?"

"I can . . . pull a trigger, if that's what you mean."

"It ain't," November said, returning to the fire with the gun. "He means can you hit what you aim at."

"Ah . . . that I don't know."

"Take the gun," Speaks said, "an' tuck it into your belt. We'll see about showin' you how to use it tomorrow."

"Yes, sir."

Fellows accepted the huge hogleg from November and tried to tuck it into his belt, then his pants, unsure of how to do it.

"Just keep it next to you for tonight," Speaks said finally.

"Yes, sir."

"Lyle and I are gonna split the watch," November said. "You can get some sleep."

"It's amazing," Fellows said, "but I'm not sleepy. Do you mind if I sit up awhile?"

"I don't mind," November said. "I got the first watch."

"I'll see you in four hours," Speaks said, and

rolled himself up in his bedroll. He'd been sleeping in a real bed for so long, he knew he was going to be sore in the morning—and he relished it.

Before long November and Fellows could hear him snoring.

"Mrs. Speaks is quite a woman," Fellows said.

"She's somethin', all right."

"Have they been married long?"

"About fifteen years," November said.

"Oh, I would have thought it was longer. She's, ah, quite a bit younger than Mr. Speaks, isn't she?"

"She is that," November said. "She was married before, but her husband was killed by Indians."

"Oh, my," Fellows said, "they had that in common, then."

"Yes, they did."

"Mr. Speaks was never married before—"

"You gonna keep jawin' at me?" November asked.

"Uh, well, it is my job, sir. I'm just, uh—"

"How about I talk and you listen?" November said.

"That would be fine," Fellows said. "What will you talk about?"

"I'll tell you a story," November said, "but you can't tell Lyle I told you."

Fellows became excited.

"What kind of story? About gunfights? Outlaws?"

"I'll tell you," November said with a little smile, "about the first time Lyle fell in love, and made a damn fool of himself over a woman."

"Oh," Fellows said, and then, "Well, I suppose we'd need that in the story, too."

"So stop jawin'," November said, "and listen . . ."

Part Two

Chapter Eight

Fort Worth, Texas—early spring, 1857

Melanie Beaufort stood at the window in her sister's small house and pulled back the lace curtain so that she could look out on the dirt street. There was precious little to look at. Two other houses were within sight, but neither was as nice as the one Ben Thompson had built for his wife, with its board sidings painted a gleaming white—now dulled with dust, but Melanie would never have mentioned that—and a white picket fence enclosing what might someday, with struggle, be a garden. Knowing her sister Sophie as she did, Melanie could not imagine why she had chosen to marry a man who wanted to be a banker in Texas. Every time Sophie looked at the hot, dusty street with no trees lining it, she had to think with longing of Linden, their Georgia home, with its towering pines and magnolias and the green lawns that stretched out beyond forever.

Some six months along in her first pregnancy, Sophie sat in a rocking chair, complacently taking neat, even stitches on a tiny garment.

"Anything worth looking at?" she asked idly, her attention riveted on the small garment.

Melanie shrugged.

"Two men on horseback. They look . . . well, unkempt, to say the least."

She stared at them again. Unkempt they may have been, with long hair spilling out under hats with wide brims and their cotton pants and boots covered with dust, but they were laughing and gesturing as though they were having the time of their lives. Melanie watched them intently and felt a twinge of envy at their freedom. Even here in the wilds of Texas, she was bound by what a "lady" should and should not do.

Sophie rose, a little laboriously, for her new shape was still strange to her, and came to the window.

"Farmers," she said, "from the west. Sometimes they come in for . . . well, I guess for some excitement, but they had to come a long way. A hundred miles or more. We don't associate with such people, of course."

Ignoring her sister's last prideful statement, Melanie asked in disbelief, "They ride for a hundred miles for excitement?"

To herself she thought she too would ride that far for a little excitement. So far, after three weeks, life with Sophie and Ben had been more than a little dull, and she had promised to stay until the baby was three months old. A long six months stretched before her.

Intent on getting a better look, Melanie pulled the curtain back even farther. She was a tall young woman, with reddish-brown hair she parted in the middle and pulled back into a chignon, though tendrils always escaped to frame her face. Her almost severe hairstyle only accented her high cheekbones and large, dark eyes. Her father always said there must have been a Cherokee in the woodpile someplace who had given his dark good looks to Melanie, while Sophie clearly took her rounder, softer blond appearance from their Celtic ancestors.

The riders were by then abreast of the house, still laughing, when suddenly the one nearest the house happened to glance at the window. Seeing Melanie, he tipped his hat in a jaunty gesture and smiled broadly.

The curtain was quickly replaced, but not before his look was burned on Melanie's memory. He was older than she—in his late twenties, she judged, and they had been years of hard living. Even at a distance she could see a certain firm set to his chin, a directness to his gaze that bespoke someone beyond callow youth. She couldn't tell for certain since he was ahorseback, but he looked tall—and there was that thick dark hair that hung to his shoulders. For a reason that Melanie Beaufort would not identify, her heart skipped a beat.

"Melanie, what is it?" Sophie asked.

Red rising in her face, Melanie replied, "Nothing. I just find such men . . . so, well, interesting. You know, they're so free to do what they want to do."

With all her fine Georgia breeding rising to the fore, Sophie said preachily, "They're not the kind of men we will ever know, Melanie. Even though we are in the wilderness, we must try to live as we did at home. And that includes the people we associate with."

Melanie was tempted to tell her she was tired of the people they always associated with, and since few of them were in Fort Worth, they'd been associating only with themselves, which was getting boring. But she held her tongue, reluctant to upset the mother-to-be.

"Ben says he'll take us to dinner at Hutchin's tonight," Sophie said. "It's probably the finest dining room in Fort Worth." Then she giggled, sounding just a bit as she had not too long before when she'd been but a girl and Melanie had liked her better. "It's the only one decent enough that Ben would take me there."

Fort Worth was not quite ten years old, a town that began as a military fort for protection of settlements from the Indians. Having never seen any Indian activity, the army soon abandoned the place and left it to civilian squatters. Now, some five years after the army's departure, the city showed signs of growth—a doctor, two lawyers, several saloons, a cotton yard, Steele's Tavern, where ladies could wait in a secluded parlor for the stagecoach that stopped there, Hutchin's Hotel, hardware and mercantile businesses, and, of course, a new bank. Newcomers these days were not squatters but men like Ben Thompson, men of wealth who came from the South and brought their slaves with them. There was even talk of building a courthouse, but so far that had not materialized. But the squatters and farmers and the drovers—those with not enough money to own slaves and drive fine carriages and build new houses—had not been driven out. They mingled easily with their wealthier neighbors in this frontier city.

They even mingled at Hutchin's Hotel. Ben, Sophie, and Melanie had only just seated themselves—they chose the table with the cleanest-looking cloth on it—when two men dressed in rough clothes entered.

"I tell you, it was Providence," one said to the other. "Meant to be that we came to Fort Worth today."

"If you say so," the second man replied, his voice considerably lower. He was dark-headed, not quite as tall as his companion, but stocky and solidly built. Now he took off his hat and held it nervously in his hands as though uncertain what to do with it. His hair bore the indentation where the hat had been sitting all day.

After one quick glance at the men, Melanie quickly turned her full attention to her dining companions, who were, unfortunately, totally silent. Then Sophie, too loudly, said the last thing Melanie wanted her to.

"Aren't those the two men we saw riding into town today, Mel?"

Before Melanie could shush her Ben turned his head, then said heartily, "That's Lyle Speaks and Sam November, new clients at the bank." He was instantly out of his chair and across the room.

Ben, Melanie thought somewhat angrily, is a good banker because he flatters his customers. But how, she wondered, had these two men found enough money to deposit in a bank? The next thing she knew, the two men were following Ben back to their table, where the banker made the proper introductions.

The taller one—the one who had raised his hat to her—was Lyle Speaks. His companion was Sam November. Speaks knew no embarrassment, probably never would in his life.

"Ma'am," he said, "I saw you at your window today. You—well, just for a minute there, you reminded me of someone—someone very special."

Was she imagining it or were there tears forming in the eyes of both men?

"I guess, then," she said haltingly, "that's a good comparison."

"Yes, ma'am, it is, a very good one," Speaks said, his voice cracking. And then, recovering himself: "Well, we won't interrupt your dinner. Just wanted to say hello. Thompson, we'll be in to sign those papers tomorrow."

Melanie felt disappointment—and a thousand questions—as the two men turned away. She kept her attention focused on her dinner

the entire evening, never—well, almost never—
looking in their direction, though the roast beef
tasted greasy to her and the potatoes were
burnt.

The two men stayed buried in deep conversation, even while they ate. Melanie did sneak
enough of a look to see that their table manners
were pretty good, somewhat to her surprise.
She also noticed that they drank more than a
little whiskey with their dinner. When Ben announced that it was time to "get poor little Sophie some rest," and they rose to go, a cheery
"Good night, folks!" followed them out of the
dining room. She knew it came from Lyle
Speaks, and on a bold impulse she turned just
enough to send him a smiling thank-you.

"Sam," Lyle Speaks said, "I'm gonna get to
know that woman. I may marry her."

Sam November laughed aloud.

"Lyle, you get crazier ideas than anybody I
ever saw. We come to town to sell our farms,
and you decide to get married. You do that and
we can't go bounty hunting for that sheriff, like
we discussed today."

"I ain't sayin' I'm for sure gettin' married. I'm
just sayin' she . . . well, she attracts me more
than any woman I've ever seen."

"Most of the women you've known have been
whores," November said. "This one's a lady, a
real southern lady. You wouldn't know how to
treat her."

Speaks sobered, and his voice softened.

"Mama was a lady, and she insisted we learn

our manners and learn how to treat women. And Beth, she was fixin' to be a lady." Suddenly, his voice had a hard edge to it. "But I don't want to talk about them."

"Man," his friend said, "someday we're gonna have to talk about them, or they'll haunt us till we die."

"They'll do it anyway." And Speaks left his companion behind.

It had been twelve years since Lyle Speaks found his family massacred. Since then, November, who'd planned to marry Speaks's sister Beth, had become his constant companion. They'd farmed, they'd wandered West Texas looking for Comanches to kill in vengeance—something Speaks had thought he'd had enough of, but found that he'd been wrong—they'd even served under General Samuel Curtis Ryan in the Mexican-American War. But none of it had brought them peace. During the day they laughed and rode and fought and carried on with the best of them, but at night both men were haunted by memories—Pa and Mama and Caleb with their scalps gone, the cabin in flames—and especially Beth, brutally treated before she was murdered on the road. Jeffrey, the youngest, whom Lyle had managed to rescue, had been sent to Tennessee for relatives to raise. It was more than Speaks could do to shoulder the responsibility of a growing brother, even while he tried to work his way out of despair.

Chapter Nine

"Melanie, where are you going?" Sophie's voice had a whiny tone to it.

"For a walk," Melanie said. "I'm feeling cooped up." She tied her bonnet under her chin and picked up her parasol.

"It's . . . it's not proper for a young woman to walk unescorted," Sophie said.

"Oh, bother, Sophie. We're not in Georgia. We're in Texas, and it's all different here."

"Well," Sophie moaned, "it shouldn't be. You wait, someday it will be just like Georgia."

Melanie resisted an urge to say, "Heaven help us!" She also managed not to slam the door as she left. She was soon aware that Sophie's words were not idle. The rutted first street was almost empty, but the few people she saw were men. Were there no women in this town? She decided to simply walk the length of the street to the bluff where one could look out over the Texas prairie forever. Then she would turn back, having had her fresh air, dusty as it was. But the going was not easy: She had to pick her way over ruts, dodge wagons careening down the street, even watch for stray dogs.

When she reached the bluff she stood for a long time, staring out at the plains, wondering that she found herself in such a strange place. But the view intrigued her, and she felt a longing to ride out into that lonesome land. It was April, and the prairie was covered with wildflowers so that from the distance it looked like a yellow carpet over the brown land. She had never seen anything like it.

"Ma'am? Are you all right?"

The voice startled her, and she whirled to find herself staring at Lyle Speaks, who stood with his hat in his hand.

"I . . . I'm just admiring the view. The flowers . . ."

"You shouldn't be walking alone," Speaks said. "No tellin', with all these ruffians in town, what could happen to a fine lady like yourself." His eyes stared directly into hers, and she felt something deep inside her jump. She didn't know if it was alarm or pleasure or embarrassment, but she sincerely hoped her face was not turning red.

"Thank you, Mr. Speaks. I'm sure I'm fine."

"Well," he said, holding out his arm, "I'm not so sure, and I'm going to escort you wherever you're goin'."

Slowly, she took his arm. "Home, I guess," she said.

And so, her hand linked in his arm, they paraded the length of what was then Fort Worth. He told her, unbidden, some about himself—though he never told her about the massacre of his family.

"We came to town to sell our farms. Didn't know what we were going to do, but farming wasn't it anymore. Just happened the sheriff was looking for bounty hunters. Now, *that* we can do—tracking men down."

"Why would you track men down?" she asked innocently. Bounty hunters were not something she knew in Georgia.

" 'Cause they done—uh, have done wrong and need to be apprehended," he said righteously. "And we'll get paid for bringing them in."

The idea appalled her, and she turned to stare at him.

"You'd turn men in for money?"

Something along his jawline hardened, and his eyes turned dark.

"Yes, ma'am, if they've killed somebody, I surely would. Wouldn't hesitate an instant."

"Something bad has happened to you, hasn't it?" she asked, having watched his face change.

Without even thinking he turned toward her, putting his hand overs hers, which rested lightly on his arm.

"Yes, ma'am, it has. But I don't want to talk about it." His eyes were dark and hard.

They walked the rest of the way in silence, his

hand all the time covering hers. She made no move to dislodge it.

At Sophie's house she thanked him for escorting her safely home and he made a funny little half-bow. Clearly, he wasn't used to such gestures.

She didn't see him again for two weeks. Oh, she saw him when she looked through the curtain—she was embarrassed now to pull it aside—but she did not see him to talk to. For days, just after the noon meal, he would ride by, and he would always look toward the house. But he never stopped. Then there would be a string of three or four days when he didn't appear. After that, he'd be back again. Once he appeared at the Sunday meeting a visiting preacher held in the tiny schoolhouse, but they had no chance to speak.

Melanie had no way of knowing, of course, that when he didn't appear he and November were off chasing this desperado or that. Nor did she know that November teased him unmercifully.

" 'Bout time to go for your ride, isn't it?" he'd say as they rose from the table at whatever saloon they'd chosen for their noon meal. Speaks would just grin and reply, "Guess it is."

What Melanie did know was that Sophie disapproved, loudly, of even a mild interest in "that wild man," as she called him. "I don't know why you keep watching out the window for him," she said, fanning herself. "He's not your type, and he knows it. He best not ever stop at this house."

Of course, that was just what he did. He boldly stopped at the house one afternoon when the two ladies sat over a cup of tea.

Sophie answered the door.

"My husband is not at home," she said loftily. "I believe you can still find him at the bank."

Hat in hand, he stood tall, straight, and not the least bit intimidated by her.

"I didn't come to see Mr. Thompson," he said. "I came to speak to Miss Beaufort."

Sophie opened her mouth, but Melanie was too quick for her.

"Why, Mr. Speaks, do come in." Her heart fluttered a little, but she kept her voice steady. "We were just enjoying tea . . . might I offer you a cup?"

Must be a southern habit, he thought. Aloud he said, "No, ma'am, I never was much for tea. If we could talk for a minute . . ."

"Of course," she said. "Sophie will excuse us."

Sophie made a broad show of picking up her cup and leaving the room, pulling the door almost but not all the way closed behind her. Then she sent Penny, the maidservant, to listen at the door, but as the poor girl reported to her angry mistress, nothing much was said except that he asked her to ride out on the prairie with him the next day, and Miss Melanie agreed. Sophie sent Penny for the smelling salts.

"I'm afraid any buggy I could find would be pretty rough," he said apologetically.

"I would much prefer to ride," she said. "Side-saddle, of course."

He grinned.

"I'll see if I can find one of those contraptions. Don't wear your best gown."

And he was gone, still grinning.

The next day he appeared, leading a fine chestnut horse with a sidesaddle on its back. Melanie, wearing a muslin morning dress and matching sunbonnet, met him at the door.

"Sophie would greet you," she said with a revealing smile, "but she's resting. She's feeling poorly."

He understood perfectly. At the fence, in a most gentlemanly manner, he placed his hands on her waist and hoisted her into the saddle, backing away as soon as he was sure she was safely situated. She hooked her knee over the horn, draped her skirts appropriately, and nodded at him as if to say, "I'm ready."

"I want you to see those flowers," he said as he turned his horse westward, away from the settlement.

Soon they were by themselves, the town a speck in the distance. The flowers, she discovered, were not all yellow but all kinds of colors—there were deep blues and bright reds, a few delicate pinks, but the biggest and boldest were yellow.

"Do they have names?" she asked.

"My mother could have told you," he said with a shrug, "but I can't. Some are Indian names."

At the mention of the word "Indian" she looked around in all directions. They were in totally open land, with only here and there a clump of mesquite or black oak, surely no cover in case of an attack. In the distance, she could see a fork of the Trinity River edging toward Fort Worth, but its banks offered no comforting trees.

"Is it safe to be out here alone?"

"Indians?" he asked. "There's been no trouble here since the army came. Indians are to the west." His eyes turned hard, a look she had seen only briefly once before and found frightening, both then and now. "Sometimes I wish they'd try," he said. "I . . . I . . . well, never mind." He smiled as if to reassure her and then said, "Only thing to worry about here is outlaws, and I can sure to God take care of them. No, you're safe."

She had known all along that she was.

They rode slowly, talking of nothing of consequence and everything of importance. He asked about her home, and she described Georgia and her family—two brothers and a sister, all younger, still at home. She told him she'd come to help Sophie with the baby and then, as though someone else had her tongue, she confessed that she was growing impatient with her sister's complaints and bored with the narrowness of their lives.

"Sometimes," she said, "I just want to ride as far and as fast as I can. Isn't that awful?"

"No," he said. "I've known that feeling a whole lot of late." Then he grinned. "But you can't do it on that saddle."

"Men," she announced, "have all the fun just because they can wear pants."

He chuckled.

"There's a woman or two around here, early settlers they were, that wear pants and ride astride just like a man." He watched for her reaction.

"Why, I'd never!" she gasped. And then, with a slight smile of surprise, she said, "Or maybe I would."

Chapter Ten

Their rides became a regular thing, two or three times a week, except when he was gone. And then he always sent a message to tell her he was leaving town. When they rode, they laughed and were silly in ways that neither of them could be in town when others were around. Once he took her to a plum thicket and helped her load her apron with the juicy fruit. Then they laughed because they had no way of carrying the plums home.

"You put them on the ground," she said, "until I'm mounted, and then I'll make a bowl of my apron again."

"It would be like riding with a lapful of eggs," he said. "One misstep and you would be purple from head to toe."

She laughed aloud again at the picture that drew up in her mind.

Another time they watched fascinated as buzzards circled farther out on the prairie.

"What is it?" she asked.

"Could be anything," he said. "Deer, coyote, probably not a buffalo, but maybe a man. Want to ride out and see?"

She shuddered and shook her head, and he said, "Don't much want to, myself."

Speaks never talked to her about where he had come from, and she knew intuitively not to ask. But he talked a lot about his plans for the future.

"Rich," he said. "I'm gonna be rich. Gonna have a big place somewhere—not in West Texas—and live like a king. Gonna raise a family just like mine was, a lot of kids, teach 'em all how to work."

"How are you going to get all this money?" she asked, eyes alight with merriment. If she had noticed the past tense in reference to his family, she chose to ignore it.

He shrugged.

"Haven't figured that out yet. If they ever put a bounty on Comanche scalps, I'll do it that way." There was that hard look again, the one that frightened her. "Meantime, I'll wait and see. Too late to go to California for gold."

What he didn't know then, of course, was that in the future Texas beeves would become a kind of gold of their own and that was where he would find his fortune. But neither of them had a crystal ball on the prairie.

*   *   *

Sam November would have been amazed by the difference between the laughing, relaxed Lyle Speaks who rode out with Melanie Beaufort and the Lyle Speaks who rode with him after outlaws. Chasing a horse thief or a suspected murderer, Speaks was cold, analytical, all business with never a smile or a joke. When he caught his prey he tended toward cruelty, and November sometimes wondered if Speaks didn't take his deep anger at the Comanches out on outlaws. On one occasion, when a sniveling coward of a stagecoach thief tried to sneak away from their campfire in the night, Speaks shot him once, cleanly, through the head.

"Got what he asked for" was all Speaks said.

"You think that southern lady is going to marry a bounty hunter?" November asked him one night.

"Not going to be a bounty hunter all my life," Speaks said. "Neither are you. We . . . we're headed for something, Sam, I just haven't figured it out yet."

Sam November was always ready to let his friend do the "figuring." He just followed along. But always, he wondered where revenge on the Comanches would fit into the scheme of things.

One day, as Melanie and Speaks were returning from a ride, they met Ben Thompson, coming home after a day's work at the bank.

"Thompson," Speaks said, raising his hat.

"Mr. Speaks," came the reply. "I've been

meaning to talk to you. Melanie, could you leave us for a minute?"

Lyle was off his horse in a second, throwing the reins to Thompson, who looked surprised and somewhat indignant at having to hold the other man's horse. But Speaks was already helping Melanie dismount, his hands around her waist, her hands on his shoulders.

Was it Thompson's imagination or did they stay that way just a fraction of a second too long? And did their eyes really meet and lock for just a minute? Before he could be sure, Melanie was thanking "Mr. Speaks" for the ride, and Mr. Speaks was bowing from the waist—a gesture he was getting better at. Then she opened the gate, went up the dirt path, and vanished into the house.

"My wife," Thompson began, "is upset."

"I heard she is in the family way," Speaks said.

"No, no, that's not it." He wanted to add that even between men such a subject was not politely brought up, but he refrained. "She is upset at this . . . this relationship between you and her sister."

"I'm finding her company delightful," Speaks said, not at all relieving the other man's anxiety. He considered adding that he intended to marry the girl but thought he'd spare this nervous banker that much.

"It's not proper for her to be riding with you unchaperoned," Thompson said, speaking through his nose, as if that gave him authority.

"Well," Speaks said slowly, as though to one

who might have difficulty understanding, "Mrs. Thompson surely can't ride with us. And I can't see that you'd want to take time from the bank to do it. Now, maybe I could ask Sam November . . ."

"That would hardly solve the problem," Thompson said. "I want you to discontinue the rides and stop calling on my sister-in-law."

Speaks was polite, but firm. "I'm afraid I can't do that, banker." With that he raised his hat again, grabbed the reins of Melanie's horse, mounted his own, and rode off, leaving an indignant banker behind him.

The next time he came for Melanie, she appeared wearing a muslin skirt and white shirtwaist.

"You're a mind reader," he said as he helped her mount.

"Why?" she asked. "And why do you have a third horse? Is someone else going with us?"

He chuckled.

"No, but your brother-in-law thinks that would be a good idea. You'll see what I have in mind."

They rode south this time, where the land dipped into culverts and hidden valleys. At a stream he called the Clear Fork of the Trinity, there were trees and shade from the sun, which was now almost summer hot. Carefully, Speaks unrolled a bundle from behind his saddle.

He watched her as he spoke.

"If I turn my back and stand on the other side of the horses, will you put these on?" He unfurled a pair of pants, many sizes too large for her. Then he handed her a length of rope. "For a belt."

She stared at him in disbelief.

"Well," he said, now uncomfortable, "I thought maybe you could ride astride, and then we could race over the prairie like you been wanting to do. If you don't think it's a good idea . . ."

Without hesitation she went to him and took his face in her hands.

"I think it's a wonderful idea," she said. "And the sweetest thing anyone has done for me since . . . I don't know when."

He was tempted—sorely tempted—to kiss her, what with her face just inches from his, but he didn't want to step beyond the boundaries of propriety.

"Get behind the horse and turn your back," she said. "I'll tell you when I'm ready."

"Yes, ma'am."

In minutes she called to him and he walked around the horse to have a look at her. At first it was all he could do to keep from laughing. The pants could have held two of her, and the rope she had knotted through the loops made them pleat so that they were bigger than some of the skirts she wore. The dainty white pleated chemisette she had worn with her skirt looked purely ridiculous on top of the outlandish pants. But not having a mirror in which to see herself, she looked inordinately proud.

He couldn't help it. He laughed, and then he couldn't stop laughing. And then she, looking down at herself, began to laugh. Finally, she had to sit down on the ground, panting. "I . . . I think the next time you should bring me a skirt," she said. "And could you find me a smaller pair of pants?"

"Those are mine," he managed through gasps. "It never occurred to me, but I guess I could go get some pants made for young boys."

"A capital idea!" She stood up, having finally regained her control. "What do we do with my clothes? Just leave them here?"

He nodded. "We'll come back to this spot, and you'll have to change again."

"What if some Indian comes along and decides he wants a muslin skirt and petticoats for his wife?" The idea set her to giggling again.

"You'll have to go home looking like that!" he said, and when he imagined the looks on Ben and Sophie's faces he, too, was off again on hopeless laughter.

Finally, they sobered. Speaks tied the side-saddle horse to a small tree, draped her clothes carefully over a bush, and held a hand for her to mount. She was awkward at first, riding astride, and had to fight the urge to sling her right leg over to the left side of the saddle. But when he slapped her horse's rump with his hat and they rook off across the prairie at a gallop, she shouted with delight.

They rode, the world whirling by them in a blur, until Speaks caught the reins of her horse and slowed them both down.

"The horses," he said, "they're gettin' winded."

"Me too," she panted. "But that was the most

wonderful thing I've ever done. You've given me a gift, and I thank you." And then, with a smile, she added, "Besides, the pants are cooler than all those skirts."

He looked at her, uncertain whether to smile or not. Even Lyle Speaks, untutored man of Texas, knew that women didn't ordinarily talk about their skirts with men to whom they were not married. He changed the subject.

"We'll walk the horses a bit, and then we can ride back to . . . to, ah, your clothes."

"And hope they're still there," she said mischievously.

The clothes were there, and so was the tethered horse. After a last hard ride across the prairie, Melanie was as winded as the horses, and when Speaks reached to help her dismount, she fell into his arms. Without Ben Thompson there to watch they stood that way for a long minute, and then, forgetting his mother's admonitions about the way you treated proper young ladies, Lyle Speaks bent down and kissed Melanie Beaufort. Her lips were cold and still, having never been asked to respond thus before, but then she answered his kiss tentatively . . . and Speaks suspected she might get a lot better at it with practice.

"You best get those clothes on," he said, pulling away. "I'll step over here and turn my back."

When they rode sedately up to the Thompson house, Melanie Beaufort knew that something had happened that would change her life forever. She would never again be the person who had ridden away from this house only hours earlier.

But when Lyle Speaks helped her dismount, he held her properly at a distance. And he said, "I have to go away. I may be gone three weeks or more. I'll be back as soon as I can."

Impishly, she looked up at him. "Will you bring three horses next time?"

He grinned. "I will."

And then he was gone.

Chapter Eleven

Bad things, they say, always happen in threes. Melanie Beaufort came to believe it in early August of that year. Lyle Speaks left for three weeks or more, and that was the first. Then Sophie's overdue baby put in an appearance that involved prolonged labor and much gnashing of teeth and screaming on the part of the new mother. And finally, Melanie received a letter from her own mother.

About Speaks, there was little she could do but worry, and worry she did. He and Sam November were trailing horse thieves to the north, up to what was called "Red River Country." She had only the vaguest idea of what that meant, but she was fairly certain it was also Comanche country.

The realistic part of her mind knew that what

Legend

Speaks did was dangerous and that he just might not come back from any of his trips. But that part of her mind also recognized that he was more capable of self-protection than most and that he and Sam November were an unusual and impressive combination.

The imaginative side of her mind constantly saw Speaks staked out on the prairie—hadn't she read somewhere that Indians did that?—or hanging from a tree limb because the horse thieves had lynched the bounty hunters, instead of the other way around. Indeed, if Lyle Speaks could have been privy to her wildest imaginings, he wouldn't have known whether to laugh at their extreme nature or to be angry at her apparent lack of confidence in his ability to take care of himself. For Melanie, it would be three long weeks and she would spend much of it pacing, albeit sometimes with a crying baby in her arms.

The baby was all reality, and her presence required no wild imaginings, although Melanie suspected that Sophie had suffered through some wild imaginings during the long hours she labored to bring the child into the world. It began late one night, when Sophie complained of indigestion. Melanie wanted to suggest that she had eaten a rather large dinner for one in her delicate condition, but she bit her tongue. Within an hour, indigestion had turned into labor pains.

Melanie had honestly tried to prepare for this moment, for she felt that to be of aid was the whole reason she had suffered through a hellish

113

long trip by steamer and stage from Georgia to Texas. She sent Ben for the doctor, hoping he could be found. And she called for Penny.

"Penny, we must get Mrs. Sophie to bed," she said, her voice calm.

"Lord, Miss Melanie, I don't know nothin' about birthin' babies. When my maw had her babies, she made us young'uns leave the cabin. Sometimes we was gone two days."

Melanie rolled her eyes heavenward, while Sophie continued to moan.

"You don't have to know anything, Penny. Just do what I say. First, put her arm over your shoulders and together we'll get her to the bedroom. Are the linens clean?"

"Yes, ma'am, they are."

Getting Sophie to bed proved more difficult than Melanie had anticipated, for she was limp, deadweight. But at last they had her in bed, dressed in a flannel gown, even though she had wailed for one of her pretty silk gowns.

"I want to look pretty for the baby," she panted between moans.

"Not now, Sophie," Melanie said, realizing she would have to be stern with her sister.

She sent Penny to boil water and bring clean sheets. At home in Georgia when her mother had the younger children Melanie remembered that one of the housemaids had tied ropes to the posters at the foot of the bed and given these to her mother to pull on. Improvising, she pulled draw cords from the bedroom drapes, allowing the drapes to hang limp over the windows, and tied the cords to the rail at the foot of Sophie's iron bedstead.

"Here," she said, "pull on these."

"I haven't the energy," Sophie said, her tone indignant.

"Sophie, you'll have to have the energy or you'll never get that baby out. It won't come out by itself. You'll have to do the work." Her tone was deliberately harsh.

"Why are you so mean to me?" Sophie wailed.

By the time Ben returned with the doctor, Melanie was tearing strips to be used for bandaging or whatever. It seemed to her a logical thing to do, but Ben was indignant.

"These are good linens!" he cried. "What are you doing?"

"I think you have enough bandages," the doctor said mildly. "Might I have a cup of coffee?"

She sent Penny to brew a pot of coffee—"Be sure to put an eggshell in it to settle the grounds!"—and sent the doctor into the room with Sophie. Ben hovered at the door of the bedroom until Melanie suggested that he go out on the porch and see if the night air didn't offer the slightest breeze.

"And leave Sophie?" He was aghast.

"You won't be far, and I'll get you if you're needed." Melanie could see that this would be a long night.

The first loud, piercing scream came about one in the morning, startling Melanie from the rocker where she'd been dozing. Her dream had been of Speaks on the prairie with a broken leg, his horse having spooked and thrown him, his companion having ridden on. She could hear Lyle saying, "No, don't worry about me. You go after them." She was almost relieved that it was only Sophie screaming in childbirth.

Things went on that way through the night. The doctor left, saying he'd be back at daybreak, and that there was nothing to do but give her sips of water and lots of encouragement.

"Urge her to pull on those ropes," he said. "She doesn't seem inclined to help herself."

Melanie spent the night sponging Sophie's forehead and praising her few feeble pulls at the ropes. By daybreak, when the doctor returned, she was more tired than Sophie. The doctor ordered Penny to take her place at the bedside and sent Melanie to sleep, but it was at best a fitful sleep punctuated by Sophie's screams.

By noon, Ben had decided that Sophie was going to die.

"It's my fault," he said. "I should never have . . ." Then he blushed, to think that he was speaking of such intimate matters to an unmarried woman.

Melanie was tempted to put him on the spot by asking, "You should have never done what, Ben?" But she didn't. Instead, she said, "Nonsense. Most women have this much difficulty with the first baby . . . and they say afterwards, with the baby in their arms, that they've forgotten all about the pain."

"Not Sophie," Ben muttered.

By suppertime, even Melanie had begun to worry. Sophie was exhausted and nearly crazy with pain. The doctor had come and gone all day, but when he returned in the evening Melanie asked, "Is there nothing you can do?"

"She's almost there, Miss Beaufort," he said. "She has not . . . ah . . . been the most cooperative patient. And . . ." He hesitated, as though not sure he should finish the sentence, but then he plunged boldly on. "Her extra weight does not make it any easier. I can hardly feel the baby."

Sophie, claiming she was eating for two, had put on more pounds than Melanie cared to think about. She had gone from gentle and round to overwhelmingly fat, and Melanie knew their mother would have had a few things to say about it if she'd seen Sophie.

The baby arrived shortly after dark, a squawling, healthy baby girl with a headful of dark hair. Melanie helped to sponge off the baby and then get Sophie into a clean gown—silk, this time, thank you—and fresh linens, while Penny stood cooing at the tiny handful.

"We done it, missy," she said in a singsong voice. "We done brought you into this world hale and hearty."

Melanie wanted to whirl and say, "What do you mean, 'we'?"

With mother and child clean and in fresh clothes Melanie invited Ben in and shooed the doctor and Penny from the room. Ben stayed no more than five minutes before he came rushing from the room, apparently still uncomfortable about the screams he'd heard. His first, indignant words were directed toward Melanie.

"It looks more like your baby than hers.

Where'd she get all that dark hair? Sophie's blond!"

Melanie gave him a withering look.

"But not everyone in our family is," she said. "Your daughter is beautiful, and I hope you told her mother that."

"Yes, yes, of course I did." Nervously, he went out the door to pace the veranda again.

They named the baby Emily, after Mrs. Beaufort back in Georgia. The doctor had said that Sophie would need to rest a day or two and then could be up and about as long as she did no heavy housework. Melanie wanted to assure him that there was no danger of that! But Sophie seemed to require more rest—days stretched into weeks, and she was too weak to rise from her bed. Ben hovered over her when he was not at the bank, and Penny labored over energy-building meals—fried chicken, mashed potatoes, stew, all the heavy dishes she'd been taught were good for building blood. Melanie was left with Emily, a responsibility she delighted in.

Sometimes Melanie would stand on the veranda, the baby in her arms, and look to the west out over the prairie, as though she'd see Speaks riding in. And she'd imagine him admiring the baby and looking deep into her eyes as though to say he hoped one day they, too, would be the parents of such a beautiful child. But then she'd bring herself up short by remembering that Lyle Speaks was probably not the marrying kind and that the differences between them were as great as a canyon that could not be jumped. And sometimes she'd look at the contented, sleeping baby in her arms and wonder how those two people had ever produced this beautiful, happy child.

"Mean, that's what you are, Melanie Beaufort," she said to herself when those thoughts came unbidden to her mind.

The letter from her mother came the day that Emily was two weeks old, which also happened to be the day that Lyle had been gone three weeks. Melanie knew better than to expect him back punctually on the day he said—his was not work that followed the calendar—but she also knew the longer he was gone, the more she would worry. So she was not in a good frame of mind when she slit open the envelope.

Dear Daughter,

We are anxiously awaiting the news of the arrival of our first grandchild. I know that you will be of great help to your sister, and I am grateful to you for undertaking that long journey to be with her. Ben will, of course, be of comfort to her, but it is not the same as having a woman from your own family with you at that hour of need. I am only sorry that I could not be with Sophie, as by rights I should have been, if that husband of hers had not seen fit to take her off to the wilds of Texas.

You should be grateful, Melanie thought, *that you are not here. Sophie would have embarrassed you—or driven you wild.*

Then the letter got down to brass tacks.

Sophie has written us about your "pre-occupation" with a gentleman from Texas. We are given to understand that you are infatuated with a man who is not your social or educational equal. While I have always had faith in your good judgment, Melanie, I know that sometimes you are given to impetuosity. I expect you to break off this friendship at once and no longer see this man. I am sure there must be suitable men in that place for you to meet. Surely Ben would not have taken Sophie to a total wilderness.

Your father joins me in sending love and wishes me to tell you that he expects you to behave in a way that will do the family credit. By that I mean, of course, no more unchaperoned rides across the prairie with this rough, uncouth Speaks person.

Your loving Mother, E. Beaufort

Melanie held the letter in shaking hands, uncertain whether to laugh or cry, whether to storm into Sophie's sickroom and accuse her of snitching—and slanting the truth—or to ignore it. Knowing that actions taken in haste were often regretted, she slipped the letter into her pocket. But every word was emblazoned on her memory, and she carried those words with her day and night.

Chapter Twelve

Lyle Speaks was not lying dead on the prairie, as Melanie imagined, but neither was he exactly the strong, invincible lawman that even he liked to think of himself as. He and November had tracked the horse thieves in a crisscross pattern across North Central Texas. One day they were headed northwest toward the Panhandle, the next they turned south to Abilene, then east almost back to Fort Worth, then north again just when Speaks thought town and a glimpse of Melanie were possibilities. Everywhere they went they were told stories of missing horses. Sometimes the horses disappeared in the night; sometimes men could point in the direction the thieves had gone. But nobody had gotten a good look at them.

"If they've stolen all these horses—must be

near fifty head by now—why haven't they sold 'em? Where they takin' 'em?" November asked, sipping at a cold cup of coffee early one morning.

Lyle Speaks was about to roll up his blankets, but when Sam spoke he stopped in midmotion.

"Comanches," he said.

November scoffed. "The one thing we know is that it ain't Comanches stealing these horses. Nobody killed. Horses stolen during daylight. And it ain't the Comanche moon yet."

"No," Speaks said patiently, "it's white men, stealing the horses and selling them to the Indians."

"What the Indians got to pay for them with?"

Speaks shrugged. "Who knows? Buffalo hides, stolen good, captives . . . I don't know. But I bet that's where those horses are going."

"Or have gone," November said. "In which case you and I aren't gonna get them, 'cause I ain't raiding no Comanche camp." He favored Speaks with a long, serious look and added, "And neither are you. I'm not lettin' your taste for revenge take my scalp."

Speaks grinned ever so briefly.

"I got good reason not to lose my scalp, no matter how much I want to kill a few Comanches. I won't be foolish, Sam."

"Good" was the reply.

"But we got to think where they're goin', track 'em, and get them before they get to the Indians."

"We been tryin' to do that!" Sam exploded.

"We weren't lookin' for a big herd. That changes things."

November agreed that it did, and the two set out following the latest direction that had been pointed out to them. At Speaks's suggestion they fanned out over an almost five-mile path, agreeing that the first man to find sign would fire his pistol once. It was November who fired, about midday.

"Headed toward the Red River," he said when Speaks rode up.

Lyle shook his head.

"Damn! We're already been there twice." Then, "Let's go!"

There were, far as they could tell, three men herding the horses, and they were moving slowly, probably so as not to lose any animals. The trail was fresh, and Speaks judged finally that they were less than three miles behind their quarry.

"Let's wait till dark," he said, and so they settled down in a clump of trees by a fresh water spring. November napped, but Speaks was too wound up to sleep. Always, in the back of his mind, was the thought that he'd been gone longer than the three weeks he told Melanie. And some unknown instinct told him that something was wrong.

It wasn't even true dark yet when he nudged November with his toe and said, "Let's move."

They rode slowly, silently, until they could see a fire glowing in the distance.

"Damn fools," November said. "They don't even have the smarts to make a cold camp."

123

"If you were that smart," Speaks said, "would you be stealing horses in a country where that might likely mean a lynching?"

November laughed.

Within yards of the fire they ground-reined their horses and, shotguns in hand, crept toward the fire. Three men lounged around it, and from the sound of their talk, they'd indulged in a bit of whiskey.

At Speaks's signal he and November peppered the air with shotgun blasts and then commanded, "Throw out your rifles and stand by the fire with your hands in the air."

The "damn fools" did everything except what they were told. Grabbing shotguns, they fired wildly into the darkness beyond the circle of the fire's light. Speaks and November returned the fire, and by the time it was over, two horse thieves lay dead and the third was badly wounded. As the two bounty hunters walked toward their fallen prey, they could hear the nervous whinnying of horses—a lot of horses— nearby. They found the horses in a rope corral, so frantic they were about to break out. It took Speaks and November a good hour to calm the spooked animals.

"Now what are we gonna do with the horses?" November asked.

"Guess we're gonna herd 'em back to Fort Worth and send word out to the owners," Speaks said.

"I'm just glad I don't have to personally deliver 'em," November said.

The third outlaw, gunshot, would not live

long. He knew it and they did, and he lost nothing by admitting they were taking the horses to a band of Comanches, supposed to meet them across the Red River in two days' time.

November forestalled what he feared would come.

"I'm not gonna take on the Comanche nation," he said. "I hired on to find horse thieves, and I've done that. No more. Period."

To his dying day Speaks believed that he could have convinced November if he himself had truly wanted to go after the Indians. But he didn't. He wanted to go back to Fort Worth—and Melanie. He simply nodded at November.

They made a travois out of logs and a blanket for the wounded man and tied the other two across two horses, which they carefully led by a rope. They loosed the rest of the animals.

The wounded man died about halfway to Fort Worth and they abandoned the travois, which slowed them down, in favor of tying him to a horse.

And that was how Lyle Speaks returned to Fort Worth: corralling a herd of fifty horses and packing three dead men on led horses.

"You want to go in another way, so you don't go by her house?" November asked at one point.

"Nope. I ain't puttin' on any pretenses."

And Melanie Beaufort saw Lyle Speaks return to town, and all that registered in her mind was that there were three dead men draped across the backs of three horses. She fingered her mother's letter in her pocket.

*   *   *

He sent word that day that he would come for her in the evening, being as the days were so hot now. When he arrived, he had only two horses.

Melanie, carefully dressed in a muslin skirt and the plainest shirt she owned, threw propriety to the winds and met him at the gate.

"You only have two horses!" she accused.

He laughed aloud.

"I'm glad you missed me, too!" Then, more seriously: "I decided it was silly to have three horses for two people. I've got a plan."

She believed him, and they were soon cantering out of sight of the town. As they rode she told him all about Emily's arrival, and she spared nothing about what she saw as Sophie's weaknesses.

"You won't be like that?" he asked.

"You bet I won't," she said. "Mama always said doctors and midwives are scornful of women who scream."

He chewed on that thought and liked what he heard from her.

When they reached "their spot" on the Trinity he handed her pants and a loose shirt and walked around the horses.

Once changed, she demanded, "Do I have to ride sidesaddle dressed like this?"

"No, I'm gonna ride bareback and you can ride my horse."

She smiled at him and, without even thinking about it, walked into his arms. He kissed her gently, then pushed her away. Lyle Speaks was a man who knew about propriety . . . and understood that if he hadn't stopped her, things could easily have gotten out of hand right here on the prairie.

They rode fast and hard for only a mile or two, and then she pulled her horse to a stop.

"I want to sit," she said.

Obligingly, he helped her dismount, ground-reined the horses, and put the saddle blanket from his horse on the ground.

"Don't want to sit on ants," he said.

"I've had a letter from my mother," she told him. "She's as much as ordered me to stop seeing you."

"Does she have some kind of second sight?" he asked. "I mean, all the way from Georgia?"

"Sophie wrote her, the snitch!"

He laughed.

"I bet Ben Thompson put her up to it. I'd pull my money out of his bank if there was another bank in town."

"I don't know what to do," she said.

His hand reached to cover hers.

"Well, you have two choices. You can stop seeing me, or you can keep on riding the prairies with me."

"It's not that simple," she replied, averting her eyes from his. "I saw you come in yesterday . . ."

"And you know we killed three men." He said it flatly, without looking at her. "I do my job. I'm paid to bring men back dead or alive. I'd rather bring them in alive, but I'm not going to risk my neck—or Sam's—to save some outlaw. Men who break the law make a deliberate choice—they know the risks. If I didn't go after them, someone else would. And if nobody did, Melanie, we couldn't live in this land."

"But couldn't you . . ." She almost smiled. "Couldn't you be a banker or something where you didn't have to kill?"

"Nope. It's not my nature."

He wondered if now was the time to tell her about how he'd lost his family, as though that would, in some way, explain the anger that almost forced him to do what he did. But Speaks wasn't used to confiding, and he particularly didn't want to talk about that day twelve years before. Instead, he asked curiously, "Do they ever kill men in Georgia?"

"Not the people I know!" she said indignantly.

"I bet you'd be surprised," he said. "What about whipping slaves? Is it worse to kill an outlaw than to whip an innocent slave?"

She grinned at him.

"Why do you presume the slave is innocent? They're people. They do bad things."

"What an admission of guilt from a southern girl!" he said slowly. "Slaves are people. Do I take it you don't approve of slavery?"

"It's not a question of approving or disapproving," she said slowly. "It's the way of life in Georgia . . . and always will be."

"Then you've not been keeping up with the news," he said. "And I suspect you've not read *Uncle Tom's Cabin*."

"That awful book," she exclaimed. "I wasn't allowed to read it. Have you?"

"No, but I'll get you a copy," he promised. "The North is up in arms about this slavery business, and I'm afraid there's more power up north than in the South. I'm no politician, but I think they'll go to war."

"They? Isn't it your country, too?"

"Naw," he said with a laugh. "I'm in Texas. That war won't touch us out here."

"You wouldn't fight?"

"Texas will need to take care of its own problems if war comes. Think about the Indians, for instance. If the army pulls its soldiers back east to fight, the Comanches will try to take over this country again."

"And you'd fight the Indians but not the Yankees?"

"Reckon so," he said.

It was a loyalty—or lack of loyalty—that she couldn't and wouldn't understand. To her, the South was her home and demanded allegiance. Texas was . . . well, frontier, not a country. How could one be loyal to Texas? She stood up abruptly. "Let's ride." It was almost an order.

She set the pace, riding so hard and fast that Lyle Speaks began to wonder about the wisdom of his bareback ride. But he kept up with her, afraid to let her go farther on her own, and at last, as winded as her horse, she pulled to a stop.

"I feel better now," she said triumphantly.

"I'm glad." He would never have admitted that he felt a lot worse.

They walked their horses back to the spot on the river, talking about nothing serious, avoiding her mother's letter, his killing of the outlaws, even the possibility of war. She told him

about the baby and how spoiled Sophie was—
"I don't know how she'll manage when I go back."

"Do you want to stay?" he asked.

She shrugged. "I don't know."

Speaks was the first to spot trouble. Melanie's skirt was not hanging on the bush where they'd left it. He looked around to make sure he had the right spot, but it was his business to note signs like bushes and trees, and he had little doubt about which bush was which. Without a word to her he pushed his horse into a fast trot. The sidesaddle was gone too.

Melanie approached to find him dismounted and doubled over in laughter.

"Whatever is the matter with you?" she asked. Her attention was so riveted on him that she hadn't noticed her clothes were missing.

When he finally straightened up and calmed himself he said, "I'm picturing you riding into town that way."

"This way? Why?" Only then did she look around. "My clothes! They're gone!"

"So's the blasted sidesaddle, and I bet the livery will charge me a pretty penny for that," he said.

She slid off the horse, took one look at him, and began to laugh, herself. Finally, choking, she sputtered, "Sophie! She'll die of embarrassment."

Lyle Speaks knew at that moment that he loved her. Any other woman would have been furious and would have likely turned that fury on him. Furthermore, most women would have thought of their own embarrassment. She didn't seem to give a fig about what people would think of her.

"We can wait till dark to go in," he suggested.

She began to giggle again.

"Then Sophie will think we've been killed by Indians, so she'll have two reasons to be angry—because we made her worry and because I'm a disgrace to the family."

Neither of them knew how it happened, but the next instant she was in his arms and he was kissing her gently on the forehead, the tip of her nose, and finally on the mouth. His gentle kiss turned to one of real longing and passion, and she responded much more than she had during their one brief kiss before. Wordlessly, they sank to the ground, locked together.

It was Speaks who stood up.

"I don't think we'll wait for dark," he said.

Over the years he and November had visited more than once with the "soiled doves" in various West Texas towns, but he had never known the desire that raced through him now. It frightened him—for himself and for her.

Equally shaken, although less understanding of what had happened, she remained sitting on the ground.

"You know those two choices you gave me before?"

He nodded.

"I know which one I want."

He drew his breath and waited.

"I want to keep riding with you."

Exhaling slowly, he said, "I'm glad." And almost added, "And I want to marry you." He didn't know what made him afraid to say the words, but he was. It was as though she were a doe that would spook easily. Instead, he said, "Well, damn, I guess I'll just have to find another sidesaddle."

She rode proudly into town, head high, slid off her horse at the fence, and handed him the reins, letting her hand linger in his just a moment. Then, with a wry smile, she headed for the door, calling over her shoulder, "I'll return the pants tomorrow."

The lace curtain moved back into place.

Sophie waited, her hands planted on her hips. In another part of the house the baby wailed loudly. Before Sophie could attack, Melanie said, "What's the matter with Emily? Why aren't you seeing to her?"

"Don't tell me how to take care of my child, Melanie Beaufort. You're a disgrace to this family."

"I knew you'd say that, and I don't want to hear it," Melanie said. "Nor will I tell you why I happen to be wearing a pair of men's pants." She stormed out of the room, leaving her sister behind, babbling to herself. But Melanie heard the words "Wait till Ben comes home!" and resisted the urge to ask, "Why, will he spank me?"

Chapter Thirteen

That night, while Lyle Speaks lay on his bunk, hands behind his head, eyes fixed vacantly on the ceiling above him, Sam November went to Steele's Tavern. When he came back two hours later, smelling of whiskey, he shook Speaks awake.

"Man, you've done it now," he said, his voice full of laughter. "Everyone's talkin' about how you brought that southern girl home wearing pants. Lyle Speaks, is there something you ain't telling me?"

Speaks sat up.

"They're talkin' about it? Who?" He reached for his boots.

"No, no," November said. "You'll go to defend her honor against a bunch of drunks. And I'm too drunk to help you."

"She's too good for the likes of them to talk about." Then Speaks's face reddened. "Besides, it was all very innocent."

"You need to go to Miss Sadie's?" November asked.

Lyle threw a boot at him.

The next morning, dressed in his newest breeches and a freshly laundered shirt, his hair clean and plastered to his head, Lyle Speaks rode up to the Thompson residence. For once in his life he wished he owned a suit like the ones banker Thompson wore to work every day.

Sophie opened the door when he knocked.

"You're not welcome here," she said.

He wondered how two sisters could be so different in looks and temperament. Politely, he said, "I came to see Miss Melanie."

"Miss Melanie is busy tending the baby," Sophie hissed.

Melanie disproved her words by appearing behind her.

"Mr. Speaks," she said formally. "May I help you?"

"Yes, ma'am, I came to talk with you, if I might . . . in private."

"Mr. Thompson has ordered me not to allow you in this house after you disgraced my sister," Sophie said, her voice rising in agitation.

He almost bowed.

"Then perhaps we can speak on the veranda. Mrs. Thompson, I have come to make amends for embarrassing your sister. It's the last thing in the world I wanted to do." He hated himself for fawning over this bothersome young woman.

"Fiddle, Sophie! If anyone's embarrassed, it's you. It didn't bother me a bit. Now go and see to Emily, and I'll speak to Ly—Mr. Speaks."

She stepped out onto the veranda and pulled the door firmly shut behind her. Then, looking at him, she had to cover her mouth to keep from laughing.

"Isn't she foolish?" she asked.

To her surprise he didn't even smile in response. Instead, looking down at the hat he held in his hands—she noticed his still-wet hair—he said, "I came, Melanie, to ask if you would marry me."

Taken completely by surprise, she leaned against the veranda railing for support. Finally, weakly, she muttered, "I don't think that's what Mother had in mind in her letter."

"Do you mean that your family would never give permission for you to marry me . . . or for me to court you?"

"I guess that's what I mean." She wanted to throw herself into his arms, tell him she didn't care about her family, beg him to take her away right then. But she stood rooted to the floor.

"And you need their approval, their permission?" He spoke formally.

"I don't know," she said slowly. "May I have time to think about it?"

"Of course." He, too, felt the strangeness of their situation. He wanted to hold her, laugh with her as he had done on the prairie. Instead, he stood before her, feeling like a wooden doll. A speechless wooden doll.

He inclined his head just a little—the best he could do toward a bow at the moment—and bid her good day, ramming his hat back on his head as he went toward his horse. Although she stared after him, he never looked back.

"Well," Sophie said when Melanie went inside, "I certainly hope you told him you'd never see him again."

"I think," Melanie said, "that I will probably marry him."

"Marry him?" her sister screeched. "You can't!"

"I can." She wanted to add, "He's a lot better than the fool you married," but she kept that thought to herself.

She sent him a message with the simple word "yes," and her name. He came, dressed in his finest and still wishing for a suit. They sat in the parlor, like strangers.

"I guess I'll have to go to Georgia," he said.

"Why?" She was appalled at the thought. It conjured up visions she'd rather not contemplate. Mostly visions of her mother, who could be as uppity as Sophie.

"To meet your parents, and ask your father's permission."

"Ah, I didn't think we'd do all that. I thought . . . well, maybe I presumed . . . but couldn't we just get married here?"

"I don't think that would be proper," he said. He was remembering his mother and imagining what she would have said to him. The one thing she never would have said was that this girl was too good for him, and that thought never occurred to Lyle Speaks. She was different, he knew that, but they could overcome differences. He didn't know, as she did, that her parents would find him wanting in education, in social graces, and in future prospects.

"Well," she said, rising impatiently, "I'm not to go until October, and it's only August now." Then she exploded. "Lyle Speaks, I don't want to sit in the parlor and speak formally with you! I want to ride and laugh and be like we've always been. Marriage comes up and look what happens!"

He was startled at first, and then began to laugh. Standing, he grabbed her hands and whirled her around the room.

"Will you be ready to ride tomorrow?"

"Will you have a sidesaddle?"

"Yes," he promised. And wondered why he felt apprehensive.

She wondered why she felt sad.

They rode on the prairie almost every day. Sometimes when they left Sophie stood on the veranda, her arms folded across her chest in a belligerent way, staring stonily after them.

"What's the old saying," Speaks asked, "about if looks could kill?"

"We'd wither like prairie grass in the summer heat," she said.

"You're starting to talk like a Texan." He laughed. "That's good."

"Is it?" she said, genuinely puzzled. She never

intended to talk like most of the Texans she'd met.

Other times they'd arrive home near dusk to find Ben Thompson sitting in the rocker, pushing it back and forth with one foot, his fingers drumming impatiently on one of the chair's arms. Once he saw them, he'd rise and enter the house without ever having spoken a word to either of them.

They'd become accustomed to their routine. Speaks brought "her" pants—a smaller boy's pair—and a cotton shirt for her, and he turned his back in a gentlemanly fashion while she changed, though he had to fight back the waves of longing that washed over him. They never did find out what happened to the stolen clothes and sidesaddle, but now they were simply more careful about hiding things. They found a plum thicket that did nicely for that purpose.

By late afternoon, now that it was September, the air had cooled, and sometimes there was enough of a breeze to ruffle Melanie's hair as she rode. They had survived the beating sun and ferocious heat of the Texas summer, but in spite of the bonnet she had worn faithfully, her face had tanned. Lyle thought she glowed with a look of health and happiness, and he told her so, in words that made her blush and look away. She thought he looked handsome as always, but she was embarrassed to tell him . . . or didn't know how.

"Next summer," she said, "I want a hat like yours."

"You'll have it," he promised.

Sometimes they rode without talking, letting the horses amble along companionably; other times they raced across the prairie, chasing each other and shouting like wild Indians. Well, at least Melanie thought they sounded like Indians. Speaks never would have made that comparison. Other times, they ground-reined the horses and watched the sky change as the sun went down and light clouds trailed across the sky.

They never talked of serious things like marriage, for they found the subject made them both speechless. Once he felt obliged to tell her about his family. He didn't tell her it was something she had to know if she married him. Instead he just said, in his blunt way, "My family was massacred by Comanches. My mother and father and one brother scalped; my sister . . . well, she was terrorized before she was killed. I saved my little brother."

She knew what he meant by "terrorized," and she knew that what he had just told her explained the hard look he sometimes got in his eyes, the look that had puzzled her all along. But it left her speechless. "I'm sorry" seemed empty and trite, though she did lay a hand on his arm and say it.

He shrugged.

"I've learned to live with it."

And then she knew he hadn't. She couldn't say, "How awful," nor could she tell him that now she had two visions in her head that would not leave: one of a family she'd never seen, lying scalped in the yard of a house she'd never seen;

the other of three dead men across the backs of three horses.

One day, as they walked their horses toward home, he said, "In October I'll go east with you. Speak to your father."

"I guess so," she said.

"You don't sound like you put much stock in the idea." He stared straight ahead, as though afraid to look at her. Maybe, if he looked at her eyes, he'd see that she didn't love him.

"I . . . I can't imagine it," she said. "Oh, Lyle, there's so much I can't imagine."

"You don't have to imagine anything," he said. "You just let what's going to happen come."

She shook her head.

"I always have it planned out before . . . and I always know if it's going to work or not."

His voice almost broke as he said, "And this isn't going to work?"

"I don't know," she said miserably.

Two days later she received a letter written in her father's bold, scrawling hand:

Dear Daughter,
    Your mother is ill. You are needed at home. Please come at once.
                                    Your Father,
                                    William P. Beaufort

When Lyle came for their ride she tucked the letter in her pocket and went to meet him with her usual smile on her face.

When she had changed into her pants, she came around the horse, grabbed his arm, and reached up to kiss him, a light, teasing kiss.

"What's that for?" he asked, obviously pleased.

"For being you, because I love you," she said. And then, without waiting for his help, she was ahorseback—a trick she'd learned over the summer.

"I'll beat you to that far tree!" And she was off, leaving him to leap into the saddle and gallop after her. She beat him, a triumph that set her to laughing.

"You're sure full of yourself today," he said.

"I have to be . . . or I'll cry." She had put the letter into her pants pocket when she changed, and now she fished it out and handed it to him.

He read, then looked at her. "You'll go?"

"I have to."

"And it's not a good time for me to go with you."

She shook her head to say no. Then: "I'll come back."

But they both knew at that moment that she would never come back to Texas.

Speaks drove her to the stagecoach. When she walked out of the Thompson house, Sophie followed, wringing her hands.

"Poor, dear Mother, whatever can it be?"

"Serious, if Papa wrote me," Melanie said shortly. "Try to take good care of Emily, Sophie."

"She's my daughter!" was the indignant reply.

To Ben, Melanie said briefly, "Thank you for your hospitality." The words were so formal they almost conveyed her distaste.

She hugged Sophie quickly and felt a pang over the distance that had come between sisters once close. Then she turned and walked around the wagon, where Speaks waited to help her up. He had already thrown her baggage behind the seat. When they drove away she never looked back. Melanie Beaufort was wondering if her mother was really sick or if she, herself, had been caught in—or rescued by?—a trap of Sophie's making. She would only know when she got to Georgia, and she couldn't risk calling Sophie's bluff in case her mother really needed her.

"I'll let you know what's wrong with Mother and when I'm coming back," she said to Speaks, and he replied, "I'll be waiting." Then he kissed her lightly on the forehead and handed her into the stagecoach. He drove off in the wagon before the driver cracked the whip over the team.

"Let's go. We're movin' on." Lyle Speaks charged into the room he shared with Sam November.

Caught napping after an afternoon beer or two, November struggled awake. Sitting up and rubbing his eyes groggily, he echoed, "Movin' on?"

"That's what I said. I told you we weren't going to be bounty hunters forever."

"What about Melanie?" November asked before he thought, and the minute the words were out he would have done almost anything to take them back.

Speaks's jaw tightened and his eyes took on that hard look that November knew better than Melanie did.

"Never would work out. We're too different."

"I hope she's not heartbroken," November said.

"She's not."

Lyle Speaks didn't believe in heartbreak, but this was the second terrible wound to his soul that he would carry the rest of his life.

They rode north at dusk, in spite of Sam's timid suggestion that they wait till morning. Speaks was determined to go then, though he didn't say where.

"Where we goin'?" November asked.

Speaks shrugged.

Sam November just sighed and prepared to follow his friend.

Sophie and Ben Thompson were among the many for whom life in Texas was too much. Within a year they returned to Georgia. With them gone and Lyle Speaks gone north, there was no one in Fort Worth who remembered Melanie Beaufort. But folks talked for a long time, and children heard the story of the wild lady from Georgia who rode astride in men's pants.

Chapter Fourteen

Montana, 1901

When they woke the next morning Speaks had made one last pot of coffee.

"Cold camp from now on," he reminded Fellows, who wrote it down.

"Are you gonna write down everything we say?" November asked.

Fellows looked bewildered by the question.

"I want to get it all right."

November looked at Speaks, who shrugged. He was surprised he could shrug. When November woke him for his watch he was sore from lying on the ground, but during the hours of his watch his muscles had relaxed. His body had not forgotten all those years of being on the trail.

When they finished their coffee they broke camp and started following the trail again.

"How do these men expect to get away with stealing your horses and killing your men," Fellows asked, "if their trail is so easy to follow?"

November looked disgusted and said, "We've been wondering the same thing. They've been working the area for months, hitting different ranches, and the law hasn't been able to find them."

"Why not?"

"Well, partly," Speaks said, "because they try to track them in automobiles. It can't be done."

"This is the only way it can be done," November said.

"On horseback," Speaks said.

"By somebody who knows what they're doin'." November looked at Speaks. "It's nice to see you back in the saddle again."

"You haven't been riding?" Fellows asked.

Speaks scowled.

"When he turned seventy," November said, "Clytie started getting after him to take it easy. That meant stayin' at home more, doin' the paperwork, and lettin' others take over the day-to-day running of the ranch."

"I thought you were the foreman."

"I am," November said, "but that never stopped Lyle, here, from gettin' on a horse."

"And what about you?" Fellows asked. "Aren't you seventy?"

"Seventy-six," November said, "but I never got married."

"What does that have to do with anything?"

145

"Sam has a theory," Speaks said. "He thinks men who get married age faster."

"And you've been married fifteen years."

"Right."

"So if his theory is correct, you're actually older than he is."

November smiled and said, "In theory."

Several hours later, November was off his horse, studying the ground.

"Chilito is still on their trail."

"How can you tell the difference in the tracks?" Fellow asked.

"Well," November said, "first of all the fifty head that were stolen aren't shod. It looks to me like there are about five or six shod horses leavin' tracks."

"And one of them would be your Chilito?"

"Right."

"How can you tell which one?"

"Chilito rides a small mustang," November said. "Small but fast, and durable. Its tracks are distinctive."

"So that leaves five rustlers?"

"Murderers," Speaks said.

"And it's just the two of you, and Chilito?"

November mounted up, looked at the writer, and said, "And you."

"That's why we gave you a gun," Speaks said.

"You mean," Fellows asked, "you expect me to . . . shoot somebody?"

"Only if you want to stay alive," November said, and gave his horse a gentle kick to get it going.

"Is he serious?" the writer asked Speaks.

"Very."

"But . . . I'm a writer."

"You got to pull your weight, son," Speaks said. "Did you think this was gonna be easy? Just ride along and write some stuff down?"

"Well . . . I thought I'd be . . . sort of . . . an observer."

"When we catch up to those killers," Speaks said, "it ain't gonna mean a thing to them if you say you're an observer."

"I—I guess I didn't think about it . . . enough."

"I guess you didn't," Speaks said.

"Perhaps we should have waited for the sheriff and his posse."

"They'll be along . . . sometime."

"I could . . . go back."

"You'd never find your way."

"You wouldn't take me?"

Speaks shook his head.

"We'd lose the trail."

"But—"

"Besides," Speaks said, "we do have more stories to tell you."

That brightened the younger man's face.

"Like what?"

"I don't know," Speaks said. "I haven't yet decided what should come next. I'll think of something by tonight, though."

"Tonight?"

"When we camp," Speaks said. "You'll need somethin' to keep your mind off the cold."

They camped the second night and Speaks handed out some dried meat Clytie had packed for them. They washed it down with water from their canteens.

"How you holdin' up, old-timer?" November asked Speaks. The affection in his tone belied the words he chose to use.

"I tell you, Sam," Speaks said, "it's like I was never out of the saddle."

"And your bones ain't rattlin' apart?"

"No."

"Clytie ain't gonna be happy to hear that."

"Why not?"

" 'Cause now that you know you won't fall apart she won't be able to keep you out of the saddle anymore, partner."

"Are you two partners?" Fellows asked.

They both looked at him, wrapped in his blanket with his notebook in his lap.

"Only for a lot of years," November said.

"No," Fellows said, "I mean in the ranch. I mean, I understood the ranch belonged to Mr. and Mrs. Speaks."

"It does," November said.

"But . . . weren't you a partner when you first started it?"

"I was."

"Then . . . what happened?"

Before November could answer, Speaks said, "If we tell you that story, we'll be gettin' ahead of ourselves."

"Then what story will you tell next?" Fellows asked.

Speaks looked at November.

148

"I'll take the first watch this time and talk to the young man."

"Suit yourself," November said, rolling himself up in his blanket. "Just don't tell him about that time we was gonna be buffalo hunters."

"Why not?" Fellows asked. He was looking at November, who turned over and gave the writer his back. "Why not?" Fellows asked again, turning his attention to Speaks.

"It wasn't our greatest hour," he said.

"If you want this story to be the truth," Fellows said, "you'll have to tell the good with the bad . . . won't you?"

Speaks thought a moment, then said, "Well, since bigmouth brought it up . . ."

Part Three

Part Three

Chapter Fifteen

Detroit, Kansas, 1868

"Why Abilene?" asked November.

"We're almost out of money, in case you didn't notice," Speaks said. "Somebody's bound to be hiring in a town that size. Anyway, I like the name."

"You can't put much store in the name of a place. Look at Detroit."

In truth, both men would have had to turn their heads to look at the tiny log hamlet through which they had ridden in less time than it took to describe it. Changing its name from Smoky Hill hadn't seemed to do much for its prosperity.

They followed Turkey Creek up to the Kansas Pacific Railroad. Sam November held his tongue as they coaxed their lathered mounts down Texas Street, but aside from its name there didn't seem to be anything in Abilene to separate it from any other town this side of the Missouri. Bigger than most, yes, thanks to the booming cattle trade, and still growing in a wheeze and clatter of saws and hammers, but generally speaking it was the same mix of mercantiles, feed stores, manure-smelling stockpens, and saloons, with the same loafers lolling about the porches, bumming smokes from one another and telling lies. If it weren't for his thirst and his sore backside, he would think they were still in Topeka.

They gave the liveryman, a solemn Negro with deep pockmarks on his face as if a mess of buckshot had been dug out of it, their last five-dollar gold piece to rub down and feed their horses and stepped into the Chinese baths to soak the alkali out of their hides. Afterward, waiting his turn in the chair at the Great Plains Tonsorial Palace across from the turrets and gables of the Drovers' Cottage, November paged through a week-old copy of the *Abilene Chronicle*.

"Here's somebody hiring." He raised his voice so Speaks could hear him through the heated towel covering his face. "Only, it ain't around here."

Speaks waited until the fussy little Italian barber unwound the towel before he replied.

"If it's Mexico, forget it. I ain't in the mood to fight in no more revolutions after Lone Jack."

"I reckon you ain't in a mood to ride up to

154

Nebraska, then. There's a senator getting up a party to hunt buffalo. They must be shy of sharpshooters in that country. He's took out a half-page advertisement offering five hundred apiece for the winter season."

"Dollars?" Speaks sat up, lifting a hand. The barber stopped lathering.

"That's what it says. He's only offering skinners a hundred. That's hard work. Even a dead buff don't give up its hide without a fight."

"And you say he's a senator?"

" 'The Honorable Cicero Philarope, United States Senate, retired.' He's hiring till the first of December."

"Where?"

"Someplace called Julesburg."

"That's a fair piece to ride. When we get through in here we won't have nothing left for a stake."

"Signori, I am told they need bartenders at the Alamo Saloon," the barber said.

"What are they paying?" Speaks asked.

"If I were you, *signori,* I would not sell myself cheap. The two bartenders they had were shot for slow service."

"Dead?"

"Just one. The other recovered and took the train to St. Louis."

"This place needs us," Speaks told November.

The Alamo boasted the longest bar between Chicago and San Francisco: forty feet of paneled mahogany with an Italian marble top. The beer pulls were solid brass, and a nude painting

155

of Napoleon's sister reclined in a gilt frame above the back bar. When on the third day of their tenure a young cowboy with Shanghai Pierce's crew hauled down on Speaks with a Starr double-action for pouring his beer with too much foam, November cracked open the man's skull from behind with a two-foot length of pool cue. One week later, Pierce himself stamped in with his *segundo* and a half-Cherokee wrangler said to be wanted in the Indian Nations for murder and rape to get a look at the "two Texas sons of bitches who cost me a top hand." Without hesitating, Speaks swept off the half-breed's hat, grabbed a fistful of unshorn hair, and slammed his face down onto the marble bar, breaking his nose and knocking out most of his teeth. When the *segundo* went for his belt gun November swung up the sawed-off from under the bar and blew off the man's left ear. Pierce helped his bleeding companions outside and never came back. The Alamo was taking too many of his men.

After that things got downright dull. At the end of six weeks the partners had earned enough for an outfit and left Abilene without regret.

Their first night on the trail they camped out on the Republican, where November watered the horses while Speaks went looking for firewood. When a band of former guerrillas on the run from a posse in Mankato surrounded November, announcing loudly their intention to kill him for the horses and provisions, Speaks stretched out on his belly on a ridge with a good view of the river, picked off two of them with his Winchester, and wounded a third before the rest wheeled their mounts and galloped east.

"You all of a piece?" asked Speaks upon rejoining his partner.

November, who had dived into the Republican to avoid getting caught in a cross fire, sat down on the bank to pull off his boots and wring out his socks.

"Next time, *you* water the horses."

On a hunch, they carried the bodies into Mankato, where the towheaded marshal identified them as two of the men who had stuck up the local express office, and informed the newcomers they had a two-hundred-dollar reward coming.

"There's another three hundred in it if you'll round up the rest," said the lawman. "The suetbellied posse I put together ran clean out of civic indignation five miles out of town."

Speaks said, "That's your wagon, Marshal. We're on our way to Nebraska to shoot buffalo."

"I can't believe a couple of men like you will stay satisfied with that. Buffalo don't shoot back."

"We done our share of hunting men. Now we're on the scout for something we ain't done."

"Well, good luck to you."

"Don't need it," November said. "I got Lyle and he's got me."

Speaks said, "I think we're in Nebraska."

November had been in a black mood for hours. They had crossed the snow line the night before, but the wind was blowing so hard none of it stayed on the ground, and with nary a tree nor a building nor a respectable hill in sight, there was nothing to stop it between them and Canada. When the wind gusted, frozen crystals struck his face like fistfuls of gravel and burned like sparks; or they did until his face numbed over, becoming a wax mask. He thought of lighting a fire in his belly with a pull from the bottle he'd bought in Mankato, but he was frozen so stiff he was afraid if he moved his arm to scoop the bottle out of his saddle pouch it would snap clean off.

"How can you tell?" he demanded. "This whole country is flat as a schoolteacher's chest. I ain't seen a tree in a week. Why they bothered to divide it up at all is a riddle to me."

"The air smells different. I got a nose for these things."

"Let me know as soon as you smell Dakota. The Badlands can't be worse than this."

Suddenly, Speaks's bay gelding let out a sharp snort and threw up its head. Speaks patted its sleek neck.

"Old Leviticus says we're about to have company. Maybe they can tell us where we are."

"If it's Injuns we'll know already: up Hell's Creek without a pole or a paddle."

"That's why I ride with you, Sam. Anytime I get to feeling too sunny I can always count on you for a gully-washer."

"I thought maybe it was because if I wasn't standin' behind you everybody would see that big ol' target painted on your back."

They were still following this line of conversation when the first of a column of riders came out of the gray overcast on the horizon. November guessed right away they were neither Indian nor road agents, unless the northern variety paid heed to the Manual of Arms. In a little while they spotted the swallowtail guidons snapping above the riders' heads, and then the white gauntlets of the U.S. Cavalry. The "Company halt" command reached them, warped by the wind. Speaks and November drew rein as well. After a space, a pair of horsemen peeled off from the column and approached them at a canter.

"Skinny one's a general," November said as the gap closed.

"Colonel, more like," said Speaks. "Generals don't go out to pick blueberries with anything less than a hundred men."

"That was just during the Rebellion. Things ain't so starchy here on the plains. I got a Morgan dollar says he's a brigadier at least."

"I'll take that bet. I can't read them collar gewgaws any better than you."

The riders stopped twenty paces short of where Speaks and November sat waiting. One was a ruddy-faced old campaigner with gray muttonchop whiskers in a kepi cap. His companion, gaunt and rifle-backed, wore black handlebars trimmed to lethal points. The brim of his fawn campaign hat was turned up on one side and pinned to the crown with crossed sabers.

"Good afternoon, gentlemen," said the gaunt

159

one. "Captain Netherwall, Company F, Fifth Cavalry, at your service. This is my aide, Sergeant Snyder."

November produced his poke, fished out a silver dollar, and handed it to Speaks.

"What can we do for you, Captain?" asked Speaks after he'd introduced himself and November.

"We're looking for a band of Northern Cheyenne that broke loose of the reservation in Colorado last month. They're dog soldiers, the worst. If you came up from Kansas, you might have seen them."

"We come up from Kansas, but we ain't seen any Injuns. I reckon you're saying we're in Nebraska. Sam and I was discussin' that when you showed up."

"You've been in Nebraska all morning. Where are you headed?"

"Julesburg."

"Are you buffalo hunters?"

"We aim to be."

"I hope your aim's better than your direction. Julesburg's in Colorado."

"Advertisement in the newspaper said it was Nebraska," November said.

"You hunt in Nebraska. You outfit in Colorado. Keep heading the way you're headed till you come to the Platte River, then follow the Platte west. It's just across the line. You'll smell it half a day before you enter the city limits." Netherwall touched his hat. "Good riding, gentlemen. Keep an eye out for those Indians. This used to be their hunting ground. They haven't made their peace with hiders."

"What's the chief's name?" Speaks asked.

"Slaughter."

Speaks smiled bitterly. "I hope it gained somethin' in the translation."

"His Cheyenne name is too long to pronounce. The whites named him Slaughter. If he's guilty of half the things he's been accused of since he left the reservation, he'll hang before Christmas. Let's go, Sergeant." The captain turned his horse.

One side of Snyder's muttonchops twisted to expose a row of tobacco-stained teeth. "You boys be sure and enjoy your stay." He swung around to follow his superior.

November rubbed feeling back into his cheeks.

"You recollect what was the rank of that fellow you blowed out from under his hat at Lone Jack?"

"He was a sergeant," Speaks said.

"I never did think much of him."

"I liked him best after I blowed him out from under his hat."

The Platte was flat and brown, with mud islands down the center. Ice crusted along the banks like torn and filthy lace. That night they camped around a buffalo-chip fire and took turns standing watch, one man walking around carrying a rifle to keep his feet from freezing while the other shivered in his blankets. November half hoped that Slaughter and his dog soldiers would show up, just to distract him from his misery; but he had learned very young that Indians were nothing if not inconsiderate.

Chapter Sixteen

Julesburg stank, all right. Hard enough and high enough to make God hold His nose when the wind blew from that direction. The stench was so bad, November got a full measure of it despite the fact that his head was stuffed tighter than a banker's valise, but he didn't mind it so much because it was warm. The steam rising from all those green hides, aswarm with flies— flies, by God, with December only a week off— made the air humid and reminded him of the Chinese baths in Abilene. Except, of course, for the stink.

The stacked hides filled rude stockades behind all the stores, even the dress shop; they trundled down the rutted main street on the backs of wagons, stood on the boardwalks, forcing pedestrians to step down and walk around them, and leaned against the outside walls of the laundry and livery, stiff as barn doors. Some, too long uncured, crawled visibly with maggots, which spilled onto the ground in bunches like squirming heaps of rice. The sight appeared not to have damaged the mystique of the trade, however, because nearly every establishment, from the Buffalo Saloon to the Skinner's Cafe, bore a sign referring to the animal that had put Julesburg on the map. A line of bearded rustics in buffalo coats had formed in front of the gunsmith shop, whose window displayed a sign advertising reduced prices on large-caliber rifle cartridges.

Speaks said, "I reckon this is the place."

"You think?" November cut himself a plug big enough to take his mind off the stink and began chewing.

The plug was half frozen. In the lobby of the Bison Hotel he worked on it till his jaws ached. His partner got directions to Senator Philarope's house from the sallow-faced clerk, and when they were leaving, November had squeezed out barely enough juice to spit in the glass eye of the buffalo head mounted next to the door.

"If that was a live buff and I was firin' powder and lead instead of Levi Garrett's," he said, "we'd have us a start on that five hundred."

Speaks said, "If that was a live buff, you'd be a dead Sam. He'd stomp you before you got that close."

"What makes you such an expert on the critter?" November swung aboard his sorrel.

"I ain't. But there's fifty million of them and only thirty million of us. If it was as easy as that, the odds'd be better."

The road they took led five miles through good pasture to a pair of gateposts joined by a board across the top. BAR 19 RANCH—NO TRES-PASSING was burned into the board, along with the brand, a straight line above the number 19. After passing through the gate they rode another mile before coming to a one-story ranch house, sixty feet long and twenty feet deep, with a porch running its entire length.

"Hello the house," Speaks called out without stepping down.

Almost immediately the front door was opened by a dusky-faced Mexican in white cotton shirt and trousers. He stared at them without speaking.

"This the Philarope spread?" Speaks asked.

After a moment the Mexican nodded.

"Tell 'em we're here to hunt buffalo."

The door closed, and stayed shut long enough for Sam November to spit out the last of his tobacco. When it opened again, the Mexican lowered his head in a deep bow.

"The senator will see you."

"Mighty white of him, seeing as how we rode all the way from Abilene to answer his advertisement," November said.

"Shut up, Sam. This ain't Texas." Speaks stepped down.

They followed the Mexican down a dim hallway and through a door at the end. This put them back outside the house, on a long porch identical to the one in front. Here sat an old man in a wheelchair with a heavy Indian rug drawn up over his knees. In front of him stood an ashwood table with a number of long-barreled rifles lined up across its top, the butts-tocks pointed his way.

"Cicero Philarope?" Asked Speaks.

"Senator, if you please. I think I earned it after five terms, on top of two in the House of Representatives." The old man's voice cracked, like lake ice breaking beneath one's feet. "Whom have I the pleasure of addressing?" His attention remained on the rifle he was fingering, a Remington rolling-block whose walnut stock glistened with oil. Rheumatism had curled his hands into calcined claws.

"Lyle Speaks. This here's my partner, Sam November."

Now the senator looked at them. His face was tanned dark brown against the blizzard white of his hair, but withered below the cheekbones, like a plant unaccustomed to too much sun and not enough water. His eyes were blue glass splinters in thickets of creases. "Speaks and November of Texas?"

"That's where we started out," Speaks said. "We been a heap of places since."

"I'm aware of most of them: Socorro, Tucson, the Indian Nations, Missouri. What possessed you to ride for Bloody Bill Anderson?"

"We was riding with him, not for him. It was on orders from General Lyons in Springfield."

"Union spies. Splendid! It goes against my grain to offer employment to Johnny Rebs. I don't care how well they shoot. Any man who would turn against his country will turn against his employer."

"We rode for the Confederacy, too," November said.

"It was a funny war." Speaks lifted his Stetson and resettled it. "Your advertisement said you was paying five hundred per man for the season. The offer still hold?"

"It does, for good marksmen. You'd be surprised how often I'm disappointed. I signed on a fellow named Hickok based on his performance at the Rock Creek stage station, where he gunned down the McCanless Gang. He couldn't hit a target as big as a buffalo beyond fifty paces. Just because you're a killer doesn't mean you can shoot."

"Just because you can shoot doesn't mean you're a killer," said Speaks. "It works both ways. But me and Sam got it coming and going. We're both."

"Indeed. Would you be willing to give a demonstration?"

"Which will you have?" November warmed a fresh plug of tobacco between his palms. "Killin' or shootin'?"

"Shooting will have to do. Unfortunately, we have an absence of game at the moment, and I like Diego's corn cakes rather too much to offer him as a target." He curled a withered lip at the Mexican standing in the doorway, whose face remained immobile. Then Philarope pointed a crooked finger beyond the porch railing. "There's a dead cottonwood I've been meaning to have cut down near the creek. This Sharps fires a three-eighty-grain slug that ought to slice the trunk in two. Does either of you think you can do it from here?" He laid the Remington on the table and picked up the one next to it, a single-shot weapon with a set trigger and a fifty-caliber bore.

Speaks took the Sharps and studied the shot. "That's only a couple of hundred yards. If Diego needs to cook dinner, there's a fine big jack washing its whiskers three hundred yards farther out."

The senator squinted in the direction the big man was pointing. He shook his head, selected a Springfield with a sniper scope attached, and looked through the scope. "Bah! No one could hit a target that small at a distance of five hundred yards. Not even with a Big Fifty."

"Well, they're having a sale on cartridges in town. What have we got to lose?" And without hesitating Speaks shouldered the rifle, lined up the sights, engaged the set trigger, and fired. The roar shook the porch.

"Astounding!" Philarope looked up from the scope. "Diego, you're serving jackrabbit stew."

November said, "It's good shooting for a fact, but you still got that cottonwood problem." He drew the big Walker horse pistol he carried on his hip and emptied the cylinder as quickly as he could cock the hammer and press the trigger. The skeletal tree shook, swayed, and fell. As a flourish he executed a dime novel twirl and returned the revolver to its holster.

"Peacock!" said Speaks beneath his breath.

Philarope returned the Springfield and the Sharps to the table.

"I can use you both. The party leaves Julesburg on the first at sunup. You'll be traveling with two skinners and Jared Lillie, my foreman. You'll take your orders from him."

"I've got no objections to taking orders if I respect the man that's givin' them," Speaks said.

"He's a man to respect, if not to like. There's too much money to be made to bother with popularity contests. You can beat my wages in Kansas City, where they're paying five bucks a hide, and Chicago, where a well-cured robe sells for a hundred; but those places are a long way off, and my offer's guaranteed. The Bar Nineteen can't compete with the big ranches in Texas until the buffalo are cleared out to make room for the cattle.

Speaks asked him why he'd named the ranch the Bar 19.

The old man's lip curled again. "I cast the deciding vote in the impeachment of President Johnson last February: nineteenth ballot against, as opposed to thirty-five in favor. We came within one vote of the two-thirds majority necessary to remove him. My vote. Mind you, I was no friend of Lincoln's. I saw more advantage to be gained by leaving a weak Republican in office rather than creating an opening for a potentially dangerous successor." He held out a crabbed right hand. "Welcome aboard, gentlemen. I'll not see you again before payday, thanks to all the chalk in my bones. But I'll raise a glass of champagne with you when the job's done, in honor of the American cattle industry."

"Politics is one bear I never wrestled," Speaks said to November on their way back to town. "I was born too innocent."

"I always thought I'd make a fine city alderman," November said. He spat tobacco at a rock. The stream froze in midair and shattered when it struck. "I seen a rotogravure of one once, riding in a parade in New York City, and I thought it was just the grandest thing. That was before I seen Jeff Davis sitting in a carriage in Richmond. He didn't look like he was in no parade."

"That's because Lee surrendered the next day. I seen him, too."

"What do you make of Philarope?"

"I think he's a Comanche in a wheelchair," Speaks said. "But he's payin' top wages, so I reckon I'll overlook it."

Sam November knew better than anyone alive what a big thing, indeed, that was for Lyle Speaks to overlook.

Chapter Seventeen

They pitched camp on the second floor of the
Bison Hotel. Their room was fitted out with
porcelain and brass and the counterpane on the
bed was a buffalo robe, soft as a down-filled
comforter and twice as warm. The flies were be-
deviling; they bit when they lighted on flesh and
hummed like drunken bullwhackers when they
rode the currents of fetid air. November bought
a fresh copy of the *Colorado Antelope* every day
to use as a swatter. In the restaurant on the
ground floor, both men discovered a taste for
buffalo hump steak and buffalo chitterlings
deep-fried in buffalo fat, which they agreed
would serve them well on the hunt.

At the end of the week the telegrapher at the
post office tracked them down and handed
them a Western Union bank draft in the amount

of two hundred dollars, the reward they had coming for the dead bandits they'd delivered in Mankato. They cashed it in at the Buffalo Bank & Trust and used some of it to outfit themselves at the gun shop. The gunsmith, a short ugly Swede named Isidnar, sold Speaks a Sharps carbine, which Speaks preferred to Philarope's heavy rifle, in a .45 caliber, which he thought would be less susceptible to wind drift on the flat Nebraska plain than the bigger slug fired by the Fifty. November elected to stand pat with his horse pistol, but bought four times as many cartridges for it than Speaks did for the Sharps, suspecting the lighter gun would require more rounds to bring down the brutes.

Buffalo coats being dear at the dry goods, they opted for fell-length sheepskins with the fleece turned inside, badger hats, and red flannels. At the bootmaker's Speaks bought a new pair of stovepipes. November dropped off his old pair to be resoled. The clerk at the emporium brought out a handsome set of binoculars with a nickel-plated frame and nubby leather case, but after admiring it they concluded that any buffalo they needed long range glasses to see was too far away to shoot. Thus they held on to the rest of their Kansas windfall for incidentals and emergencies.

December first dawned, a thin edge of fire on the grassy tabletop to the east, quickly extinguished by the leaden overcast. They woke up the sallow-faced hotel clerk and settled their bill. In the lobby they met a tall stretch of braided rawhide in a bearskin coat and wideawake hat with a feather in the band, who in-troduced himself as Jared Lillie, Senator Philarope's ranch foreman and leader of the hunting expedition. He had a stubble beard and smiled when there was nothing to be amused about. He ducked his head too much, November thought, like a coyote trying to ingratiate himself with wolves until he got behind them, when he went for their hamstrings.

"I observe one rule, and one rule only," Lillie said when they'd put the pleasantries behind them. "I make the rules."

Speaks said, "Somebody has to, I reckon."

Lillie smiled and ducked his head. "We may get along. That your weapon? I prefer the Rem-ington." He raised the rolling-block rifle he was carrying. "The Sharps' reputation is just talk to keep buffalo hunters from admitting they got skinned. Washington City unloaded them after the war for a buck apiece to every post trader betwixt here and California. The traders turned around and sold 'em to the runners for twenty-five."

"What's a runner?" November asked.

"Well, you and me and Speaks are three. Buf-falo runners."

Speaks said, "I thought we were hunters."

"A horse can't throw a shoe in this country without hitting a curly square on the head. There's no hunting to it. We just run 'em around and shoot them down like sardine tins off a fence. Unless we're lucky enough to get a stand."

Neither Speaks nor November felt inclined to

stand there asking questions all day. Finally, Lillie got tired of waiting.

"A stand's when you come on a herd resting. If the wind's with you, they don't even know you exist till they start to drop. Sometimes not even then. Jayhawker from Kansas City got himself a stand last year outside Omaha; shot better'n a hundred before the rest stampeded. Buff are dumb as clodbusters."

"Sounds more like butchering," Speaks said.

"Just like. Only we don't mess with the meat. Hides are what brings in the money." Lillie ducked his head and smiled. "Well, let's go out and meet the rest of our little party."

They accompanied the foreman to the emporium, where a pair of men in cold-weather gear were loading supplies onto the back of a heavy elm wagon with iron-reinforced wheels. Speaks and November shook hands with Oscar Pin, as small and thin as his surname, with fair hair and whiskers under a dirty bowler and a thick German accent; and a brute of a man with a childlike grin, whose huge hand enveloped each of theirs in a moist grip. Lillie introduced him as Chicago Ed.

"That where you hail from?" Speaks asked.

"Where, Chicago?" The man hoisted his brows, and with them his thick, sloping shoulders under a balding buffalo coat. "I never been, though I'd admire to. I talk about it so much I reckon that's why they call me that."

"Ed and Pin are skinners." Lillie made it sound as if they cleaned spitoons for a living.

"Who's cook?" asked November.

Oscar Pin said he was, if they didn't mind their buffalo cooked German style. "Plenty onions. You've not lived a lick till you smell onions frying in the open air."

"Takes your mind off the fact you're fixin' to eat buffalo." Chicago Ed laughed.

Speaks said, "Me and Sam like buffalo."

Lillie said, "You'll change your minds after you eat it every day for a month."

November asked how long they expected to be gone. The foreman shrugged and socked his Remington into its scabbard behind the saddle of the blue roan hitched to the back of the wagon.

"Month, six weeks, two months; we could be out till spring. It all depends on how quickly we fill the wagon with hides."

"I wouldn't be too fast about it," said Chicago Ed. "It takes a heap longer to skin a buff than it does to shoot one. If the weather turns warm and you shot too many, half of them could rot while we're still stripping the hides off the first half."

Lillie said, "If that happens I'll shoot you myself. You represented yourselves as the fastest in the territory."

"We're fast for a fact," said Oscar Pin. "But we're only four hands between us, and one team of horses to do the pulling. You wanted to break the record, you should have hired more men and animals."

"The more you have, the slower you move. I didn't sign on with this party to watch no hides get away for moving too slow." Lillie jerked loose the roan's reins.

"How many hides you figurin' to take?" Speaks asked.

"Every damn one in the state of Nebraska."

They spotted their first small herd close to sundown the first day. First they saw the dust, and when Lillie and Speaks and November spurred their mounts ahead of the wagon driven by Chicago Ed and Oscar Pin, they caught them running on the other side of a low hill. Lillie counted fifteen of them strung out in a line as he swung down to bring them up in the Remington's sights. Speaks dismounted also and worked a bottle-nose cartridge into the breech of his Sharps. November alone remained in the saddle, quirting the reins back and forth across his sorrel's withers as he charged into the midst of the running beasts.

"What the hell is he about?" demanded Lillie.

Speaks said, "Sam's got his own way of doing most things. I've found it's wise to just let him have his head."

Whooping like a Comanche, November came abreast of a large bull and drew his big horse pistol. The animal skinned one eye in his direction, then abruptly changed course, wheeling and running perpendicular to its original path. But the sorrel was a cutter, obtained with the aid of a pair of Jacks from a top hand in Amarillo, and stayed with it. November could hear the bull's lungs heaving, expelling breath each time its hooves pounded earth, could feel the condensed moisture on his exposed skin. It steamed as thick as milk in the frigid air. He aimed the revolver at the triangle of skin that stretched and folded between the buffalo's left foreleg and its chest as it ran, and fired three slugs through into the bull's heart. His prey kept going for fifty more yards on momentum alone before its legs folded. It skidded an additional twenty feet, gouging up a ridge of earth and snow, as if by burying itself it could avoid surrendering its hide to its conqueror.

November reined in and leapt down, keeping his pistol ready in case the bull still had fight. Immediately he knew it didn't. It had come to rest with its great woolly head turned around as if to peer back over its shoulders, but the dust on its spilled tongue, as big as a spatula, and especially the wet-velvet sheen in the one eye that remained open told November it wouldn't look at anything ever again. As with any kill, man or animal, he allowed himself the painful luxury of regret for a life taken before its time.

He forgot it in the next instant, because he was forced to hurl himself headlong over the buffalo's rounded back when something small and deadly sped past him with a sharp crack of heated air, followed a hundredth of a second later by the hollow report of a rifle. He landed with a grunt behind the animal, and looked around just in time to see another bull somewhat smaller than his fall to the ground twenty yards away; for some reason, lameness perhaps, it had lagged slightly behind the rest of the herd, which vanished over the next rise just as November had caught up to his quarry. Now, with his own kill serving as a breastwork, he came up on his knees and rested the heavy barrel of the Walker Colt in the groove where the beast's neck curved into its hump, sighting along it to find out who had chosen to shoot so close to him.

As he watched, Jared Lillie rose from a crouching position near where he had dismounted when they sighted the herd, lowering the Remington as he reached his full height. Even from that distance November could see the patch of gray smoke scudding away from the rifle's muzzle.

At that moment Lyle Speaks dropped his Sharps, closed the gap between himself and the foreman in one lunge, and swept his big right fist up all the way from his heels. November heard the crack of bone on bone an instant behind the actual impact; time enough to Lillie to fall spread-eagled in the snow, like a boy making angels. It was as true a blow as he had ever seen his partner throw.

Lillie was just starting to sit up when November rejoined them, leading the sorrel, which faithful to its training had remained ground-hitched even with a bullet slicing past. Speaks stood over him, ready to knock him down again. Oscar Pin and Chicago Ed caught up to them with the wagon then and set the brake with a creak.

"What the hell did you hit me with, a single-tree?" The foreman spat out a tooth.

"No, just my right. I'd've used my left, but I

didn't want to make a ghost out of you. I'll use it next time you let off a shot close to Sam."

"I'm all right, Lyle," November said. "I only went down to get out of the line of fire."

"I figured that when you got back up." He was still glaring down at Lillie.

"He didn't have anything to worry about," Lillie said. "I ain't missed a shot in five years."

"That makes you just about due."

Lillie got to his feet, brushed himself off, and looked around for his rifle. When he found it he picked it up and knocked snow out of the muzzle. "I don't like the way your friend hunts buffalo. We could have shot five of 'em long-range in the time it took him to ride in and kill one."

"You should have made that rule before Sam broke it."

"Next time you lay a hand on me I'll kill you."

"Next time you won't be able," Speaks said.

Chicago Ed jumped to the ground. "Time enough for you boys to bump horns later. Right now me and Oscar can use a hand with these here hides."

"Cut 'em yourself," said Lillie. "I ain't no skinner."

"What kind of help you need?" November asked.

Chicago Ed drew two coils of rope from the wagon bed. Each was knotted to an iron hook filed to a wicked point.

"Me and Oscar'll make the cuts if you boys can hitch these here to the back of the wagon. Then we'll sink the hooks into the hide and use the team to haul it off the carcass."

"That's your job, I said." The foreman swung aboard his roan. "We got us a herd to catch up to. Join us when you're finished. We'll have more work for you by then."

Speaks spread his hands. "He makes the rules."

"No skin off our ass." Oscar Pin stepped down to help with the ropes. "You and November can pitch in when we get our first big harvest. There is no daylight between runners and skinners when the work piles up."

Lillie said, "It ain't daylight that separates runners from skinners. It's the stink."

"There's stink and stink," Speaks said. But he and November mounted and spurred off behind the foreman.

Chapter Eighteen

November borrowed Speaks's Winchester and the next time they came upon a herd, crossing the Platte, gave as good an account of himself with the shorter-ranged carbine as the other did with their heavy artillery; together they shot two more bulls and three cows. Oscar Pin and Chicago Ed, who caught up with them just before sundown, skinned the animals after dark by torchlight.

They went three more days without success, then as they were breaking camp on the fifth morning, had to saddle up fast to catch a swiftly moving band of sixty or so, spooked by wolves or another hunting party in the vicinity, thundering past close enough to shake the wagon. Since there was no time to pick a spot, all three runners used November's technique, running alongside and firing pistols into the herd. Old Leviticus, the great bay Speaks had paid a hundred dollars for in Kansas, outran not only the sorrel and the roan, but the buffalo as well, despite their head start, stretching out its long legs to overtake and turn the leaders and give the runners another crack. They emptied their cylinders, reloaded on the gallop, and resumed firing, stopping at last only when the clouds of snow and pulverized earth rose so thick they couldn't distinguish their targets from their partners' mounts. When their vision cleared, twenty-one buffalo lay dead or dying. The three men walked their horses among the hunched forms, shooting through the heads of those that showed any sign of life.

The rest of the day, Speaks and November helped out with the skinning, propping up carcasses with sharpened sticks as demonstrated by Oscar Pin and Chicago Ed, cutting the hides from brisket to tail and up the legs, then sinking the sharp hooks into the skins where they'd torn them loose from the meat, and standing back while Pin drove the team and wagon away from the carcasses, dragging the hides away from their original owners. Then they used more sharpened sticks to stretch and stake out the hides to dry in the sun. It was hot, sweaty work, and the sunlight glaring off the snow burned their faces deep red. Their clothes, soaked though with perspiration, turned clammy at dusk. They huddled shuddering around the buffalo-chip fire to keep from freezing to death. Lillie chuckled and leaned back against his sad-

dle, smoking a cigar. He had spent the afternoon cleaning his weapons and snoozing with
his hat over his face.

"Don't pay him no mind." Chicago Ed pulled
the cork from a pewter flask and handed it to
Speaks. "You and November did a man's work
today. Any fool with eyes can shoot a buff. Making 'em give up their hides takes muscle and
sand. I've known railroad section hands to quit
in the middle of their first harvest. Compared
to skinning, swinging a sledge all day is sport."

Speaks sniffed at the raw whiskey and took a
swig. It burned all the way down and lit a fire
in his belly, warming him to the soles of his feet.
"It's a chore for a fact," he said. "I believe I'll be
a mite stiff come morning."

November said, "I'm stiff now. I can't feel my
ears."

"Pass him that flask," Chicago Ed said. "That
tanglefoot'd make a corpse stand up and take
off its coat."

November hesitated before accepting it. "Oscar's missed a turn."

Oscar Pin, smoking a charred blob of pipe
with a short stem, shook his head. "My father
was a deacon in the Lutheran Church of Phil-
adelphia. When I was fixing to come west he
made me swear on the Book never to touch a
drop. I lost two toes to frostbite on the Rocky
Ford last February because I wouldn't stick my
feet in sour mash."

"Well, I may go to hell, but I won't go limping." November tipped up the flask. It was like

183

swallowing a strand of rusty barbed wire, but it took his mind off his ears.

Speaks said, "I didn't see any marksmanship today. It was like fishing with black powder."

"You'll see it comes in handy when we get our first stand."

"You ever get one?" November asked the foreman.

"I came close once, on the Missouri. I shot six before this pregnant cow went down bawling. Rest of the herd spooked and took off like a flock of birds from a Western Union wire. I missed the heart and shot through the lungs, that was my mistake. Didn't take time to set it up. That won't happen again. Next time I mean to take the record."

"What's the record?" Speaks took back the flask and gave it to Ed.

"That jayhawker up by Omaha shot a hundred and two. I reckon if I pass that by forty or so I'll not have to worry about giving it up soon."

Pin blew smoke. "That's if the buffalo hold out. They won't be long if runners keep killing them at that rate."

"I reckon they'll hold out long enough to get my name in the history books. After that I don't much care."

Chicago Ed corked the flask. "If you do and it includes a trip to Chicago, I hope you'll take me along. I'd admire to put up my feet in a private room at the Palmer House before I die."

Speaks said, "We'll never skin a hundred and forty buffalo before the sun goes down and the wolves come in. We'd waste more'n half."

"Half a hundred and forty's still seventy." Lillie rolled himself into his blankets and slid his hat down over his eyes.

Oscar Pin changed the subject. "That's some horse you have."

"Old Leviticus?" Speaks glanced back over his shoulders to make sure the bay was still picketed with the others. "I wouldn't sell him for a thousand. He may save my life someday."

"That may be today." Chicago Ed was looking past November.

The others turned. A big moon lay on the horizon, looking as if a buzzard had covered it. A line of horsemen appeared against it briefly, then vanished. It might have been a trick of the shadows.

"Another hunting party, maybe." November didn't manage to sound any more convincing to the others than he had to himself.

"Not at night." Oscar Pin rapped out his pipe against the heel of his boot. "Nothin' moves around at night out here except wolves and Indians. Those aren't wolves."

"Comanches camp at night," Speaks said. The years had done nothing to soften the hard look that came into his eyes whenever he spoke of Comanches.

"Cheyennes, too," said Chicago Ed, "unless they're riled."

Pin said, "I cannot think why they'd be riled. We're only hunting them out of everything they live on. Buffalo's like a general merchandise to them. Without it they starve."

November said, "This cavalry general we met

on our way up from Kansas told us to watch
out for a renegade named Slaughter."

"He was a captain," Speaks corrected.

"Let's us all just hope this ain't Slaughter."
Lillie was sitting up now, his hat slid to the back
of his head and his Remington across his lap.
"That's one butcher you don't want to meet in
broad daylight."

"Nor night neither," Chicago Ed put in.
"Mothers in Julesburg get their babies to go to
bed by tellin' 'em Slaughter'll scalp anyone he
catches still awake."

Lillie said, "Lucky thing Injuns don't attack at
night."

Speaks grinned without humor. "Who told
you that?"

"Everybody knows they're afraid if they get
killed in the dark their souls won't find their
way to the happy hunting ground."

"That's only if they think they'll get killed. If
they outnumber us by enough braves they won't
worry about it."

"How do we know they outnumber us?" Lillie
asked.

November said, "Because they let us see 'em."

Speaks took the first watch. November
spelled him after two hours, followed by Lillie
and then Chicago Ed, filling in for Oscar Pin,
who suffered from night blindness. In the
morning none of them was dead, but the Indians were still there, strung out on horseback
facing them in a line of thirty, not bothering to
conceal their presence. Their feathers bristling

against the sky reminded November of Spanish bayonet cactus growing in bunches on New Mexico. He had never liked Spanish bayonet, or New Mexico, either.

Lillie blew dust out of his rifle's rolling-block action. "Injuns can't shoot for sour apples. We could pick off ten or twelve of 'em before they get within bow-and-arrow range."

"That leaves eighteen," said Speaks, "and we're just five. I wouldn't bet a nickel against a hand like that if I was rich as Vanderbilt."

"Beats sitting here while they take target practice."

"We don't know they're looking to fight." Speaks unbuckled his gun belt containing his Army Colt and laid it on the ground.

Lillie stared. "What the hell?"

November said, "They might not be the parleyin' kind, Lyle."

"I don't see as the odds against us are any worse if I go up there and find out." He went over and untied Old Leviticus from the picket line.

Lillie said, "They pick you off on the way there, we're out one shooter."

"That's why Sam's stayin' here with my Sharps. One of them bucks scratches his nose, he's going to blow it clean off."

November said, "Luckily, Injuns got big noses." He picked up the heavy carbine and checked the load.

"What you fixin' to bargain with?" Lillie asked.

"Twenty-one dead buffalo."

Chicago Ed frowned at the hides they'd staked out. "Well, I worked harder for uglier bosses."

Lillie said, "I'll see my scalp on Slaughter's lodge pole before I'll let one of his damn savages touch one of my kills."

"See, that's the thing of it." Speaks mounted. "You won't see it."

Oscar Pin bent down and removed a pepper-box pistol from his bedroll. "Don't give Lillie a thought. If he raises that rifle I will make a punchboard of him."

The foreman glared at him. "This here's mutiny."

"You be sure to tell Senator Philarope when we see him," November said. "We won't none of the rest of us say a word. Our standing there will be evidence enough on our side. Watch your topknot, Lyle."

"That's your job, Sam. Always was." He gave the bay a kick.

The leader wasn't hard to spot, which wasn't always true with Indians. This one had the best rifle, a Winchester with a brass receiver, called the Yellow Boy by those who were lucky enough to have seen one in a frontier flooded with surplus cap-and-ball weapons from the late war; the others had single-shot Springfields and one old flintlock that someone must have been using to prop open a door. Speaks steered his mount toward Yellow Boy.

When he got within twenty feet, the Indian worked the lever of the repeater, jacking a shell into the chamber. That was his signal to draw rein. The leader had a pumpkin face made up of bunched ovals, his eyes slitted like gun ports in a shuttered window. His face was painted in slashes of ocher. Despite the biting cold of that bright winter day, he and the others were stripped to their breechclouts and leggings so that any wounds they suffered would bleed clean.

Speaks considered this a bad sign.

"Anybody here talk American?" he asked after a moment.

The icy prairie wind whistled through a long silence, stirring feathers and plaited hair.

Finally the brave mounted to the right of the man with the Winchester stirred. He was very young, maybe sixteen, and his hair was cropped at ear level, reservation-school style.

"I speak American," he said. "The teachers in your missionary school taught me English."

Speaks waited while the young brave translated the exchange to the others. None of them changed expression.

"What's your chief's name?" he asked then.

"Our chief is many miles away, talking to your chief in the city of Washington. The man we follow is at my right. His name is Ho-ist-o-ha-a—what you say Smoke Rising. Your people in Nebraska call him Slaughter."

The leader said something and gestured Speaks's way with the Winchester.

The young Indian said, "He wants to know why you steal our buffalo."

"Strictly speakin', they ain't yours."

When this was translated, Slaughter spat a

reply. The young Indian assumed an expression of contempt.

"You say this because you are white, and believe that everything you covet belongs to you."

"I said that because you're red, and believe nothing belongs to nobody. That being the way you look at it, I don't see where stealing enters in."

Slaughter appeared to consider this before he spoke.

"He asks how it is you know what our people believe."

"I growed up in Comanche country. You all think the same about most things, just like folks in Ohio and Kansas."

"Why, then, did half your people go to war against the other half?"

Speaks smiled. "That your question or your father's?"

The young brave's composure fluttered. Then his chin came up. "Who told you Slaughter is my father?"

"You favor him. Also you paint your face the same, which means he's the one taught you how. I'll answer your question with one of my own. Why does the Cheyenne fight the Crow, or the Arapaho or the Pawnee? Just because folks think the same about most things don't mean they won't kill each other over things they don't think the same about. We're all of us just as dumb as all the rest, red and white."

He watched Slaughter while this was being translated. He suspected the leader knew some English and was taking advantage of the delay to put his thoughts in order before he spoke.

"He says there is one thing all the red men think the same about. They all hate the white man and want to kill him. All of us here have lost something because of him. My mother and my two sisters were killed in the raid that rounded up the people of our village and sent us to the reservation. Your cavalry cut them to pieces with their long knives."

Speaks listened to these hot words in cold calm. "You ain't alone in that," he said. "Except you still got your father."

"We all have reason to hate." The young man spoke without consulting Slaughter.

"Question is, how do we get out of this here situation without someone else gettin' killed?"

An animated discussion followed, in which several of the Indians took part. Slaughter cut them off with a slashing movement. He spoke quietly and at length.

"My father says you will give us the buffalo you have slain. You will give us the hides. You will give us also your arms and saddle horses. You may keep the wagon and the horses that pull it, so that you may leave. In return for these things he will give you your lives."

"Unacceptable," Speaks said. "Tell your pa he can have the buffalo and nothin' else."

"This is not a trading session. Our terms are final."

"Not as final as killing, and we all done our share of that."

"We outnumber you six to one."

"We'll whittle down those odds."

They conferred. The young man said, "My father is a great man, whose heart is generous. He says we will take the buffalo and the hides and the horses. You may keep your weapons."

"You can have the buffalo and half the hides. We keep our horses, too."

"His heart is not that generous."

"I ain't offerin' anything you can't take," Speaks said. "I'm just saying here's a way to keep others from losing folks they care about and hating them that took them and the whole thing happenin' all over again. I'm offering him a chance to say the killin' stops here, for one day. For that he can have the buffalo and all the hides."

The young man translated. Slaughter pointed again with the Winchester. Speaks didn't like where he was pointing.

"He says he will take what you offer. But you must give up your horse, as well."

"Nope. A man don't give up his horse."

"He says he will kill you and take it, then."

"He can do that. Then my partner will blow him back to Colorado with my Sharps gun. Or he might miss and hit the horse. Either way, your pa don't get the horse."

The next conference was longer.

"My father says you are a muleheaded son of a bitch."

Speaks showed his teeth. "His words or yours?"

"What he said doesn't translate. He accepts your offer."

Chapter Nineteen

Jared Lillie cursed all the time they were breaking camp. "We bust our butts killin' and skinnin', and those lazy red bastards waltz in and grab the whole kit and kaboodle. If you was Dutch, the Injuns'd still have Manhattan *and* the damn beads."

"To start with," Speaks said, "you didn't skin so much as your elbow. Next, there wasn't a thing but my flapping chin to stop them from killing us and taking our gear along with the meat and hides. Third, if we don't stop talking and start skedaddling, they might just figure that out for their ownselves. Injuns got no better history than white men for keeping their word."

"Wasn't for that damned squarehead and his pepperbox, we'd be closer to even."

"You'd best speak to Sam about that. He's been watchin' my back since before you got your second set of teeth."

They finished loading their gear into the wagon and pulled out. The scene of their kill was still in sight when the Cheyenne dog soldiers rode in and began butchering the carcasses.

They spent the rest of the day putting distance between themselves and Slaughter, just in case he changed his mind. When they camped, Lillie sat apart from the others, drinking from Chicago Ed's flask and muttering to himself. When November's turn came to watch, he wasn't sure if he was guarding the others from Indians or their foreman.

Late the next morning they discovered the unmistakable signs of a big herd. The frozen ground had been churned up and worked by hundreds of hooves into frothy mud. Lillie, his hunter's instincts getting the better of his resentment, recalled that there was a big wallow a few miles to the north and charted a looping course that would bring the party down on it with the wind on their side.

"The water's frozen," November said. "They might stop there."

"It's a deep wallow. Buffalo's dumb about some things, but they're smarter than cattle. They know if they bust the ice they'll have plenty to drink."

The detour took them miles out of their way, but toward midafternoon, Lillie came back from a scouting expedition on foot to report he'd sighted the herd below the next rise.

"It's as big as I seen since I came out from Michigan," he said. "If we work this right, we might just have us a proper stand."

Speaks and November accompanied him up the slope, crawling on their bellies and elbows as they neared the top. From there the earth declined gently, ending in a large, perfectly round depression, in which five or six hundred buffalo of every size and condition stood up to their chests in water or lay sunning themselves on the adjacent ground or rolled around in the mud. There were deep-chested bulls and nursing cows, young calves chasing one another or suckling, graying old veterans with beards worn short from decades of dragging on the ground and horn scars all over their bodies, decorations of countless battles won and lost. The heat from their bodies rose in clouds of steam.

Forked sticks, packed as carefully as the weapons in that treeless plain, were brought from the wagon and shoved into the earth. They spread the wagon sheet on the frozen grass, stretched out side by side upon it, rested the barrels of their rifles on the forks, and began killing. The first three shots, from the Sharps, Remington, and Winchester, were almost simultaneous. Three bulls fell, groaning and heeling over without a kick. The echo of the combined reports growled forever across the level land. The rest of the herd went on drinking and suckling and playing and resting.

November thought he was dreaming. "Why don't they run?" he whispered.

"I said they was dumb." Lillie rolled a fresh cartridge into the block. "The shots sound like thunder, and they're used to that. So long as they don't hear voice nor smell people nor see nothing they don't expect to see, they'll just stand around waiting to be killed. They watch each other fall and think they're resting."

"I wouldn't believe it if I wasn't seein' it," November said.

"Just aim for the heart. The quieter they die, the better for us."

Three more animals fell, then two more. Speaks shot what he thought was a young bull, but when it went down he saw its calf standing on the other side. Lillie shot the calf.

"It'd starve anyway," he said. "We don't want it crying for its mother and spooking the rest."

Fourteen, twenty. They were taking their time now, letting their barrels cool. Lillie explained that in half an hour or so he'd signal to Oscar Pin and Chicago Ed to fill a canvas bucket from the water barrel and fetch it to soak the muzzles. "We don't want 'em melting off true."

Number forty-two was barely a heifer, shot by Lillie. It fell to its knees, then rolled over with a moan that was almost human. A young bull turned its head to look, then resumed drinking. Speaks and November exchanged glances.

After sixty, the foreman realized he was the only one still firing. He turned his head just as Speaks rose to his feet. "Get down!" he whispered. "They'll spook if they see you."

"It don't matter. I shot my last one." He

196

started back toward the wagon, carrying his Sharps.

"What's the matter with your friend?" Lillie asked November.

"Nothin' that ain't the matter with me." He got up and followed Speaks.

"Where do you two think you're headed?"

"That's up to Lyle."

"You leave this party, you leave the hides. No payday for you in Julesburg."

"We'll see what the senator has to say about that. We cleared some space for his damn cattle, just like he wanted."

"Suit yourself, you gutless bastards. I'll take the record alone."

"Not today." November retraced his steps to the top of the rise. He changed hands on the Winchester while he stripped off his sheepskin coat, then took the coat by the end of one sleeve and swung it over his head, raising his voice in a shrill rebel yell.

Alerted, an old cow turned her head in his direction, then let out a loud bawl of warning. November had heard somewhere that the females took charge during emergencies. The rest of the herd threw up their horns and, without bothering to confirm the alarm, abandoned the wallow in an explosion of water and a thunder of hooves. Cursing, Lillie managed to get off two shots, fumbling to reload in between, but if he hit anything vital the momentum of the stampede carried the casualties along with it. He turned a face black with hatred upon November, then fumbled inside the sack where he carried his cartridges. November jacked a shell into the Winchester's chamber and pointed it at the foreman.

"Throw the sack at my feet."

Lillie hesitated, his mouth moving to form silent curses. Then he picked up the sack of ammunition and hurled it at November's boots. November picked it up and walked down the hill.

Oscar Pin and Chicago Ed, who had been busy breaking out skinning knives and uncoiling the ropes from the wagon bed, stopped to watch Speaks and November step into leather. November put the sack of cartridges in his saddle pouch.

Speaks said, "Sorry to leave you boys with all the work. Me and Sam just found our limit."

"The smell ain't for everyone," said Chicago Ed.

"It ain't the smell. Not of the skinning."

Oscar Pin said, "Don't worry about the hides. We haven't missed one yet."

"You boys can do better than Lillie," November said as he gathered his reins.

Chicago Ed twirled the skinning hook at the end of the rope he was holding. "Buffalo running's full of Lillies."

They rode east, away from Indians and buffalo. They'd made a quarter mile when something made a loud thump and Speaks's big bay fell without a sound but that of its own body thudding to earth. The rider threw himself clear.

"Lyle, you hit?" November's horse pistol was

in his hand. He didn't remember drawing it.

Speaks got up and tested an ankle. "I'm all of a piece." He went over and looked down at Old Leviticus. Then he knelt and stroked its muscular head. He felt no pulse.

"Serves me right for gettin' to likin' something." He rose.

The echo of the report was still rolling toward Canada. Both men turned their heads toward the wagon. It wasn't where they had left it. They saw Oscar Pin leaping down from the driver's seat where the vehicle had come to rest a hundred yards farther north, Chicago Ed standing not far from the tailgate, looking down at something on the ground. They couldn't see what it was. Jared Lillie was nowhere in sight.

November gave Speaks a hand up and they rode back to the wagon. The foreman lay on the ground behind it, half rolled onto his side, his rifle and the wideawake hat with the feather in its band lying near where the wagon had been standing earlier. One of the razor-sharp skinning hooks was buried deep between his shoulder blades. It was still attached to the wagon by a dozen feet of rope.

Chicago Ed bent down, grabbed a fistful of Lillie's hair, and wobbled his head back and forth. "Busted neck. You didn't have to whip the team that hard."

Oscar Pin said, "I didn't have time to consider it. You didn't tell me you were going to let fly with that hook."

"I didn't have any more time than you." Chicago Ed straightened, looking at Speaks sitting behind November on the sorrel. "He had a box of cartridges in the wagon. I didn't know what he was about until he had one in the breech. I just wanted to throw off his aim."

Speaks stepped down.

"We'll ride into Julesburg with you. I reckon Lillie's roan won't mind a stranger on its back. There'll be an inquest, but I don't reckon they'll have much truck with either of you when they hear your story."

"Not unless the jury's all buffalo runners." Oscar Pin filled his pipe.

Montana, 1901

"That was also the only time I ever let myself get attached to a horse," Speaks said.

Fellows looked up from his notebook. He was writing by moonlight, making do with what he had.

"I thought you loved horses?" he said. "I mean, the way you complain about automobiles . . ."

"I don't love 'em," Speaks said. "I prefer them, I trust them, I have more faith in them . . . but after that time I never again got attached to one. Man's a fool to give a name to somethin' he might someday have to eat."

"Eat a horse?" Fellows was aghast.

"It's been done," Speaks said. "You better get some sleep."

"Mr. November talked with me longer last night," Fellows complained.

"Well," Speaks said, "at least my story was

more excitin' than that foolishness he told you last night."

"What was foolish about the Melanie story?" Fellows asked.

"I'm gonna check the horses," Speaks said, getting to his feet. "Get some sleep. I'll see you in the morning."

He walked away from Fellows over to where the horses were picketed.

Chapter Twenty

November held his hand up for them to stop.

"What—" Fellows started to ask, but Speaks silenced him with a chopping motion of his hand, then held his forefinger to his pursed lips.

November turned in his saddle and made a "stay" sign with his hands, then rode ahead.

Speaks leaned over and said in Fellows's ear, "He heard somethin'."

"I didn't hear—" Fellows began, but Speaks silenced him again.

They sat there, remaining mounted, and waited nearly twenty minutes until November returned with another man on a horse.

"Chilito," Speaks said.

"Is it safe to talk now?" Fellows asked.

"Talk," Speaks said, "and dismount," and stepped down from his horse.

Fellows found Chilito a fascinating specimen. The man was barely five and a half feet tall, but he was extraordinarily muscled. He looked as if he could wrestle a bear—and had enough scars covering his body as proof that he might have done so a time or two. The writer was hard-pressed to guess the man's age.

Chilito was wearing calfskin pants and a leather vest with no shirt beneath it. Fellows noticed also that the man wore moccasins. He was armed only with a rifle that, to Fellows's untrained eye, looked like Speaks's Winchester, possibly newer.

"How did you hear him?" Fellows asked November.

"Damned if I know," November said. "It's just an instinct."

"Chilito," Speaks said, clapping the man on the shoulder. "Tell us."

"Five men," Chilito said. "They travel with the horses."

"Have you gotten close enough to see them?" November asked.

"Not yet," the Mexican said, "but soon. They are not far ahead. I waited."

"For what?" Fellows asked.

Chilito looked at the writer and didn't answer.

"It's all right, Chilito," Speaks said. "He's with us."

"Yeah," November said with a wry grin, "he's writin' Lyle's story."

"Story?" the Mexican asked.

"His life," Fellows said. "His legend."

Speaks winced when Fellows said the word "legend."

Chilito simply looked at the three men as if they were mad, and shook his head.

"What were you waiting for?" Fellows asked again.

"For Speaks and November."

"You knew they'd come?"

The Mexican nodded.

"But how? I mean, why did you expect them? Mr. Speaks said he hadn't ridden the trail in years."

"I knew Speaks would come," Chilito said, "when he heard about Clay."

The moment became somber, and then passed.

"All right," November said, "we're here now. Where do you think they're going, Chilito?"

"They have crossed the Powder River."

"Still headin' south?" Speaks asked.

Chilito nodded.

"Wyoming," Speaks said, looking at November.

"Maybe the Black Hills."

"That might be why the law can't find them," Speaks said. "They're takin' the horses across the border and sellin' 'em there."

"If that's the case we better stop 'em before they cross."

"They might follow the Little Powder River down," Speaks said. "That'd be a direct route."

"What about the Dakotas?" Fellows asked.

"No," November said, "they'd have to go around the Powder River Range. It would take too long. Lyle's right. If they hug the Little Powder it'll take them right into Wyoming."

"They have to pass between two mountain ranges," Speaks said. "If we stay with the Powder and cross ahead of them, we can be waiting when they come through the pass."

November looked at the Mexican.

"You got to call it, amigo," he said. "If we commit to this they're gonna have to stay with the Little Powder. If they veer off, we'll lose 'em."

Chilito didn't hesitate.

"I say they go straight to Wyoming."

"We just have to hope that when they get clear of the Powder River Range they don't hook up with the Little Missouri and go east," Speaks said.

"Too long," November said.

"We better split up," Speaks said. "Chilito, stay behind and track them. If they do somethin' we don't expect, at least you'll be able to follow them. November, the writer and I will get ahead of them and cross the Powder. When they get to that pass we'll have them covered, front and back."

He looked at November for support, and his old partner nodded.

"Go now, my friend," Speaks said to the Mexican, "before they get to far."

The two men shook hands, and then Chilito shook hands with November.

"Good luck," November said.

"*Vaya con dios,*" Chilito said, and then he was on his small mustang and gone.

"Is this wise?" Fellows asked.

"When we catch them we're outnumbered," Speaks said. "We need an edge. This is it."

"But . . . you're Speaks and November. There's only five of them."

November looked at Speaks and said, "The boy's eyes are not very good."

"He's young."

"That's my point."

"All right," Fellows said, "I get it. You need to compensate for your, uh . . . ."

"Age," Speaks said. "Get mounted, writer. We're movin' out."

They rode long and hard. Their reward when they camped was a fire, hot food, and coffee.

"We're far enough away from them for it not to make a bit of difference," Speaks said.

"Besides," November chimed in, "we got to keep our strength up for the fight."

"The fight," Fellows said. "Yes. Just what would my part be in this, uh, fight?"

"Don't worry about it," November said.

"Is there any chance that they'd just, uh, give up?" The writer's tone was hopeful.

"I doubt it," Speaks said. "This has been a big business for them. They're not going to give it up without a fight."

"A fight," Fellows said, shaking his head.

"Take it easy, Fellows," Speaks said. "You've managed to hold your own so far. You've kept up."

"Does that mean I get a real story tonight?"

"A real story?" Speaks asked. "What did you have in mind?"

Fellows looked at both men and said, "The Devereaux gang."

"Oh," Speaks said, "that one."

"It's one of the most famous—"

"It's exaggerated," Speaks said, cutting the young man off.

"Tell it to him, Lyle," November said. "Tell it to him just like it was, so he can write it all down in that little book of his."

"I'll write it just the way you tell it to me," Fellows said.

"Son," Speaks said, "you'll write it down just the way it happened, because that's what I'm gonna tell you. . . ."

Part Four

Chapter Twenty-one

Colorado, 1876

The lynching was just about to get started good when Speaks and November rode into town.

They drew rein at the end of the dusty street, two big men on good horses. Speaks was riding a rangy, mouse-colored stallion with a dark streak down its back; November was mounted on a buckskin gelding. Speaks rested his hands on the horn and leaned forward in the saddle, squinting a little as he looked at the gallows, the crowd around it, and the man standing on the trap with a noose around his neck and a nervous expression on his face.

"That's him?" asked November.

Speaks grunted. "Looks like." He reached for the stock of the Henry rifle snugged under his right leg in a saddle boot. "Come on."

With a weary sigh November pulled his own rifle from its sheath and heeled his horse into a walk just behind Speaks.

A man in a dusty black suit was standing next to the prisoner on the gallows, but he wasn't a preacher. The tin star pinned to his vest said he was the local lawman. The mustache that dropped over his wide mouth was mostly white and the hands holding the shotgun were spotted with age. He still had some bark in him, though. Speaks could tell that.

The star packer saw them coming and angled the barrel of the shotgun in their general direction without actually pointing it at them. The members of the crowd, anxious to see the hanging, didn't notice the arrival of the newcomers until Speaks and November were practically in their midst. Men stepped back hurriedly, taking their women and kids with them, as the horses pressed forward.

"What the hell do you men want?" the local law demanded. The twin barrels of the greener moved a little more toward Speaks and November.

Speaks grinned, but the expression didn't look too pleasant on his craggy face. "Looks like we're interrupting a necktie party," he said.

"This ain't no lynchin'," the lawman said, drawing up straighter and stiffer in his injured dignity. "It's a perfectly legal hangin', bein' carried out by a duly appointed officer of the law, namely me."

"Well, we don't like to interfere with the law,"

said Speaks. He glanced over at his companion. "Now, do we, Sam?"

November shook his head. "Nope."

Speaks nodded toward the second man on the gallows, the one with the noose around his neck. The one with the scared look on his narrow face.

"But my partner and I need to talk to your prisoner, there, and I don't reckon he'll be sayin' much once that rope's good and tight. So we'll have to ask you to postpone this here legal hangin' for a spell."

The lawman's white mustache rose and fell as he puffed air through his lips in a noise of disgust.

"The hell with that. This fella tried to hold up the mercantile, and when the clerk didn't jump fast enough to suit him, he shot the poor lad. Killed him dead. He didn't see me come up behind him, though, so I laid the barrels of this scattergun over his head." The lawman spat off the gallows. "He had a fair trial. Now he's goin' to hang."

Speaks lifted the Henry rifle just a little. He'd only recently switched from his old Winchester.

"Not just yet."

One of the townies spoke up, brave in a crowd.

"Who do you think you are, mister, ridin' in here like this and tellin' us what to do?"

"His name's Lyle Speaks," said November.

That simple pronouncement quieted the angry muttering of the crowd. Not everyone here in this little Colorado town had heard of Lyle

Speaks, but enough of them had so that a few seconds of whispering filled in the others. Speaks was from down Texas way, an Indian fighter, bounty hunter, scout for the army, lawman—for a very short time—and assorted other professions that tended to attract the smell of powder smoke. The lawman standing there on the gallows was one of those who had heard of Speaks, and he swallowed hard before he said, "I thought you rode on the side of the law."

Speaks wasn't smiling anymore.

"I ride where the trail takes me." He moved his gaze to the prisoner, who was trembling slightly now from standing stiff and still for so long. "Your name Harrigan?"

A head jerk of a nod. "Yes, sir, th-that's me. Harrigan."

"Too bad," November said dryly. "We was lookin' for a fella named Palmerton." He started to turn the buckskin. "Reckon we can ride on and let these folks get on with what they're doin', Lyle."

"Wait a minute," the prisoner practically screamed. "I'm Palmerton! I'm the man you were lookin' for."

"How do we know that?" asked Speaks. "You just told us your name was Harrigan."

"Listen, damn it! I'm Ed Palmerton. I'm the one you want. I was with . . . with Devereaux down in Castle Rock a week ago."

The eyes of the local law widened. "You mean I was about to hang one of Devereaux's bunch?" The exclamation was startled out of him.

One of the townsmen, not the one who had

214

challenged Speaks earlier, said urgently, "If Devereaux finds out we hanged one of his men, he's liable to wipe the whole town off the map."

The lawman nodded, slowly and solemnly. "Yeah." He lowered the shotgun, let the butt rest on the floor of the gallows while he held the barrels with one hand. With the other hand he reached for the noose around the prisoner's neck. "I don't know what you want with him, Mr. Speaks, but I reckon you can have him."

"Much obliged," said Speaks.

Palmerton suddenly looked like maybe it would have been a better idea to keep his mouth shut and go ahead and hang.

Using both hands because they were shaking, Palmerton lifted the glass to his lips and tilted it up. The whiskey went smoothly and quickly into his mouth. He lowered the glass and looked a little steadier.

"Where's Devereaux?" asked Speaks.

Palmerton shoved the glass across the bar. "Can I have another?"

November stood behind the bar. Nobody had been in the saloon when Speaks, November, and Palmerton entered except the bartender, and he had cleared out in a hurry. The three men still had the place to themselves. November poured more whiskey into the glass and pushed it back across to Palmerton, who snatched it up and drained it. This time he only had to use one hand. He dragged the back of the other hand across his lips.

"I can't tell you that," he said. "It'd be worth my life."

"Your like ain't worth much at the moment," November pointed out. "We ride off and leave you here, and that sheriff or marshal or whatever he is out there might still hang you."

Palmerton sighed.

"Rope might be better'n what Devereaux would do to me if he thought I double-crossed him."

"Take us to Devereaux," said Speaks. "Chances are you'll die, all right. But you might not. Anything can happen."

Speaks knew the truth of that, right enough. It was pure chance that he had been away from his family's cabin down on the Brazos when the Comanches had come to call. He and his little brother Jeffrey were the only ones who had survived that awful day. Pa and Mama, his sister Beth and his brother Caleb, all of them had died. More than thirty years had gone by since then and it still hurt to think about it.

Speaks pushed the pain away. He had a job to do.

"What about it?" he prodded Palmerton.

The outlaw was rubbing the back of his hand across his lips again. "Some kind of break," he said thickly. "You got to give me some kind of break."

"You ain't dancin' on air right now," said November. "If that ain't a break, I never seen one."

Abruptly, Palmerton nodded and slapped his palm down on the bar. "All right, I'll do it. Leastways, I'll try. I don't guarantee I can even find

Devereaux." He laughed humorlessly. "He moves around a mite."

"You'll find him," said Speaks. He turned toward the door of the saloon and without looking back added, "Bring him along, Sam."

" 'Nother drink first?" Palmerton implored November.

"Take the bottle." November handed it to Palmerton and dropped a coin on the bar to pay for the whiskey. "You're liable to need it."

The white-mustached lawman was standing on the boardwalk not far from the saloon's entrance as Speaks pushed out through the batwings. The shotgun was tucked under his arm. "Through with him? We still got a hangin' to get on with."

"Thought you changed your mind about that," said Speaks.

"This fella was tried legal-like and sentenced to hang," the lawman said stubbornly. He had given in to his fear earlier, and now he was ashamed of that moment and determined to make up for it.

Speaks shook his head. "Sorry, but Palmerton's got to go with November and me."

The mustache quivered a little.

"That ain't right. What about poor Calvin?"

"Who?"

The lawman looked like he wanted to fall back a step, but he didn't. He stood his ground instead. "The fella Palmerton shot. The clerk in the mercantile. He left a wife and a baby girl."

"I'm sorry about that," Speaks said as November and Palmerton came out onto the boardwalk. "But he's got to go with us anyway."

Most of the crowd that had gathered earlier to watch the hanging was still in the street. The lawman glanced over his shoulder at them, and the men nearest to the boardwalk started to back off. They had the decency to look shamefaced about it, but they still melted away like snow in the bright sunshine.

"This is a mighty sorry thing you're doin'," the lawman said as he looked at Sparks. "I thought you was a good man. That's what I always heard. Now you're takin' a killer and a desperado out of the hands of the law. That don't make you any better'n him."

Speaks shrugged and turned toward the horses tied at the hitch rail. He didn't say anything as he yanked loose the reins of the dun and swung up into the saddle.

"Need a horse for Palmerton," November said mildly to the lawman.

"He's got one, down to the stable." The lawman's voice was savage now as he unleashed his anger, even though he was unwilling to do anything to stop what was happening. "Or maybe you ought to just take one from the street."

"We ain't horse thieves," said November. "Come on, Palmerton. Let's go down to the stable."

Speaks led November's buckskin. November and Palmerton went into the livery stable and came out a few moments later with a saddled bay mare. Speaks looked at the horse and nodded in approval. The ride facing them was liable to be long and hard, and the horse looked like it had sand.

The lawman had followed them, some of the townspeople trailing after him. "A mighty sorry thing," he said again, raising his voice.

None of the three men looked back at him as they rode out of town.

Chapter Twenty-two

Palmerton blew on the cup of hot coffee and said, "I never killed nobody."

"What about the clerk back yonder in that town?" November asked from the other side of the campfire.

Palmerton sipped the coffee, then nodded and said, "Well, yeah, I reckon I did for him, all right. But he startin' cussin' me. Before that, though, I never killed nobody. All the time I rode with Devereaux, I never killed nobody."

Speaks was hunkered on his heels, facing outward away from the fire. He said, "Devereaux has."

"True enough," said Palmerton with a nod. "Devereaux's always liked killin'. Reckon it must've been something he learned in the war."

"War mostly just brings out what a man's already got in him," said November. He was propped against his saddle, long legs stretched out in front of him and crossed at the ankles. He had a cup of coffee in his hand, too, and a belly full of bacon, beans, and biscuits. Life could be worse.

"What about the money?" asked Speaks, still not looking around. If a man watched a fire too long, his eyes were useless when it came to looking for enemies in the dark.

"What about it?" asked Palmerton.

"How much do you reckon Devereaux's got stashed away?" The question came from November.

"Oh, hell, I don't know. Eighty, ninety thousand, maybe?"

"He got twenty at the bank in Pueblo," said Speaks. "Ten more in Castle Rock. At least eight down in Raton. That's just in the last month. The gang's been riding together for half a year."

"We cut a wide swath, all right," Palmerton said, a note of pride in his voice. "Down through Nebraska and Kansas, across Indian Territory, up through New Mexico, and into Colorado." He paused. "I figured it was all about the money."

November chuckled. "You figured that, did you?"

"Why else?"

Speaks straightened, put his hands on his hips as he stretched his back. "Yeah. Why else?" He half turned. "Bank that fire, Sam, and get some shut-eye. I'll stand first watch."

November drained the last of his coffee and

tossed away the grounds in the bottom of the cup.

For two days they rode north across the plains toward Wyoming, the front range of the Rockies looming off to their left. Devereaux had a hideout somewhere up in the wild country along the Colorado-Wyoming border, or at least that was the rumor Speaks had heard. The same man who had told him that had also said that one of Devereaux's men had been captured in some jerkwater town north of Denver and that had turned out to be true, so Speaks was inclined to believe him about the hideout, too.

On the first day, November had asked Palmerton, "How'd you come to get left behind?"

"Horse came up lame out in the middle of nowhere. Just my luck," Palmerton had said bitterly. "It was a good while before I found a mount I could steal, and by that time it was too late to catch up to Devereaux and the rest of the boys. I ran out of what little pocket change I had, too, so that's why I decided to hold up that store."

"Yeah, that was bad luck, all right," November said, but he didn't sound overly sympathetic.

"You just admitted to being a horse thief, Palmerton," Speaks pointed out.

The outlaw shrugged. "You gents already took me away from one hangin'. I don't reckon you're gonna get too worried about a little horse thievery. Not with all of Devereaux's loot waiting somewhere up the trail." Palmerton gave an ugly laugh. "Should've knowed it. All you so-called heroes ain't any better than you have to be. The right chance comes along, you grab for it, just like any other man."

Speaks hadn't denied it, and neither did November. Now, on the morning of the third day, they had been riding for about two hours when they heard a thin, popping noise. Speaks drew rein, and the other two followed suit.

"We could sit right here for a spell, Lyle," November said after all three listened for a moment to the distant gunfire. "Maybe it'd pass us right by."

Speaks grunted. "Maybe. But I'm curious." He heeled his rangy mount into a run.

"Curiosity's always been one of Lyle's failin's," said November, as much to himself as to Palmerton. "Come on."

Palmerton hung back. "Ride right into trouble? I'll be damned if I'll—"

November turned toward him, and his hand came up with his Colt in it, the hammer eared back. "I can always shoot you in the head and leave you here if you don't want to come," he said.

Palmerton turned pale under his deep tan. "Speaks wouldn't like that. How would you find Devereaux with me dead?"

"We'd find a way," November said simply.

"I'm coming, I'm coming," muttered Palmerton. He put his horse into a fast trot, keeping pace with November. Speaks was a couple of hundred yards ahead of them by now, not looking back.

The gunshots were louder as Speaks rode to the top of a little knoll. On the other side, at the bottom of the gentle slope, a wagon had stopped. A man and a woman were crouched next to the wagon, using it for what meager cover it might offer, as four men on horseback rode around the vehicle in a circle. They were shooting, but not to kill. Not yet. They were just hoorawing the man, Speaks saw, having a little fun before they got down to business.

Speaks had a feeling their business would be ugly.

He put his horse into a walk and headed leisurely down the hill. The riders saw him coming, broke off tormenting the couple from the wagon, and came to meet Speaks. The four of them lined up side by side, guns still drawn.

When he was about twenty feet from the men Speaks reined in and nodded. "Howdy, boys," he called out.

"Best get the hell out of here, mister," one of the men replied. "This ain't none of your affair."

Speaks lifted his left hand and prodded at his ear.

"Mighty noisy doings around here. You'd think, what with all this open air and big sky, that gunshots wouldn't be so loud. But they are. And my hearing's sort of sensitive."

The woman screamed, "Help us, mister! Oh, God, you've got to help us."

Speaks seemed to ignore her. He didn't turn when someone rode up behind him, either. That would be Sam November. Speaks focused all his attention on the four riders in front of

224

him. "I'd appreciate it if you boys could sort of quiet things down until me and my friends have passed through."

Another of the riders demanded harshly, "What the hell is wrong with you, mister? Didn't them sensitive ears of yours hear us when we told you to get out of here?"

The woman sobbed loudly. Speaks could hear the frightened breathing of the man who stood next to her, an arm protectively around her shoulders. He was young and so was the woman, neither of them much more than twenty, Speaks judged. He turned his horse slightly and called to the woman, "Ma'am, what's your name?"

The question surprised her, and it dumbfounded the four hard-faced riders. "Are you leavin', or do we have to kill you?" one of them shouted at Speaks.

"Ma'am? Your name?" Speaks asked again.

Tears streaked her face. She swallowed once, then said, "It . . . it's Rosalie."

Speaks nodded to her. "Pleased to make your acquaintance, Miss Rosalie. Are these men botherin' you?"

She nodded shakily.

"Would you like me to ask them to stop?"

Wide blue eyes. Another nod.

The rider who had done most of the talking yelled a curse, then jerked his gun and said, "That's enough!"

Speaks thought so too.

He went out of his saddle, drawing and firing as he fell. The horses shielded him for a second, and he rolled and came up firing again. A rifle cracked once, twice, three times. That would be November. Speaks saw that two of the riders were down, another hunched over in his saddle and out of the fight, but the fourth man was still blazing away. The Colt bucked hard against Speaks's palm as he fired again.

The fourth man jerked back in his saddle, his arms going almost straight in the air like he was surrendering. They stayed that way as he toppled off to the side.

Hoofbeats rattled. Speaks looked around and saw Palmerton lighting a shuck off to the east. November raced past on the buckskin, angry words thrown over his shoulder. "Damn it, Lyle! Now I got to go after him!"

The man who was shot but still on horseback let out a groan and slid out of the saddle. He fell loose-limbed, like a rag doll. Speaks strode over to him, saw the blood soaking the man's middle. Air rattled hoarsely in the man's throat and his face went slack where it was pressed against the ground.

"Gut-shot like that, it could've been worse," Speaks told dead ears.

He checked the other three men. They were dead too. He thumbed fresh shells into all the empty chambers of his gun except one, and he let the hammer rest on that one. Then he holstered the Colt and turned toward the couple beside the wagon.

"You folks all right?"

"I . . . I reckon so," the man said shakily. "They would've got around to killin' me sooner or later, but they wanted to have some fun first."

Speaks nodded. "Way it looked to me, too." He nodded to Rosalie and tugged on the brim of his hat. "Ma'am."

"Don't you even want to know why?" she asked as he started to turn toward his horse.

"Does it matter?"

Evidently it did, because the young man said in a rush, "I was takin' Rosalie away from them. That one there, he's got a bawdy house in a settlement over east of here. He swore he'd kill me if I took his best girl away from him, and he came after us to do it, too."

Rosalie was blushing furiously. She was pretty and even younger than Speaks had first thought. Her hair was dark red and parted in the middle. It hung in waves to her shoulders, framing a freckled face.

"Son—" Speaks began.

"Joshua. Joshua Tate."

"You aim to marry this woman, Joshua?"

"Yes, sir, I surely do," the young man said with an emphatic nod.

"Then don't go around tellin' people she used to work in a bawdy house. Folks out here on the frontier are pretty forgiving about a person's past, but you might as well not give them any more to forgive than you have to."

"Thank you," Rosalie said softly. "Mister . . . ?"

"Speaks. Lyle Speaks."

"Thank you, Mr. Speaks."

Hoofbeats again, not hurrying this time. Speaks looked around and saw November and

Palmerton riding toward him. Palmerton was in front, head down. November rode behind him, the barrel of his Henry rifle centered on Palmerton's back.

"That was a damn fool play, Lyle," said November as he and Palmerton rode up. "I had to chase this son of a buck near a mile before I caught up with him. And then I had to slap him out of the saddle with the barrel of this Henry before he'd stop."

"Best be careful about that," advised Speaks. "You bend the barrel, you'll ruin that gun." He could see the bloody lump on the side of Palmerton's head now.

Joshua Tate cleared his throat and said, "Do . . . do we just leave . . . them . . . here?" He was looking at the sprawled bodies.

"Ever done any cowboying?" Speaks asked him.

Joshua nodded. "Yes, sir. Still doin' it."

"Then you've seen your share of buzzards and wolves. They keep the prairie clean. Sam and me and this other fella, we've got places to go." Speaks grasped the saddle horn and swung up onto the back of the roan. It seemed odd to him to think of this now, but he still missed a horse he'd owned for a short time in 1868 called Old Leviticus.

"You don't even intend to . . . to bury them?" asked Rosalie.

Speaks looked at her.

"I reckon you've known them the longest, ma'am," he said. "Would you take the time, if you had somethin' better to do?"

228

She took a deep breath and then laid her hand on the young cowboy's arm.

"Let's go, Joshua."

Speaks and November and Palmerton rode north. Rosalie and Joshua got into the wagon and headed west. The dead men stayed where they were.

Chapter Twenty-three

Speaks still had the smell of burned powder in his nose as they made camp that night. Just to look at him, killing didn't seem to bother him much. He had done his share of it over the years, beginning with the Comanches who had been responsible for the deaths of his parents and brother and sister. Since then he had killed whenever there was no other way to handle a situation, but he had never liked it. He hoped to God that he never did.

"You shouldn't have taken off for the tall and uncut like you did today," he said to Palmerton as the three of them sat around the campfire enjoying the flapjacks and bacon November had fried up.

"Hell, I thought I saw a chance," said Palmerton. "You were busy trying to get yourself killed because you had to stick up for some whore and her cowboy."

Speaks grunted. "Don't like it when the odds are that uneven, that's all."

From the other side of the fire, November said, "That Melanie gal down in Fort Worth, back in the fifties . . . she had reddish hair, too, didn't she, Lyle?"

Speaks's eyes narrowed.

"What happened today didn't have a damned thing to do with Melanie," he snapped.

November chuckled. "Didn't say it did."

"I knew what you meant."

"You damn well ought to by now. We been ridin' together, off and on, for more'n thirty years."

Palmerton laughed. "And after all this time, you've turned outlaw."

Speaks glared at him and was about to say something when November sat up straighter. "Somebody comin'," he said softly.

Speaks had heard it too. The clip-clop of hooves, and a squeaking noise that could only be wheels and springs. A vehicle of some sort of was approaching.

A moment later, Speaks wasn't too surprised when a familiar voice called out, "Hello the camp! All right to come in?"

"That boy Tate," said November.

Speaks nodded. "Come on in," he said. He didn't sound happy about it.

The wagon rolled into the circle of firelight. The glare from the flames made Rosalie's hair seem even more red as Joshua hopped down

231

from the seat, then turned back to help her to the ground.

Speaks stood with his legs spraddled a little, coffee cup in his left hand, the thumb of his right hooked in his gun belt so that his hand hung near the forward-angled butt of the Colt. "Thought you two headed west," he said.

"We did," Joshua said as he turned toward Speaks. "But we got to talking about it, and we decided to go north instead. There's some big ranches up Wyoming way, and I reckon I can get me a riding job on one of them without much trouble."

"When we saw the fire, we knew it must be you," Rosalie said. "We hate to impose on your hospitality . . ."

November stood up. "No imposition at all, ma'am. You and your fiancé are welcome to join us." He gestured toward the skillet and the coffeepot sitting on the edge of the fire. "We've got a little supper left."

Rosalie sat down on a log near the fire while Joshua unhitched the pair of horses from the wagon and tended to their needs first. Speaks was glad to see that.

The two of them dug into the food November gave them, and they ate so hungrily that Speaks wondered if they were running low on supplies. Palmerton watched the girl, his gaze so intent and so openly admiring that Speaks almost told him to keep his eyes to himself.

But before Speaks could say anything Palmerton smiled and said, "Pretty girl like you must have a story, Miss Rosalie. How'd you come to be out here on the frontier?"

She stared down at her mostly empty plate and looked embarrassed. Speaks said roughly, "Don't pay Palmerton any mind, ma'am. He's got a habit of poking his nose in where it ain't wanted."

Rosalie shook her head. "No, that's all right," she said. "My folks have a farm over in Kansas, but I didn't like it there. I didn't want to stay. This fella came through the settlement. He said he was a gambler. He wanted me to come with him." She sighed. "So I did."

"And then he sold her to that son of a bitch you killed earlier today, Mr. Speaks," Joshua said indignantly. He put his arm around Rosalie's shoulders. "I'm just glad I came along to take you away from all that, sweetheart."

Only problem with what the boy had just said, thought Speaks, was that you couldn't really take somebody away from their past. They carried it with them, no matter how far they went.

He was living proof of that.

"Cold camp tonight if you want to travel with us," Speaks said the next morning as they got ready to go. "We're getting close enough to where we're going that I don't want to risk a fire anymore."

"Where's that?" Joshua asked innocently.

Speaks just looked at him for a second and then turned away to saddle the dun. Joshua had the good grace to look embarrassed. He wore that expression a lot . . . but then, he was still a yonker, Speaks told himself.

"Up ahead about two days' ride, the trail forks," said November. "One side goes to Cheyenne. That's the one you young folks will want to take."

"You're not going to Cheyenne, Mr. November?" asked Rosalie.

November shook his head. "No, ma'am. We got business off in that rough country to the west, over the Bald Mountain."

"But there's not any settlements over there," said Joshua.

"Nope. But we ain't lookin' to settle down, neither," November replied dryly.

Speaks swung up into the saddle. "Let's go." His tone didn't leave any room for argument.

During the day thunderstorms rumbled over the prairie, luckily passing to the east of the trail Speaks and the others were following. The storms were close enough, though, that they could see the lightning forking across the sky, brilliant against the black clouds, and feel the earth vibrate as the thunder rolled. The wind whipped up grit from the trail, and Speaks might not have minded a little rain to settle the dust. None of it fell where they were, although they could see the gray curtains of the stuff in the distance.

Rosalie sat next to Joshua as he drove the wagon, and she shivered every time the thunder roared.

Night fell early because of the thick overcast. As Speaks had promised, they made a cold camp near the foothills, with Bald Mountain hulking darkly in the distance. For supper they gnawed on hard biscuits and strips of jerky and washed the food down with water from canteens. In the last of the fading light, Joshua spread blankets underneath the wagon for Rosalie. Normally he slept under the wagon while she made her bed in the back of the vehicle, but they were trading places so that Rosalie would have some shelter if it started to rain.

Speaks stood on the edge of the camp and watched the lightning fading in the distance. It looked to him as if the storm was moving on.

He heard a small rasping sound, smelled sulfur. November said, "Damn!" Speaks wheeled around in time to see November slapping a lit quirly out of Palmerton's mouth.

"What the hell!" Palmerton yelled.

"Somebody could've seen the flare from that lucifer when you struck it," said Speaks. "You're lucky Sam didn't knock that quirly out of your mouth with the butt of his Colt."

"Damn it, we're still a long way from Devereaux's hideout!" Palmer said.

"Devereaux?" repeated Joshua. "The outlaw Devereaux? That's who you're looking for?"

Speaks's jaw tightened. He would have just as soon the two youngsters didn't know anything about what he and November were really doing here, and why they were traveling with Palmerton. But it was too late now. He realized he should have warned Palmerton to keep his damned mouth shut.

"I told you last night, don't pay him any

mind," said Speaks. "Tomorrow you two will be going your way and we'll be going ours."

"I've heard about Devereaux," said Joshua, ignoring what Speaks had just told him. "They say he's the most bloody-handed killer since Quantrill."

Rosalie said, "And they say he's stolen thousands of dollars."

Palmerton snicked. "Closer to a hundred thousand, I'd say."

"Nobody asked you," said November as he put a hand on Palmerton's shoulder and pushed the outlaw down into a sitting position on the ground.

"Nobody asked anybody anything," Speaks said heavily. "And I think we all ought to be quiet and turn in. Sam, you all right to stand first watch?"

"Sure."

"Fine." Even though he could barely see her in the darkness, Speaks nodded to Rosalie. "Good night, ma'am."

"Good night, Mr. Speaks," she said. Joshua led her toward the wagon.

"You're worrying about nothing," Palmerton said to Speaks in a low voice. "Devereaux's thirty or forty miles from here, at least."

"You'd better hope you're right," Speaks advised him, his voice equally low. "Because if you're trying to lead us into a trap, you're the first man I'm going to kill. . . ."

Speaks had thought the storm was going away, but instead it came back during the night, and this time it brought the rain with it. The sky opened up and blinding sheets fell, the drops so large and falling with such force that they felt like tiny fists striking the skin. Everyone scrambled around digging out slickers, and Rosalie huddled under the wagon, wrapped in a blanket and hugging herself. Bolts of lightning slammed into the prairie only a few hundred yards from the camp. The horrible racket and the flashes of light spooked the horses—even Speaks's dun and November's buckskin, and they were accustomed to loud noises. Soaked to the skin despite the slicker he wore, Speaks hurried over to the animals to try to settle them down. He wasn't sure how he was going to go about it.

Another flash of lightning suddenly showed him men on horseback who had ridden to the camp under the cover of the storm. Speaks grabbed for his gun and yelled, "Sam!"

Thunder drowned out his warning. Man-made flashes split the night, alternating with the lightning until Speaks couldn't tell which was which. He sprinted around the horses, using them for cover as he looked for something to shoot at. He heard Palmerton yell, "Damn it, it's me!" A horse with a man on its back loomed in front of Speaks. He tried to get out of the way, but the animal's shoulder slammed into him and sent him spinning off his feet.

Somewhere in the middle of the storm and the shooting, Rosalie screamed.

That sound exploded in Speaks's ears even louder than the thunder as he struggled to get up. The rain had turned the ground to a quagmire, and it sucked at him as he tried to plant his feet. The rider who had knocked him down was still there, a few feet away, fighting to control his horse. Speaks lifted his gun.

Somebody else rode out of the chaos and drove a rifle butt into the back of his head. Speaks went down hard, face down in the mud. As blackness claimed him, he hoped that somebody would turn him over before he sucked in enough of the stuff to kill him. A bullet was better than drowning in mud.

But a man was just as dead anyway. That was his last coherent thought for a while.

Chapter Twenty-four

"And who might you be?" asked a pleasant voice. It was deep, powerful, the sort of voice a preacher or a politician might have.

Speaks forced his eyes open and looked up into a lean, bearded face with a high forehead and piercing, deep-set eyes. He had never seen the man before, but he had heard the description often enough. Folks who had been unlucky enough to see him and survive said that the man was half saint, half devil.

"Devereaux," Speaks rasped.

The man shook his head. "I'm afraid you can't be Devereaux, my friend." Firelight painted a red glare on the right side of his face. "I'm Devereaux."

Speaks looked past him, saw an arching stone ceiling. He rolled his head to the side, even though it hurt like hell to do so. He saw that he was in a cave, lying on the rough stone floor. It was a good-size cavern, with a large fire leaping and crackling some yards away. The smoke from the flames rose to the ceiling and vanished, so there had to be at least one natural chimney up there, probably more. A dozen or more horses shifted and stamped their feet in a makeshift rope corral on the far side of the cavern. A narrow tunnel opposite the corral had to lead to the surface.

Old habits made Speaks count the men sitting around the fire. Eight of them, all hard-faced and dressed in range clothes. Devereaux's men.

Not far away, sitting on a large, flat rock with their arms around each other, were Joshua and Rosalie. Neither of them seemed to be hurt, but they looked very frightened.

They had reason to be, thought Speaks. This was obviously Devereaux's hideout, and the outlaw leader wouldn't be likely to let any outsiders leave here alive.

A groan made Speaks roll his head the other way, and to his huge relief he saw November lying on the ground, trussed up as Speaks was, wrists and legs bound with rope. But at least, also like him, November was alive.

Speaks didn't see Palmerton anywhere.

Devereaux was still hunkered on his heels beside Speaks. "I believe I asked you a question, my friend," he reminded Speaks gently.

"I ain't your friend," growled Speaks. "And I don't like to talk to a man while I'm lying down."

"Then by all means, allow me to give you a hand."

Speaks's wrists were bound together in front of him. Devereaux grasped the rope and came to his feet, hauling Speaks up with him in a surprising display of strength. Devereaux was a slender man dressed in a black suit and a string tie, and he obviously possessed more power than his frame indicated.

A wave of dizziness swept over Speaks for a moment before his head settled down. When it had, he looked again at November. "He all right?"

"Just knocked out, like you. I told my men not to kill anyone unless it was absolutely necessary."

Speaks grunted. Those words sounded mighty hollow coming from a man who was known to have been responsible for the deaths of at least twenty people.

"Now, for the last time—" Devereaux's voice hardened. "Who are you?"

"Lyle Speaks."

Devereaux's bushy eyebrows lifted in surprise. "The famous lawman and manhunter? Is that Sam November, then?"

"It is."

"You and your partner came to beard me in my own den, just to bring me to justice?"

"I'm not packing a badge now. Palmerton had it in his head that November and I were after all that loot of yours."

"Ah, yes, Palmerton." Devereaux glanced toward a blanket-shrouded shape on the floor of the cave that Speaks had taken to be some supplies. "Poor Edward. He should have spoken up sooner. He might still be alive if he had." Devereaux shook his head. "On the other hand, I probably would have killed the fool myself for bringing you up here."

"I told him I'd kill him if he led us into a trap," Speaks sad heavily. "I reckon that match he struck was what tipped you off."

"One of my sentries saw the light from our lookout post, yes. But I already knew someone was behind us. I sensed it, you see. I can feel pursuit, like an animal."

He had the animal part right, thought Speaks. Devereaux was an animal—a killing animal.

November groaned again, started up as much as he could against his bonds, and said, "Wha—"

"It's all right, Sam," Speaks told him. "Just rest easy."

November slumped back. He blinked rapidly, and when his eyes focused, he looked up at Speaks and said, "Lyle?"

"I'm here, pard."

November's eyes flicked over to the tall, bearded man. "That'd be Devereaux."

Devereaux smiled. "Guilty as charged."

"That damn Palmerton—"

Devereaux turned from November back to Speaks. "Well, that seems to have accounted for everyone except those two young people over there."

"Leave them out of it," Speaks said quickly. "They're just a couple of pilgrims who met up with us on the trail. They don't have anything to do with us—or you."

Speaks knew he was wasting his breath, but he had to try anyway.

Devereaux frowned. "But they do have something to do with me. They have accepted my hospitality. That puts an unfortunate complexion on the matter."

The bandit leader was just toying with them. Speaks and November both knew it. November's nerves cracked a little, and he said, "Damn it, why didn't you just shoot us and get it over with? Why'd you drag us into this cave in the first place?"

"I have an insatiable curiosity," said Devereaux. "One of my weaknesses, I suppose."

November closed his eyes. "Said the same thing about somebody else not that long ago," he muttered

Speaks didn't ask him what he meant by that. Instead, he asked Devereaux, "What happens now?"

"We wait for the storm to pass," Devereaux said.

Speaks and November sat on the floor of the cave, their backs propped against its cold, hard wall. Both men had bruises and scrapes, but neither had caught a slug in the brief fight during the thunderstorms. They talked together in low voices. Some of Devereaux's men had rolled up in their blankets and gone to sleep, while the others were playing cards. Devereaux himself sat off to one side of the fire, a book in his lap, reading by the light of the flames.

Speaks thought about what he knew of Devereaux. The man had been a banker back east before the war, then had served as an officer in the Union army. He had a lot more education than Speaks or November did, that was certain. But book learning wasn't enough to fill up the hole in a man's soul, and after the war Devereaux had started robbing banks instead of working in them. For many years, from Missouri to Texas, across the plains and into the mountains, Devereaux had spread his shadow. Speaks should have come after him before now, just on general principles.

The rustle of skirts made Speaks look at Rosalie. She had gotten to her feet, and she started walking toward Devereaux. Joshua half stood behind, holding out a hand to her, saying, "Rose, honey . . ."

Rosalie planted herself in front of Devereaux. "I want to talk to you."

Devereaux looked up from his book, and even though his bearded face was composed, Speaks thought he was surprised. "Yes, my dear?"

"You don't have to call me dear," said Rosalie. "You don't even have to be nice to me. A few days ago I was a whore, and I'll be one again if that's what it takes to get me out of here alive. You can have me if you want."

Joshua said, "Rosalie." His voice cracked and shivered with pain.

Devereaux smiled thinly. "Under the circumstances, your kind offer is rather unnecessary,

I'm afraid. Your fate is mine to command." He gestured at Joshua. "Besides, you're upsetting your husband."

"He's not my husband," snapped Rosalie. "I never figured on marrying him. I just wanted him to get me away from the place I was. I'd have left him soon as I got the chance."

"Rosalie." Joshua whispered it this time.

She pushed back a wing of dark red hair that had fallen in front of her face. "I want to throw in with you," she said to Devereaux. "What about it?"

"Can I trust you?" asked Devereaux.

"Of course."

He slipped his pistol from the cross-draw holster he wore under his frock coat. "Prove it," he said as he held the gun out toward her. "Take this and kill your young swain."

Speaks and November were watching tensely. Rosalie hesitated, her hand halfway to the smooth walnut grips of the revolver. Speaks didn't know whether he wanted her to take it or not. A wild idea surfaced in his head. Rosalie was trying to trick Devereaux, he told himself. She was going to take the gun and shoot the outlaw leader, then try to free them. It wouldn't work, Speaks knew. She might kill Devereaux, but then his men would just shoot her too, and then the other three captives.

Rosalie's hand jerked out, closed around the butt of the gun. She turned, earing back the hammer like someone who knew what she was doing, and lifted the barrel toward the stunned

Joshua. "Rosalie!" he cried as he started to stand up from the rock.

She fired.

The sound was deafeningly loud in the cavern. The slug took Joshua in the chest and flung him backward. He sprawled next to the fire, forcing some of the cardplayers to jump out of the way. The outlaws who had been asleep were jolted awake by the shot. They came up out of their bedrolls, guns in hand.

"Hold your fire!" Devereaux shouted, as if he were back in the war and issuing commands to his troops again.

Rosalie swung back toward him and handed him the gun.

"Satisfied?" she asked.

"Very," murmured Devereaux.

"Damn," November said under his breath, shocked at what he had just seen.

Speaks didn't say anything. He felt too sick.

Chapter Twenty-five

They dragged Joshua's body over next to Palmerton's and threw a blanket over it too.

An hour later the sun came up and Devereaux walked up the tunnel and out of the cave for a few minutes. When he strode back in, he announced that it was a beautiful day.

Rosalie had been siting with him ever since she had killed Joshua, and the two of them had been talking in low tones. Sometimes they laughed quietly.

Now Devereaux came over to stand in front of Speaks and November and ask, "What are we going to do with the two of you?"

"Kill us, more'n likely," said November.

"Not until you tell me the truth. Are you genuinely not after me because you're working for the law? You really came after my money?"

"I told you," rumbled Speaks. "I'm not packing a badge."

"Neither am I," said November.

Speaks said, "A man gets damned tired of riding all those lonely trails. Cold in the winter, hot in the summer, and you never know when somebody's going to shoot at you."

"All for wages that ain't much better'n cowboyin'," November added bitterly. "Lyle an' me, we finally had enough of it. Didn't we?"

Speaks nodded.

"Figured if we were going to cash it in, we'd best do it now, before we got too old to enjoy it."

Devereaux looked from one to the other of them, studying them intently for a long moment. Then he said slowly, "Well, I will be damned. I believe that both of you gentlemen are telling the truth. That puts a different light on things."

Rosalie came up behind him.

"You'd better kill them anyway. They may be getting on in years, but I never saw anybody who could shoot like them. Especially Speaks."

Devereaux looked back over his shoulder at her, his eyes narrow.

"Then perhaps if I'm going to take on a new partner I've chosen the wrong person."

Rosalie caught her breath, then gave a nervous laugh.

"Don't even joke about that," she said. "I can make you a lot happier . . . than these two!"

"You could certainly warm my blankets better, I'll grant you that." Devereaux looked back at the two prisoners. "But with these two at my side . . . my God, the entire West would be mine for the taking!"

"But . . . but I killed Joshua for you!"

"You certainly did. And quite efficiently, too. But let's face facts, darling Rosalie. Your usefulness to me is rather limited."

Devereaux was just playing with her, tormenting her for the hell of it. His eyes were sparking with amusement as he turned toward Speaks and November. Speaks saw that, plain as day. But Rosalie didn't. She didn't know he didn't mean it.

Her hand dipped into her skirts. Devereaux's men had probably searched her, but they had missed the knife she slid from its hiding place and drove deep into his back with a grunt of effort.

Devereaux's eyes went wide and his mouth opened, but no sound came out. His men weren't really paying attention to what was happening in this corner of the cave, so they didn't know what was going on until Devereaux slumped forward, falling right on top of Speaks.

Speaks reached for Devereaux's gun. His fingers closed around it as one of the outlaws yelled, "Hey! The boss—"

Even with his wrists bound together, Speaks was able to throw Devereaux aside and lift the gun in one smooth motion. His thumb looped over the hammer, drew it back. He squeezed the trigger.

The man who had sounded the alarm was

thrown backward by the bullet slamming into him.

November rolled into Rosalie's legs, knocking her down out of the line of fire. He lunged toward Devereaux's body and ripped the knife from the bandit leader's back. Speaks fired again and dropped another man while November was using the blade to slash through the ropes around his legs. Bullets smacked into the wall above Speaks's head as he squeezed off a third shot. This one missed, but it came close enough to make the man it was aimed at dive for the nearest cover, which in this case was the narrow tunnel leading out of the cave. The other men followed him, running into the tunnel as they fired wild shots at Speaks and November.

Speaks hunched over and threw himself forward on his belly to make himself a smaller target. He didn't want to empty Devereaux's gun, but he fired one more shot, just to give the outlaws something to think about. November leaned over with the knife and Speaks held out his hands as far apart as he could. November sawed through the ropes. They fell away from Speaks's wrists.

Instinct had guided the shots Speaks had fired. His hands had been half numb from his wrists being tied for so long. But he had taken care, all through the long night, to wiggle his fingers and move his hands as much as he could, just in case he got a chance to try something.

That chance had come, and so far Speaks and

November had made the most of it. But any second now, Devereaux's men were going to realize that they outnumbered Speaks and November four to one. Speaks's deadly accurate fire had spooked them for a minute, that was all.

Speaks and November used that minute the best they could.

Pins and needles shot through Speaks's hands, but that didn't stop him as he took the knife from November and slashed the ropes on his legs. Then he cut the bonds on November's wrists.

Rosalie was nearby, sitting on the ground and shaking her head groggily. November grabbed her under the arms and hauled her upright, then threw her down behind the rock where she and Joshua had been sitting a few hours—a lifetime—earlier. He sprawled beside her.

Speaks said, "Sam," and tossed the revolver toward his partner. November reached up and caught it deftly in midair. Speaks lunged toward the gear the outlaws had left behind when they fled the cave. His hands caught up a Winchester.

As he heard a rush of footsteps from the tunnel, he hoped the rifle was fully loaded.

Bringing it to his shoulder, he started firing as fast as he could jack the lever of the Winchester. He poured lead into the tunnel and heard the deadly whine of slugs ricocheting from the stone walls. Someone gave a high, thin yell. November popped up over the rock and added a couple of shots to the storm of bullets coming from the rifle in Speaks's hands.

Speaks stopped firing. He couldn't hear a thing. The thunderous noise of the rifle fire had deafened him. He crouched, keeping the barrel of the Winchester trained on the tunnel mouth. Nothing moved there.

". . . gone?"

Speaks realized that his hearing was coming back. November had just asked him a question.

"Could be," said Speaks, "but they'll be back."

"You think so?"

He could hear November clearly now.

"I reckon so," Speaks said. "Unless I miss my guess, there's a pretty good chance Devereaux's loot is stashed somewhere in this cave."

Devereaux was dead.

Speaks checked on that as soon as he got a chance. Rosalie's knife thrust had gone between a couple of his ribs and right into his heart. She was good at killing folks, Speaks had to give her that much.

"What are we going to do?" she moaned as she lay behind the rock with November. "They're going to kill us!"

"Maybe not," said Speaks. He had found some ammunition and reloaded the rifle, then tossed the box of .44 cartridges over to November, who had filled the cylinder of the Colt. "Devereaux was an officer in the war," Speaks went on. "He wouldn't get himself penned up in a place like this unless there was some other way out."

November looked at the smoke still rising from the fire, which had burned down some but not gone out. Then he glanced meaningfully at the ceiling of the cave and said, "That smoke's goin' somewhere."

"That's what I thought," agreed Speaks. He was still rummaging through the gear left behind by the outlaws, keeping one eye on the tunnel as he did so. The survivors of the gang had to be just outside, gathering their courage for another rush. Not only was the loot from all the robberies probably hidden in here, thought Speaks, but the horses were still in the cave, too. Those outlaws wouldn't be going anywhere without them.

Suddenly, Speaks ripped the top off a small wooden crate. A grin split his face. "We're in luck," he told November. "Some of that newfangled dynamite."

"Reckon Devereaux maybe planned on using it to blow safes open," commented November.

"Likely." Speaks took five of the small cylinders wrapped in greasy red paper and stuck them inside his shirt, along with a handful of blasting caps and a length of fuse. "Now all I've got to do is find a way out of here . . ."

Rosalie spoke up again. "We could trade them some money and the horses," she said. "They'd let us go, as long as they got what they wanted."

"You don't really believe that, do you?" November asked. "Those boys don't figure to let any of us out of this cave alive."

Speaks took a burning branch from the fire and prowled around the rear of the cave, using the light from the makeshift torch to search. It took him only a few minutes to find a handhold carved into the rock wall.

"This has to be it," he told November. He went over to his partner, handed him the Winchester, and took the Colt in return, tucking it into his belt. "Keep a close eye on that tunnel while I'm gone."

"Where are you going?" Rosalie asked frantically.

"To get us out of this rat hole."

Speaks went back to the rear wall. He reached up, grasped one of the carved holds, and eased the toe of his boot into a lower one. He hauled himself up and started to climb, working by feel now.

He was a big man, and not nearly as young as he used to be. Sweat popped out on his forehead as he strained to pull himself up. Smoke from the fire drifted around his face and made him cough as he climbed higher, but at least that told him he was on the right track. He followed the handholds as darkness closed in around him, and after a few minutes he realized that he had entered a shaft of some sort. One of those natural chimneys he had thought about earlier. He kept climbing.

The shaft narrowed, its rough walls pressing on Speaks's shoulders. Devereaux would have had no trouble making it through this bolt-hole, but Speaks began to fear that he was going to get stuck. He pushed on, because that was all he could do. The rocks tore his shirt and scraped his skin.

Suddenly, he realized that it wasn't as dark

around him as it had been a few moments earlier. He climbed some more, and the shaft turned, angling toward the surface. Light spilled down the tunnel, almost blinding Speaks at first. He pulled himself on up.

Minutes later he reached up out of the shaft, caught hold of the ground, and hauled himself out into the daylight. It was screened by some brush that also provided concealment for the opening of the shaft. Speaks pushed up onto his knees and looked around.

He was on one of the shoulders of rocky ground that heaved out from the base of Bald Mountain. The slope around him was steep but negotiable. About a hundred yards below him was a small ridge. Speaks slid down to it, trying not to dislodge too many rocks along the way. He didn't want to start a small avalanche and warn Devereaux's men that somebody was up here.

When he reached the ridge, he lay down and eased his head up so that he could peer over. As he had hoped, he could see down into the rocky ground in front of the cave. He could see Devereaux's surviving men, crouched behind some boulders. Their rifles were trained on something, no doubt the mouth of the tunnel, and the men were arguing among themselves.

Speaks couldn't make out everything that they were saying, but he understood enough. Some of the outlaws wanted to rush the cave again right now, while the others wanted to wait and maybe starve out the people trapped inside. That idea was contemptuously dismissed by most of the outlaws. Enough food and water was stored in the cave that anyone holed up in there could last out a long siege.

One of the man snapped, "I say we go get 'em and I say we go now!"

Speaks heard mutters of agreement. He knew he and November and Rosalie had been lucky that the men had held off as long as they had. Speaks couldn't afford to wait any longer.

He slipped the sticks of dynamite out of his shirt, then cut the fuse into short lengths and attached them and the blasting caps to the red cylinders. When he was finished, he reached into his pocket for the little waterproof packet of lucifers he had taken to carrying. He scratched one of the sulfur matches into life and held the flame to the length of fuse curling from one of the sticks of dynamite. The fuse caught with a splutter.

Speaks came up on his knees and threw the dynamite, watching with satisfaction as it tumbled end over end, trailing the burning fuse, until it bounced right smack in the middle of the cluster of boulders where the outlaws were.

One of them had time to yell a terrified warning before the dynamite blew him to kingdom come.

Speaks had another fuse lit already. He threw that stick, too, and followed it with two more, bracketing the boulders so that as the outlaws scrambled away from the second stick, they ran right into explosions from the third and fourth sticks. When the smoke and dust cleared Speaks saw that only two men were still on their feet, and they were staggering around, bloody and dazed.

Below Speaks, the Winchester cracked from the mouth of the cave and the two remaining outlaws spun off their feet. November had heard the blasts and came to see what was happening.

Glad that it was finally over, Speaks slid down the hill to the bottom and joined November and Rosalie as they emerged from the cave.

"We get all of 'em?" asked November.

Speaks prodded each of the bodies in turn, the Colt held ready in his hand in case any of the outlaws were shamming. None of them were.

"They're all dead," Speaks told November.

Rosalie looked around at the carnage. "You . . . you wiped out the whole gang," she said.

Speaks nodded. "That's what we came up here to do."

"I thought you were after the money."

"Well, there's that, too." November had the barrel of the Winchester canted back over his shoulder. "We got to take it back to the bank where it came from."

Rosalie's eyes widened.

"You told Devereaux you wanted it for yourselves! You said you weren't carrying badges anymore!"

"Fella don't have to be carryin' a badge to be workin' for the law," said November.

"We're special deputies, workin' out of the U.S. marshal's office in Denver," Speaks explained.

"And I don't figure to lose a minute's sleep over lyin' to Devereaux about it, neither," added November.

"Come on, Sam. We've got to find that loot." Speaks turned toward the mouth of the tunnel, then stopped and added to Rosalie, "And you're under arrest for murder, so you'd better come along too."

They tied Devereaux's body on one of the horses, along with the saddlebags containing a little over seventy-seven thousand dollars. Palmerton had overestimated how much of the loot was left, but not by much. The rest of the bodies were left where they had fallen. The chief marshal could send somebody up to retrieve them if he wanted to, Speaks decided. Not that there would be much left to retrieve by then.

Rosalie's hands were tied too. November lifted her onto a horse. Joshua's wagon had been abandoned where the gang had captured them.

As the three of them rode away from Bald Mountain, Speaks and November dropped back a little, so that Rosalie was riding in front of them where they could keep an eye on her. She was slumped in the saddle, her head drooping forward in despair.

"I feel a mite bad about takin' her back to face those charges," November said.

"Maybe I would, too, if the only one she'd killed was Devereaux." Speaks kept his eyes straight. "I keep remembering how surprised that boy looked just before she shot him."

"Yeah, there's that. Still, it's a damned shame."

"Most things are," said Speaks.

Chapter Twenty-six

Montana, 1901

The next morning Aubrey P. Fellows was more chipper than he had been since they left the ranch. He finally had the kind of story he was looking for. So the various versions of the Devereaux legend he had heard weren't true. Some had Speaks killing fifty men, some forty, some had both of them killing twenty each. None of that mattered. Fellows had the real story, and it *was* impressive—even if it *had* been a woman who actually killed Devereaux himself. Now he could praise Speaks in print for telling the true story.

"Fellows!" Speaks called.

The writer realized that his name had been called several times.

"I'm sorry," he said. "I was thinking."

"Well, think about dousing the campfire and gettin' your horse ready," November said. "We're pullin' out in five minutes."

"Make that fifteen, Sam," Speaks said suddenly.

"What?"

"I think it's time to see if this here writer can hit anything with that hogleg you lent him."

The idea both amused and appealed to November.

"All right. Let's try him."

November got an empty can, one of the few cans of fruit Clytie had included for them. He paced off twenty feet and set the can on a rock, then walked back to where Speaks and Fellows were.

"Where's the gun?" Speaks asked the writer.

"In my saddlebag."

"Get it."

Fellows fetched the gun. His first instinct had been to resist this test, but suddenly he felt a rising excitement, Lyle Speaks was going to teach him to shoot. What a sidebar this could be! And he could probably sell it to his publisher for extra money.

"Okay, check the loads," Speaks said.

"What?"

"Make sure the gun is loaded."

They let the easterner fumble for a few moments, and then Speaks showed him how to check the loads.

"There's an empty, uh, thing here . . . there's only five bullets."

"That's all you want," Speaks said. "You want the chamber the hammer is sittin' on to be empty, so you don't blow off your own foot."

"Oh."

Speaks showed him how to close the gun, and then spent a few minutes explaining how to carry it tucked into his belt, since they didn't have a holster for him.

"All right," Speaks said, "we're ready to shoot."

"Which one of you is the better shot?" Fellows asked.

The two old friends looked at each other.

"We've never put it to the test," November said.

"Who's faster?"

"Ain't tested that, either."

"Don't you want to know?" Fellows asked. "Aren't you curious?"

Again the two friends exchanged a look and then said, in unison, "No!"

"It ain't important," Speaks added. "What's been important all these years is we've always had someone we could count on to watch our backs."

"Just seems to me you'd want to know—"

"Sorry, kid," November said. "That's somethin' you're not gonna get to write about."

"Okay," Speaks said, "hit the can."

"From here?"

"This is close," November said, "as close as we'll probably want to be to those rustlers."

Now Fellows's eyes widened. Suddenly, his bladder was making demands on him.

"How did you do this?" he asked.

"Whataya mean?" November asked.

"How have you spent all these years facing another man with a gun, intent on killing you, standing *this* close to you?"

"It's not somethin' we've given a lot of thought to, I guess," Speaks said.

"When a man *is* that close," November said, "and *is* intent on killin' you, you best not pause to think about it."

"Let's just see if you can hit the can," Speaks said, "and go from there."

Fellows raised the gun, aimed at the can, and pulled the trigger.

"Nothing happened," he said.

"You'll have to cock it," November said. "It ain't double action."

"Oh."

Fellows raised the gun again, cocked it, aimed at the can, and fired. The bullet kicked up dirt about three feet in front of the target.

"Well," Speaks said, "you were in line with it, just a little short. Try holding the gun with two hands."

"Okay."

Again the writer raised the gun, this time with two hands, cocked the hammer back, aimed, and fired. This shot was off line, three feet to the left, and still three feet short.

"You're aiming," November said. "Just point the gun. Pretend the barrel is your index finger."

"And don't close one eye," Speaks added.

"All right," Fellows said, and went through his motion again, raising, cocking. This time he kept both eyes open and pointed the gun, then pulled the trigger. The bullet struck the rock the can was sitting on, causing the can to shake precariously, then slide off the rock to the ground.

"I got it!"

"Not quite," November said.

"It fell to the ground," Fellows complained.

"I said hit the can," Speaks said, "not the rock. If that can was a man, he'd be down but not out."

"Let me try again."

"That's enough for one day," Speaks said. "We've got to break camp and get moving."

Speaks went to get his horse. November took a moment to show Fellows how to reload the gun, then sent him off to douse the fire and saddle his own horse.

Fellows felt uncomfortable. The barrel of the old Walker Colt was so long, but he figured he'd get used to carrying it in his belt. He was very glad they had told him about the empty sixth chamber.

"You load that one," Sam November told him, "right before the fight."

Thinking about what was ahead, Aubrey P. Fellows shuddered, then took a moment to empty his bladder before saddling his horse.

He emptied it on the fire.

Fellows had seen the long green grass on some of Lyle Speaks's land, where the cattle fed. All he had seen since leaving the ranch, however, was rocks and dust, and he felt as if the dust had crawled into his clothes and caked up.

Legend

"What are the chances of a bath?" he asked as they rode along with the Powder to their left.

"More a swim than a bath," November said, "but it would cut through the dust."

"You can take care of that when we stop tonight," Speaks said, "but let me warn you, that water will be damned cold."

"It sounds good to me," Fellows said, "cold and wet." He thought that he had sweated more in the last three days than in his whole life. The soreness in his butt was just beginning to relent. The two legends had told the truth when they said this was no Central Park. Still, it was all the riding he had done back east that kept him from now being crippled by being on horseback in this terrain.

Fellows could see what Speaks had meant about not being able to make this trip in an automobile. Tires and axles would have long since given up the ghost and left their riders on foot. These wonderful horses they were riding were taking it all in stride.

"You take care of your horse," November had told him at one point, "and it will take care of you. You don't push 'em too hard, you rub 'em down and feed 'em well, let 'em get the rest they need, they'll go on forever for you."

"Do they have names?" Fellows asked.

Speaks scowled and November said, "Remember the buffalo-hunting story."

"Oh, yeah," Fellows said, and that ended the discussion about horses.

* * *

Later in the day Fellows asked, "Will we catch up to them today?"

"No," November said, "we won't cross the Powder until tomorrow."

"What if they get there first?" he asked. "What if we miss them?"

"We won't," Speaks said. "They're moving fifty head. If we'd wanted to we probably could have caught them by now."

"But we need the element of surprise," November added.

Fellows was impressed by both men. He had to admit he'd been disappointed when he first met Speaks. The man had looked ancient sitting there on the porch, and appeared to have very little life left in him. However, since they started this journey on horseback Lyle Speaks and Sam November both seemed to grow younger and more spry with each passing day.

He was also impressed by their admitting to needing an edge in order to compensate for their age.

"The eyes ain't what they used to be," November said at one point, "and neither are the legs. We can still shoot, though, eh, Lyle?"

"Long as we can see what we're shootin' at" was Speaks's reply.

"Don't worry, lad," November said. "We can still see far off. It's close up that gives us trouble."

Now Fellows could see why the two men did not want to get very close to the rustlers.

He thought how happy his publisher was going to be with his live account of this addition to the legend of Lyle Speaks, or of Speaks and November, of Texas.

They camped by the river and built a fire. Fellows went down to the river's edge and removed his clothes, even his drawers. As he started to wade into the river, the cold was like a shock to his system. He was determined, though, to wash away the dust and dirt that had baked into his skin. When he returned to the camp the fire was going strong and he sat by it to dry, with a blanket around him.

"What about you two?" he asked. "Don't you w-want to bathe?"

"What for?" November asked. "On trips like this you need the second skin dirt gives you."

"It's extra protection against the elements, son," Speaks said.

Fellows took this information with a grain of salt. He had the feeling that the two old-timers simply didn't want to take a bath. He had no way of knowing if what they were telling him was true.

He would find out later when, red from the sun, his skin would itch much more than it ever had from the trail dust.

November was the unofficial cook, and Fellows had to admit the man made the most of what he had. He fried up some bacon and then put some of the dried biscuits Clytie had packed into the pan with the grease, turning it into a delicious pulpy mass that washed down real smooth with hot trail coffee.

"Maybe I should take a watch tonight?" Fellows suggested.

Speaks and November looked at each other, then shook their heads.

"I don't think so, Fellows," Speaks said.

"Why not?"

"You don't know what to look for," November said.

"Or what to listen for," Speaks added.

"You could teach me."

"Look at what you're doin' right now," November said.

"What?"

"You're lookin' into the fire," Speaks said. "Destroys your night vision. Now you got to wait for your eyes to adjust to the dark again, and by the time they do you could be dead. Somethin' could come from out of the dark—man or beast—and you'd never see 'em until they was on you."

"I see," the writer said, averting his eyes from the fire. Moments later he looked into it again, and he realized how difficult it was to ignore the brilliant flames, especially when you'd been told to.

"Lyle and I will split the watch," November said, "and one of us will tell you another story."

"Which one?"

Speaks looked at November, who said, "I'll take first watch. Hmm, let me see. Which one?"

"I'm turnin' in," Speaks said. "Tell him any damn thing you want."

Speaks rolled himself into his blanket and turned his back to them.

"What's wrong with Mr. Speaks?" Fellows asked.

"Ah, we had a talk about what to tell you next, and we didn't agree."

"Why not?"

"I think you should know what kind of trouble he got into whenever we split up."

"You split up?"

"Whataya think, boy? We been joined at the hip all these years? Yeah, sometimes we split up."

"And what would happen?"

"Without my common sense around," November said, chuckling, "ol' Lyle would get hisself into a heap of trouble."

"Like what?" Fellows asked, groping for his notebook.

"Like meeting Clytie," November said. "Now, there was somethin' I could have saved him from."

"His marriage?"

November nodded.

"A three-day courtship is all those two had. You ever hear of such a thing?"

"But . . . they're still together fifteen years later."

November made that rude sound with his mouth that he hadn't made the past few days.

"You want to hear this story or not?"

"Yes, yes," Fellows said, "I'm ready. . . ."

"Well, I ain't," November said. "Get yourself dressed. I don't relish sittin' here talkin' to a naked man all night. . . ."

Part Five

Part Five

Chapter Twenty-seven

Montana, 1888

The wind came out of the north long and low and level, and with it came snow, lightly at first, then heavier, blotting out the rise and fall of the plains, making the earth indistinguishable from sky.

Lyle Speaks sank his chin into the collar of his coat, pulled his hat low over his eyes. May in Montana! In Texas the blue bonnets would be out, the flycatchers buzzing, the rivers running fast and full, colored red like the dirt that contained them. Here there was only earth and sky, and the mouth of the wind that sought to swallow him.

Maybe he'd been foolish to agree to this venture, even if cattlemen were flocking to Montana, lured by the prospects of land for the taking, free graze and good water, even if, after all these years, something in him he hadn't wanted to recognize kept urging him to stop moving, to leave a mark that said he'd been more than simply a man quick with a gun, deft with a deck of cards.

He'd been brought up to know better, except all that early training had been of no use to him at all with his family lying slaughtered like so many sheep, their blood soaking into the ground and him standing there swearing a man's vengeance.

At times like this he felt cut in half, with a curtain pulled down between the boy and the man, a curtain that denied him feeling and bred caution, that had made him what he was—a man without fear or any emotion he could name. Yet here he was, headed for a second chance, and in a country cold enough to freeze the ears of a mule.

He'd come on ahead of Sam and the boys who were driving the cattle simply because he'd wanted to be alone, to stake his own claim on the place and learn it without advice or intrusion.

He and Sam had come up the fall before to look over the country—the rolling plains, naked except for a blanket of curling buffalo grass, the river and the creek that flowed to the Yellowstone with its breaks and lush stands of bluejoint, and always, west and south, the horizon defined by mountains, invisible now as if they'd been blown away by the wind and the driving snow.

Somewhere up ahead was the home place and a cabin. Somewhere . . .

"Best stay put awhile," the bartender in the last town, an old prizefighter whose nose was too mushed to support his spectacles, had warned that morning. Or had it been the morning before?

Time out here had a way of slipping past, one day into another, the red dawn erupting into the volcanic purple and gold of sunset, obliterating the miles traveled as if they'd never been.

The bartender wore a skullcap of tightly woven wool that had a string attached to the bridge of his spectacles, giving him an appearance halfway between a badger and a bulldog, and his eyes glinted like pebbles behind the thick lenses.

"A spring blizzard's just as bad as a winter one," he'd said. "Mark me."

Impatient, Speaks had ignored the advice and headed out into the grayness of morning, across the rise and fall of the naked plains, with here and there a snowdrift like a white shadow on brown earth, and all the while the wind coming stronger, with an edge to it that warned of worse to come.

His big roan raised its head, snorted, blew steam out of ice-crusted nostrils. It was a good horse, steady, muscled, broad-chested—worth the ninety-five dollars he'd paid back in Miles City, with the packhorse thrown in. Glancing back, he saw that it, too, was staring off into the

275

whiteness through eyelashes coated with a heavy fringe of ice.

On the back of the wind came the faint blue scent of wood smoke, and like the horses, Speaks lifted his head. Smoke meant people, and he wasn't in a position to be particular about what kind of people—buffalo hunters, trappers, maybe just a bunch of out-of-work cowhands holed up for the winter in a line shack. What the hell? The numbness in his fingers and toes was a warning, like the steady snow screen that made a mockery of a man's sense of direction.

He wasn't about to die out here, wasn't about to let his life get buried in a drift, though maybe that was all he deserved. Maybe.

He urged the roan on, following the smoke that laid a trail of warmth, beckoned like a mirage seen at a distance. Even so, he nearly missed the cabin, half dugout, half logs that sprouted out of the side of a hill; would have gone on past except for the roan, which stopped dead, nickered, and was answered by a faint whinny.

Then he saw the pale light, like a will-o'-the-wisp, seen, then not seen, moving slowly away.

"Hello the house!" he called, and the wind took his voice, sent it off in fragments.

The light swung once, then stopped, and he called again, riding toward it through drifts up to the roan's belly.

"Stop right there." The shotgun was aimed at his midsection, and the woman holding it had

the yellow eyes of a lynx, unblinking, unread-
able.

Automatically, he lifted his hands.

"Sorry to frighten you, ma'am."

The gun didn't waver.

"What do you want?"

What in hell did she think he wanted on a
night like this? He choked down the question.

"I was hopin' I could put up 'til the snow
stops. Your shed'd do me."

She came a step closer, and he saw she was
tall, and good to look at in spite of those eyes,
which were narrowed now, squinting up at him.

"Get out." The two words came like the spit
of a cat. "You and your kind aren't welcome
here."

She meant it. She'd turn him away, drill a
hole through him without hesitation if he was
any judge, and he was. What did she mean,
"your kind"?

"Just what kind am I?" he said, failing to keep
the beginnings of anger out of his voice.

She gave a snort.

"Just git. You whiskey peddlers have caused
enough damn trouble."

The roan shifted under him, restless, turning
toward the shelter of the barn, and the anger
that was always there danced under Speaks's
skin. Cautiously he swung down and stood facing her, knowing he could take the shotgun
away in one quick move, knock her down in the
snow. But he'd never hit a woman and didn't
intend to start now.

"I'm no whiskey trader. Me and my partner

filed on a place north of here, but I'm not going to make it tonight."

She stared at him.

"Just what we need. More homesteaders turning the grass upside down."

Probably deliberately she misunderstood, intended to stand here trading insults until they both turned to ice.

"It beats whiskey peddling."

"Not by much." She gestured with the shotgun. "All right. Put up in the barn. I don't want a neighbor on my conscience. But you better not be lying. And stay away from the mare. She's ready to foal."

His mouth quirked in a smile. Just like a female to choose the worst possible time. But what was this woman doing out here alone, no husband in evidence?

She had a long braid of yellow hair that came down over her shoulder—a thick braid, big around as his wrist and turning white with snow.

"You'd best get inside," he said. "I'll be fine in the shed. And if it'll make you feel any better, my name's Lyle Speaks. I'll be running cattle and horses, and that's all."

She stared at him as if she was memorizing his face or trying to see behind it. Then she said, with the smallest hint of humor, "It beats homesteading."

"Yes, ma'am." He picked up his reins.

"My name's Clytie Beck," she said.

He liked the sound of it—hard and soft together—wondered if she wasn't like her name, soft under the shell she wore like a turtle, like the oversized buffalo coat that hid all but her face.

"Lyle Speaks. A pleasure," he said, tasting the irony of it—the two of them at odds, him banished to a barn when in the house there was a fire and warmth, escape from the wolf howl of the storm, and the woman, brittle, yellow-eyed, guarding her door.

The barn was as tidy as a kitchen, bridles on wall pegs, worn saddle beneath, hay stacked where the horses couldn't get at it. There were two of them, both mares, both several cuts above the usual range horses and well cared for. They watched him with bright, intelligent eyes as he unsaddled, and again he wondered what the woman was doing here, so obviously alone and used to it.

"And you won't tell me," he said to the mares. "You're all in it together." He saw nothing strange in his one-sided conversation, a habit with him as with most riders—talking to his horses and to himself.

He rubbed down his own animals, then threw each a good forkful of the sweet-scented hay. It was good hay, the perfume bringing back memories he'd tried to block. The long light of summer evenings and the music of women's voices—his mother's and Beth's, and himself a boy again, trusting, innocent of the future.

It had been a long road from Texas to here, and nothing to show for it but ugliness. He'd never thought to harm a living thing until that day, but after that he hadn't cared, not for himself nor—with one or two exceptions—anyone else, and now he was here, the future unknown, the night ahead full of storm and the moan of wind around the corners of the barn.

One of the mares pawed the straw with a powerful hoof, turned around, then lay down with a grunt. It was her time, regardless of weather. Would the woman, Clytie, want to know, to be here instead of safe behind the barred door?

He knew the answer, just as he knew what he was doing was an excuse to go out across the yard, bent against the wind, toward the dugout and Clytie with amber eyes the color of lantern light.

Chapter Twenty-eight

"Now what?"

She stood peering at him through a crack in the door. Prickly she was, in spite of their being neighbors.

Behind her he glimpsed a fire where a pot hung cooking, tempting, fragrant.

"Your mare's foaling. I thought you'd want to know." He resisted the urge to push the door open.

"I'll be right there." The door closed and he was standing like a goddamned beggar on the step; like a homeless pup, a goddamned fool.

"Bitch!" The word came out sharp, and he turned on his heel and went back to the barn, ignoring his hunger aroused by the scent of the stew, and another, subtler wanting he had no intention of satisfying. He'd never begged in his life, never had to, and if the rest of his neighbors were like her, he'd be out of here and back in Texas before spring.

She pushed open the barn door, her lantern held high.

"How is she?"

"Fine. So far." He'd be damned if he'd give her an inch. "Is this her first?"

Clytie shook her head.

"No. She's a good mother. I . . . we've had her a while."

He noted the substitution and how she'd smothered here words, but he made no response. In his life he'd always waited to see how the wind blew, to estimate the position of whomever he was facing. It had always paid off.

"Shouldn't be too long now" was all he said as he hunkered down at the entrance to the stall. "But it's a good thing she's in here. It's no night for a foal to be out in."

Clytie hung her lantern on a peg, and he saw the set of her chin and something that looked like desperation in her eyes.

"I can't afford to lose any more stock," she said. "You'll find out how it is, and then you'll understand why I didn't want you here."

"Tell me."

She knelt down and stroked the mare's neck, an oddly gentle gesture, unlike the woman she'd seemed, and again he was curious at what appeared to be contradictions in her—hard and soft, jagged and smooth—so a man didn't know where he stood. When she spoke, her voice was rough, as if she was swallowing tears.

"We've got rustlers, Indians, whiskey traders, nothing but trouble. The traders sell their rot-gut to the Indians. It's illegal, but they're smart and greedy. They take horses as payment, run them into the badlands, change the brands, then sell them in Canada. They don't care how many horses the Indians steal to pay them for their damned whiskey, or who they steal from. They don't care about dead cattle or dead ranchers, either. All they know is that they're getting rich off the rest of us, and we're help-less." She sat back on her heels, her hands clutched in her lap.

"The Indians in Canada come down here, get drunk, rob and kill, and then go back, and the British don't do anything about it. Our own agents won't do anything about the Montana Indians, and the damned soldiers at the forts just sit there and watch us honest folks go broke. You'll find out, Mr. Speaks. You'll find out when your cattle are dead and the Indians blame you because they're hungry and they say that you, all by yourself, killed off the buffalo. And when your horses disappear and nobody will lift a finger to help. I've lost half my herd and can't afford any more. It's a sorry state when you can't trust a person. When what you've sweated for gets taken, and you're back where you started with nothing left but the back end of a dream."

He listened carefully, making note of the fact that once again she referred only to herself, but when he spoke, he ignored the fact.

"What about our Indians? Seems to me they can be kept in line."

She snorted. "They're worse than anybody—stealing, going on drunk rampages, and the agents support them. You need their permission to get on the reservation, even to look for your own property, and they won't give it. Every damn one of 'em's a gentleman from the east, handpicked not to cause trouble, to protect the red man and, incidentally, to line their own pockets, and they don't give a hoot about us ranchers getting back what's ours." She emphasized the "gentleman," making it sound like a curse word.

Trouble. Wherever he went. And Montana wasn't going to be any different. One thing he knew, no Indian was about to take what was his. Never again. He said, "Sounds like you folks need a little help."

Her laugh was brittle.

"You're welcome to try. The government just ignores us, like we're at the root of the problem."

"And your husband?" He took her off guard, watched her hands clench tighter, so he could see the white knobs of bone, the curiously small wrists that stuck out from the ragged cuffs.

"He's dead. A year now. He went out after our horses and never came back." The yellow eyes were once again without expression—secretive, flat, hiding an emotion too dreadful to be exposed. "The Indians got him. I found him when the snow melted. Buried what was left."

He was back again in Texas, the boy propelled into manhood, seeing the mangled bodies, the grimaces of death. With one sentence she'd managed to rip aside the curtain he'd kept closed, the veil between himself and the memory too agonizing to be borne. See it again and go berserk, remember and puke until there was nothing left but the hatred. There was always hate. It kept him going, fueled the reason for what he was.

He said, "Comanches massacred my family. I'm all that's left—me and a younger brother I managed to save."

Her expression didn't change.

"When?"

"I was eighteen."

"Goddamn the varmints. Goddamn them to hell."

"Livin' is hell," he said, knowing the truth of it.

"The trouble is, dying's worse. I've seen enough of it to know. And when you're left, you wonder why."

"I knew why."

She looked at him with that curious way she had of seeing under his bones, and nodded once.

"You got them," she said. "Then you found out you couldn't stop. Am I right?"

"That's how it was."

"I'd do it too, but I'm a woman. It's hard for a woman, even though the need is there."

"It doesn't get easier," he said. "Man or woman."

Her hands lay loose in her lap, as if she'd expended all her energy reliving tragedies hidden away but not forgotten. "Reckon that's so," she said softly. "And I'm sorry for it. For you and me."

"It's done now."

She shook her head.

"Things like that, they stay with you. Mark you. I know, and I wish I didn't. Sometimes at night I see him . . . what there was after the wolves got done, and it's like it's happening all over, like I'm digging the grave and putting him in it. Mostly bones, you know, not the man I knew."

He said, "They even killed our chickens. Wrung their necks and let them lie where they fell."

"It makes you wonder, doesn't it? We're taught that killing is wrong, but sometimes it's what you have to do to make something right."

"There's folks who'd argue that."

She looked up at him, her mouth twisted.

"There's folks who can't tell what direction they're going in even with a signpost."

Beside them the mare grunted, arched her back, and grunted again, and then the foal slid out, shining in its sack, and lay still, a butterfly wrapped in delicate gauze.

The wind keened around the corner of the barn, rattling the door, threatening the flame in the lantern, and the mare lurched to her feet, nuzzled the newborn, and began licking it, learning its taste and scent, warming the frail body with her own.

Clytie sighed. "It's always magic. Seeing this, I always believe."

"In what?"

She shrugged.

"In good things. This is one. There have to be others."

In the pale light she seemed too fragile to take on the life that she was leading, that waited to crush her and her beliefs. He didn't want to see her broken, old before her time like so many others, but he guessed that if he reached out now and took her in his arms, the lioness in her would fight. She was proud, with the memory of the dead husband still fresh, and he was only a stranger come in out of the storm, the link between them too newly forged.

With an effort, he turned back to the mare and the colt that was struggling to stand on its too-slender legs, on hooves that were hard rubber.

"You ought to name him Storm," he said, and was amazed that he sounded like himself, with none of the ragged edges of desire in his voice.

A smile shattered her face.

"I will. He'll grow into it. He's already a fighter."

"Like you."

"I do what I have to do." She reached for the lantern. "Best leave them to it. You come back to the house. You must be hungry."

He was, and not just for food. Not even just for a woman. A whole segment of his life was missing, used up, gone. He was Lyle Speaks, but he wasn't sure who that was or who he'd been.

There wasn't much good to remember, now that he reflected on it. Not much good at all.

To cover his emotion he said, "Just don't point that shotgun at me while I eat."

She smiled again, and he saw fine lines beside her eyes where the smile lingered.

"I won't. And I'm sorry I acted like I did. I just have to be careful."

"You did right. You're alone, and you shouldn't be."

She ignored that, struggling to open the door against the wind. He put his shoulder to it, pushed, and felt the force take him, wipe out the feeble lantern flame so they were alone in the whirling dark.

She took his hand.

"Come on!"

The drifts were over his knees. By morning they'd be lucky to be able to walk. He'd have to stay. Make sure she had enough wood for the fire, a path shoveled between the barn and the house—a man's work, even if she did wield a shotgun with the best of them.

The cabin was one large room, the sleeping part separated from the rest by a blanket hung over a line. He saw clothes hanging neatly from pegs, the shotgun replaced beside the door, and a big stone fireplace where flames still flickered, casting warmth and light and shadow.

She poured water into a basin.

"You can wash up."

The water was warm, having stood on the hearth, a luxury, he thought, as this little room was a luxury, with its pine table, rag rug, and

Clytie moving briskly from kettle to cupboard. All that was lacking was a stiff shot of whiskey, peddlers or no.

As if she'd read his mind she put a jug and a glass on the table.

"It's legal. I keep it handy as medicine, though Drew liked a drink now and again."

"Your husband?"

She nodded, her back turned.

"How long were you married?"

"Not long enough." She jerked her shoulders straight.

He saw her quick movement and understood. You fought for what you wanted, believed in, and then it was taken without your knowledge or acceptance. And then you fought again, regardless of circumstances or sex.

He said, "You could go back, you know. Someplace easier than this."

She turned on him, yellow eyes fiery.

"To what? To being an orphan? To being somebody's slave? You can talk all you want, Mr. Speaks, but there's no way in hell I'll go back." The light in her eyes softened. "Out here I'm free. Working for myself. You ought to be able to understand that, being a man. And besides, I'm not built for towns, and I don't much like company, especially the female kind." She gave a short laugh. "And I find that females don't care much for me, either."

Maybe it was the whiskey, maybe it was how she looked—defiant—or maybe it was the thought of her ready to blast him with a shotgun. Whatever, Speaks threw back his head and laughed.

"Don't you laugh at me!" She slammed a bowl down in front of him.

He stopped as quickly as he'd started. She had a temper, and Christ knew what she'd do if provoked.

"I'm not laughing at you, Clytie Beck. I was laughing at all the city females I've known. There's not a one could hold a candle to you."

Painted women, whores, churchgoers, schoolteacher, and every one had wanted to tame him, change him, put him in a suit of clothes to fit their image, just as they'd try to do to Clytie Beck, and with as much chance of success. Even Melanie, God bless her, all those years ago, would have tried to change him.

"I don't fit," she said. "Except out here."

She'd fit in his arms. The whole golden length of her, supple as a cat and just as untamed. In his courting of Melanie he'd been bold. Now he held back. A woman like this couldn't be taken. She had to come on her own, had to be courted, but not in the way it was usually done, with flowers and poetry and cautious hand-holding. Even though she was probably fifteen, maybe twenty years younger than he, she was much too old for that—too old in spirit, surely, if not years.

For a minute he wondered if he was crazy, if he was equal to the task, and then he chuckled.

"You fit fine," he said. "How long 'til supper?"

Chapter Twenty-nine

She woke with a start in the middle of the night and lay still, listening. The wind howled, but the house was silent except for Lyle's steady breathing beyond the curtain that was all that separated them. Judging from the sound, he was asleep.

She relaxed then, amazed at herself for actually permitting him to stay in the house—a stranger, and a dangerous man if she was any judge. *But not to me*, she thought. *He'll never hurt me*, and then wondered why she was so certain of that.

Nothing he'd said, exactly. More the way he'd acted, how he listened when she talked, understood her need for caution, even what appeared to be her bad manners but was only self-defense. And several times she'd caught him watching her with something like sadness in his eyes—and something else that made her catch her breath and turn away to hide the leap of her own heart.

She was, she admitted, lonely for talk with someone other than herself, her horses, and Lyle's presence had eased the emptiness, the threat of storm.

They had talked about everything, though she suspected he'd left out a large chunk of his life, glossed it over as if he was ashamed or wanted to spare her. That was all right. Half the people out here had lives they never mentioned, secrets that they kept, names they hadn't been born with. Even she didn't know her own true name. They'd found her at the door of a church and taken her in, called her by the name sprawled on a torn piece of brown paper. "Clytie," the message said. "One month and six days." No more.

Well, someone had cared enough to give her one name and a birthday, to leave her where she'd be found and cared for. Somewhere she had a mother and a father, a family she'd imagined over and over throughout childhood; a house with high ceilings and polished wooden floors, a house filled with love and the scent of cookies baking, as unlike the orphanage as heaven was unlike hell.

She'd been tall for her age, and strong. At fourteen she'd been taken by a farmer and his wife who needed cheap labor, and labor it was. They worked her hard. Sometimes she was almost too tired to eat the food that was, at least, plentiful. Sometimes she dreamed of running away, but she had no place to run to, no safe haven except those she created in her mind.

From the woman she'd learned thrift and how to run a house. From the man the ways of a farm and its animals, and she found she had a knack with animals, something more than a simple liking, as if she and they shared a language not understood by others. That was how she'd met Drew and changed her life forever.

The wagon train had stopped near the creek at the bottom pasture to make repairs and give stock a chance to graze. Andrew Beck had been with the train, a man with a purpose. He was going to Montana to raise horses, and he was bringing his own stud, a black Thoroughbred from Kentucky that he'd named Roamer. An apt name, as it turned out, for he'd broken loose and come to the barn where she'd been milking, come with flashing eyes and raised tail, following a scent on the evening air.

She'd never seen anything more beautiful, more powerful, more sure of itself than the stallion, but unafraid, she'd gone out and picked up the frayed rope that dangled from the halter.

"Where'd you come from?" she asked, and grinned when he arched his neck and blew.

"Think a lot of yourself, don't you? Think you can just come up here and raise Cain. Well, you can't. I bet somebody is missing you and fit to be tied, so come on. I'll take you back." And she wasn't surprised when he followed her, didn't have the sense to realize she was leading potential death on a string.

It was like it had been meant from the beginning, Drew coming out to meet her, to take the stallion and tether him, and then to ask her questions, all the while looking at her as if he couldn't get enough.

She hadn't known about passion. What she wanted, had always wanted, was to belong somewhere, to someone. So when Drew asked her, she'd made up her mind in an instant, had gone with him and never looked back. Until now, with the stranger asleep by the hearth, the man she'd taken in because he was as lonely as she and didn't know it. Because they were both drifting, even though she was rooted here in this place she'd helped to build, drifting like smoke, belonging to no one, and aching inside.

How would it be to be with a man again? *This* man, lean of body, with cheekbones she wanted to touch? How would it feel not to sleep alone anymore, to give up her secrets at the moment of joining?

Lyle Speaks. Her lips formed the words. *Lyle Speaks*. A name, a sound to hold to in the dark.

The wind died as she lay thinking, replaced by a silence as deep as the bottom of a well. She listened, heard Lyle's steady breathing, and snow sifting against the small window. Far off, a wolf howled, hungry and hunting in spite of the storm, lured by instinct to those struggling in the drifts, weak, trapped, dying.

She hoped Drew was dead before they'd got to him. Hoped he'd not spent his last minutes fighting them off, calling her name, and her too far away to hear.

The howling was closer now, and her thoughts turned to the foal. Had she shut the barn door, or had they left it open in their struggle with the wind?

Wolves had come in before, after her chickens, come right up to the house on padded paws, and she met them with her shotgun. Just as she was going to do now. She slipped out of bed, searched for her moccasins, grabbed the buffalo coat that doubled as a blanket, and moved toward the door.

No need to wake the stranger. She'd handle this herself like always. The door opened easily on leather hinges, and she saw that the snow had stopped, leaving only a few horsetail clouds and a moon reflecting off the ground.

Her shadow moved before her, black on silver and long, as if she were a giantess moving soundless toward other shadows that materialized out of nowhere.

The path she'd made earlier was obliterated. In one step she was up to her waist, floundering, trying to keep from falling, to keep hold of the shotgun that was her only defense against the wolves moving stealthily across the yard.

Now where was she going at this time of night, tiptoeing past him like a slender ghost?

Speaks watched her pick up her shotgun and open the door, saw the moonlight beyond and the path it made to the house, saw her silhouetted against it, a proper target if she'd stopped to think.

In one quick motion he was out of his bedroll

and on his feet, pistol in hand. She hadn't asked for any help, but that was how she was made—independent as a hog on ice.

When he reached the door he saw her fighting the snow, saw the wolves, six of them, drawn by her struggle, sure of an easy kill, and he shot—once, twice, three times—heard the yelps as they leaped and went down. Then he was pushing toward her as best he could through the drifts.

"What in hell do you think you're doing?" Fear turned his voice harsh.

Her teeth were chattering when she answered, as much from shock as from cold.

"I couldn't remember if we shut the barn. Help me out before I freeze."

"What if I hadn't been here?"

"Well, you were."

"And that's no answer."

Damn, she didn't weigh much more than a bird, he thought as he hauled her up and carried her to the house.

"It was the best I could do," she said, shivering in spite of herself.

"I'll check the barn. You go warm up. Take off those wet shoes." And if she got sick, what would happen? She'd be here alone tending the animals, killing herself to do what she had to do.

He stopped to inspect the wolves. They were big ones, with fine pelts. In the morning, after the fleas had jumped off in search of a better home, he'd skin them. They'd make a warm coat, or a rug for beside her bed.

Her bed. He'd wanted to be in it, but had forced himself to move slowly. If he hadn't, none of this nonsense would have happened. With that, he made up his mind. When he left here, she was going with him, though how he was going to convince her he couldn't figure.

The door to the barn was closed, but he opened it and peered in, waiting for his eyes to adjust to the darkness. The mares were both on their feet, alerted to danger, but the foal, curled up in the straw, slept the deep, dreamless sleep of the very young.

"Reckon they won't be back tonight, Mama," he said. "You and your baby are safe." She nickered at him with a gentle flaring of her nostrils.

He slogged back to the cabin. Clytie had been right to go out and defend. The loss of brood mares like these, even without the foal, would indeed have been a disaster. But dammit! Why hadn't she called for help?

She was standing by the fire in her stocking feet. The hem of her skirt was wet, and her hair had come loose from its tight braid, giving her the look of a girl, young and vulnerable.

"That was a damn fool stunt." He closed the door behind him and drew the bar. "You should've called me."

"You needed your sleep."

"I've gone without before. Did you stop to think what would have happened if I hadn't been around?"

"Yes." Her voice was small.

He folded his arms across his chest and looked at her.

"I have a suggestion."

"What?"

She returned his look with a hint of suspicion, as if she knew what he was going to say and was ready to counter it.

"Come with me when I leave."

She opened her mouth, then closed it and turned away and stared into the fire for a long moment.

It struck him that she might be hiding tears, and he went to stand beside her.

"I didn't mean . . ."

When she turned back her eyes were bright, but with anger.

"I know what you meant. You're not the first or the last to ask me, Mr. Speaks. But I'll be no man's whore. I've done fine on my own, and I don't need you to feel sorry, to feel you can just walk in here with your hands out and think I'll fall into your arms." Then she was quiet, chewing on her bottom lip, hating herself for being at cross-purposes.

He sighed. He might have known she'd take it that way, should have realized she'd reject what he hadn't said right in the first place.

"Clytie . . ."

"What?"

"I'm sorry."

She sniffed.

"You'd better be. Coming in here acting like all you have to do is snap your fingers and I'll follow you. Like I haven't any brains or self-respect.

298

"You've plenty of both."

"So you say now." She poked at the fire and watched it, ignoring him.

He'd lived most of his life in the company of men—and liked it that way. He'd not wanted to be tied down, leg-shackled to some female who expected him to be different from what he was. Nor had he ever wanted to give his heart to anyone. Not after losing it once. Yet in a few brief hours, all that had changed, on account of this woman who'd opened up his past and shared her own, and in doing so had laid it all to rest.

And, damn, she was beautiful, with the spill of yellow hair catching the firelight, and her determined little chin set hard, trying not to show her hurt.

He'd come to Montana for a second chance, a new life, and here she was, the woman he wanted to share it with, only he'd made a mess of the whole thing.

"We'd make a pair, Clytie," he said slowly, reaching deep into his head for the right words. They were slow in coming. He put his hands on her shoulders, expecting her to pull away, but she didn't, just stood where she was, still as a hunted animal, waiting.

"I came here to start over," he said finally. "To find a little peace and to settle. To build something I'd be proud of and maybe pass on. But I can't do it alone. A man needs a woman. A wife. Just like a woman needs a man. It's good not to fight alone, to have somebody watching your back who cares, who's there in bad times and good ones. You and me, we're both loners, but maybe we've had enough. Maybe it's time to try another way. That's what I meant in the first place, only I haven't had much practice askin'."

Her tears came then, big ones, along with a chuckle.

"That's about the prettiest proposal I've ever heard." She wiped her face with her sleeve. Actually, it was only the second one she'd ever heard, but best not to admit that. She wiped her face with her sleeve again. "I need time to think. We only just met."

Oh, she knew her answer. It just wasn't seemly to accept too fast, like you hadn't an alternative, were so man-hungry you'd take anyone that came along.

His hands tightened on her arms, then went around her.

"How much time?"

"A month?" Her words were muffled against his shoulder.

"Too long."

She fit against him like a hand in a glove. He tilted her face to his. "I'm not a patient man, Clytie. I've waited most of my life, but no more."

When he kissed her, she thought that she'd been waiting too—for the surge of fire deep in her belly, which was so strong she was startled and drew back.

He felt her response and tightened his hold. "Well?"

A few hours before she'd been drifting like smoke, and now she was flame, and suddenly she recognized that without it there was nothing between a man and a woman, only words and meaningless couplings, and that she could grow old, embittered, out of simple pride.

Even knowing her answer, she held firm.

"A month. That way you'll have time to change your mind."

"I won't," he said.

She shrugged.

"It's a possibility."

"You're stubborn."

"See! You're finding fault already." She turned away so he couldn't see her regret. "Drew never minded."

Was she comparing them? he wondered. Making a saint out of a dead man, and himself falling short?

"Neither do I," he said. "Sometimes stubbornness is a good thing."

"If I wasn't, I wouldn't be here," she said, acknowledging her efforts to keep what she had, to keep going, regardless. "So you can add pride to the list."

"Anything else I should know?" He was laughing now, and she heard it, risked a look over her shoulder.

"You'll have to find out for yourself," she said, flirting a little before turning prickly again. "Now I'm going back to sleep, and so should you."

"Alone?"

"Mr. Speaks . . ."

"Lyle."

"What happened before wasn't an invitation." Though she wished it were, wished the night and the storm would go on forever, and the two of them here, the world with its rules and regulations nonexistent.

She was tough, honest, straight talking. What was generally called "a good woman."

He said, "You drive a hard bargain."

Her eyes caught the gleam of the fire.

"Things that come easy usually aren't worth it."

"You have an answer for everything."

Did she? And was shutting him out an answer or only a temporary retreat? "Not everything. Not for this. I don't even understand what happened, or if I can trust myself."

"Do you trust me?"

She looked at him a long time before answering with a quick nod of her head. "Yes." That was all. She pulled the blanket that divided the room, closing herself in, shutting him out.

He sat looking into the coals, fighting the heat of his desire. It would be easy to go to her, wrestle her own, take her. But what then? He'd never make it up to her. She'd never forgive or forget, and he'd have lost what he knew he wanted above any momentary passion.

"Damn you, Clytie," he murmured, and he had the suspicion it wasn't the last time he'd say it. One thing was sure, with her around, he'd never be bored. He wondered what Sam was going to say when he found him hitched, and to a lady who not only knew her own mind but said it, straight out. And then he wondered what he'd do if, at the end of the month, she turned him down.

Chapter Thirty

From the top of the rise he looked back. She stood in the yard, hands clasped, a small figure, too small to be left alone. By chance or luck he'd found her, the woman he'd been waiting for without knowing it, and to lose her now would be like killing that part of himself that had just come to life.

"It's only a month," she'd said that morning when he tried once more to change her mind. "You have things to do, and so do I, so stop fussing."

But anything could happen in a month. Hell, life could change from one minute to the next. Courage and determination were well and good, but she was female, a target for any Indian, any horse thief that came along, even if she was good with that shotgun. And of all the women in the world, he had to pick one who didn't know the meaning of fear.

He lifted a hand. Waved. She waved back, her arm high in the air in a gesture that seemed triumphant.

He nudged the roan and went on, following a faint trail beside the river. The worst of the snow had melted, turning the ground to mud, the prairie grasses green, and in spite of his worries, Speaks responded as any cattleman would.

Here was all the grass anyone needed—miles of it, unfenced, unsurveyed, free for the taking. Here was his future, spread out around him and full of promise.

A bunch of antelope, startled at his approach, bounded away, white rumps flashing, and in the muck at the river edge, frogs twanged, croaked, shrilled, a pulsing chorus, urgent and insistent. It seemed the whole earth was in a frenzy of regeneration.

He put the roan to a swinging trot, eager to get to what he now thought of as home. Yet when he saw the cabin in the distance, his heart sank. Compared to Clytie's snug place this was a disaster, a windowless shack, lacking a door and leaning at an angle as if a good wind could push it over. Hardly a place to bring a bride, a woman whose own house boasted a fireplace, a wooden floor, a window of real glass.

Working alone, felling enough timber, always conscious of the threat of Indians and taking precautions, he'd be lucky to get a few logs laid in a month. And if at that time she refused him, what then?

No matter how you looked at it, women created problems. Come to it, life was full of problems, regardless of where you were or what you did. He had expected starting a cattle operation would be easy, but all by himself he'd introduced complications.

He looked around the little valley, rimmed by hills, cut by the river, with a creek to the east. The frogs still twanged like a thousand Jew's harps, and a lark rose up out of the grass singing. It was a fine place, peaceful in itself, well-regulated. It was humans and their greed who brought trouble into paradise, and he expected that sooner or later he'd see more than he wanted.

For now, he'd sat dreaming too long. "Reckon I'd best get started," he said, and swung down off the roan.

The shot went over his head, missing him by inches. A second earlier and he'd have been dead.

The horse shied, but he held on to the rein, keeping the animal between himself and whoever was out there—someone who had every intention of killing him.

Cautiously he maneuvered around the side of the cabin, thinking fast. Once behind the shack he'd be able to get to his rifle in its scabbard on the other side of the roan. Then with luck he'd cut through the brush and locate his attackers.

They had obviously been there awhile, judging from the churned-up ground and horse droppings. Three of them, he decided, and white, riding shod animals. Maybe Clytie's whiskey peddlers working a still.

"But not for long," he said, tying the horse and slipping the Winchester out of the scabbard. He'd switched to Henrys at one point in his life, but had long since gone back to Winchesters. Soft-footed as an Indian, he ducked into the brush and crouched down, listening.

Frogs. The sound of the creek running over rocks, his own breathing, slow and steady. *Come on, you bastards.*

Somewhere up ahead a horse blew. Still he waited. Sooner or later they'd move, show themselves, and he was patient, the hunter waiting silent behind a scream of elders, primed for the kill.

Clytie watched him disappear over the rise, then stood a long time examining the turn her life had taken without any warning at all. Only two days before she'd been someone else, a woman without hope or feelings, going through the motions of life by rote, seeking only the rude means of survival, talking to herself to break the silence, falling asleep out of exhaustion and ignoring the emptiness of bed and heart.

And then Lyle Speaks had come out of the storm, a man like any other, or so she'd believed until that moment when he looked at the mare, and she'd seen compassion in his eyes, a rare understanding of nature and the pain of living.

He was tough, with a hard shell around his pain that was similar to hers. She'd sensed that, known it through instinct, the way an animal recognizes its likeness and responds.

There was a bleakness in him, well-hidden except to her who had tasted bitter despair, the finality of death, the horror of it. Even now she remembered how Drew had looked. Mouth open in what was a last cry of agony, the bones of his face and body plainly visible, brown bleaching to ivory, returning to dust.

Standing there in the yard, she shuddered, clenched her hands into fists. Just like this, she'd waved Drew off and then had gone about her chores with a will. Just like this she'd been certain he'd come back, sure of the rhythm and continuing of her days.

Did actions repeat? Had she, because of her pride, her doubts, sent Lyle off to a similar end?

"You stop right now," she said, and even to herself she sounded puny, a lone voice staving off terror.

This was what happened when you let down your guard, allowed yourself to feel. Oh, she should never have let him in her house—or her heart. She'd made a mistake and now would suffer for it.

"Damn you, Lyle Speaks," she said, and was pleased that she sounded herself again, the Clytie with her head on straight.

She turned on her heel and went to the barn, let the mare and foal out, and watched as the youngster tried his legs, investigated the piles of drifted snow and jumped at the sight of his own shadow.

"Storm," Lyle had named him, right after his birth.

Lyle again. In three days he'd stamped everything with his mark. Even her. Especially her. And now a month seemed infinity—thirty years instead of thirty days, and each one more worrisome than the last.

In the house, too, were reminders—the whiskey jug, the remains of breakfast, wood he had carried in and stacked by the hearth—and something else, the scents of leather, tobacco, maleness.

Would he come back? Or would she be left waiting, faithful, all the long years of her life, looking out over the plains for the sight of one who never came?

She cleared the plates, swept the crumbs from the table, then attacked the floor with a broom, and her thoughts danced like dust motes in the light from the open door. A part of her was riding with him on the trail north, where the future lay in wait, a panther crouched, ready to spring.

Her hands clenched on the broom handle. She had never been superstitious, never believed in the spiritualism that had taken such a hold on so many, but she had learned to trust her instinct, that mysterious sensing of people and possibilities which was warning her now.

Quickly she undressed, pulled on Drew's trousers and shirt, a wool jacket, heavy boots. The old pistol was stuck in her belt, and the shells put into deep pockets. She saddled the brown mare, threw hay for the new mother and grain for the chickens in the coop next to the house, then she picked up the shotgun and closed the door.

"I'm coming."

The wind took her voice, carried it off like a tumbleweed, split it into syllables, untranslatable sound.

Lyle's trail was plain. She found where he'd stopped and rested the horse, and where a party of Indians had crossed behind him, hesitating, then gone on their way. The brown mare had an easy, ground-covering jog and was tireless, but it was midafternoon before she pulled up on the hill that looked down into the valley and heard the shots—the crack of a rifle answered by a flurry of bullets from her side of the creek and a second rifle shot.

Lyle, she thought. And not in the cabin, but hidden somewhere. She scanned the course of the creek, steep-sided and overgrown, and on the wind, faint but unmistakable, she caught the scent of fermenting grain.

"Goddamned whiskey traders! Goddamned murdering bastards!" And Lyle was out there alone, probably across the creek, judging from the sound of the rifle.

A flash of blue caught her eyes, and she squinted, straining to see through the under-growth. They'd chosen their hiding place well, No one passing by would notice the little camp, not unless the smell was obvious.

"The odds just got a little better," she said, and smiled grimly. Then she led the mare downstream, tied her, and walked cautiously back up the rise.

Her choices were plain. She could swing around and find Lyle, or she could come up behind the bastards, catching them unawares. Without hesitation she chose the latter, slipping into the underbrush like a shadow, finding and following a narrow but well-used trail.

Obviously they'd been here over the winter, spreading their trash around, replenishing their supply of rotgut, thumbing their noses at the law. And on Lyle's place! She clenched her jaw.

"I'll see you in hell. Every last one." The words were soundless but felt; a cold anger that steeled every muscle pulsed in her veins, urged her on so she had to force herself to go quietly.

Intent on watching where she put her feet, she almost walked into the small clearing where the three men were crouched, their attention on the opposite bank. Behind them she caught sight of a rude still, and farther back three horses, probably stolen. They were fine animals, too fine for the likes of these.

Cautiously she backed away, ducked behind a boulder, and considered her options once more. She could go back in shooting and hope to get them before they turned on her, but that seemed foolish. Dying wasn't part of her plan, or being held hostage, either.

Heavy footsteps and a crackle of brush turned her mouth dry. Had they found her out already? She flattened herself against the stone, drawing the pistol. One of the men, tall, with a filthy red beard, came around the bend carrying a rifle.

Because of trash like him, Drew was dead, and who knew how many others? She lay still, holding her breath, as he passed without a glance. All of his attention was on the opposite bank where Lyle was holed up. Probably his rifle fire had given him away, and now this man was intending to circle around, cross the creek. Well, not if she had anything to do about it! Silently, she followed, realizing that if her prey went too far downstream he'd find the mare and come back looking for the rider.

"You just do that," she muttered. "You just come on back. I'll be here waiting."

Chapter Thirty-one

Speaks waded across the creek, which was running high in the spring runoff. Cover was thinner on the eastern side, but he found a cottonwood with a double trunk and crept behind it.

He'd been in worse situations, but few as uncomfortable as this one. The ground was damp, the wind was rising, his boots were soaked. The night would be long and cold—and sleepless if he couldn't pick off his attackers in daylight. There had to be a way to bring them out into the open.

A movement that wasn't part of the brush caught his eye. Either they'd gotten careless, or they figured he was gone. A mistake, he thought as he sighted down the barrel of the Winchester, taking his time, aiming at the target that was now still, and squeezing. A volley of shots answered his fire, all going wild. He squeezed off another, then sat back, assessing his options. Now at least he had them located, could make a move instead of sitting here wasting shells. He looked downstream in search of a better place to cross, and saw Clytie walking slowly up the hill, coming into trouble sure as she was born. And there was no way he could warn her, call out, without putting her in greater danger.

She had to have heard the shots, must know she was walking into a rattlesnake den. For a long moment she stood looking around, searching both sides of the creek, and it seemed that her eyes met his, that he could see their yellow light, fearless, as if she knew his predicament and had come to help.

Cat-footed, carrying the shotgun, she disappeared, moving in the direction of the still, and he took comfort from the stealth of her movements. She wasn't a fool, and she was well-armed. But she was on her own. All he could do was trust her judgment. But how many times was it possible to lose what you loved before even the future had no more promise and you gave up, quit living? If anything went wrong, he'd take her killers apart with his bare hands. With that, he waited, his thoughts bitter, his intentions fueled by controlled rage.

Suddenly, a man stepped partway out of the brush, and behind him, off to one side, was Clytie, pistol in hand. Speaks fired a second before she did, and watched his quarry fall, facedown in the muck of the creek.

"Clytie!"

She threw up her head, then motioned for silence and faded back, Indian-like, into the weeds.

Admiration for her replaced his anger. With a woman like this a man could take on anything—Indians, outlaws, a platoon of peddlers. And she was his. Or was she? Damn! Her very presence was a distraction, with at least two of the bastards still holed up like bears in a den. But if he was any judge, they'd soon come to find out what had happened to their partner, and get shot down for their trouble. So again he waited, this time knowing he had an ally on the other side—a yellow-eyed woman dressed like a man, with a braid down her back as thick as her arm.

Only one of the men came creeping down the trail, searching the woods on either side, forgetting caution when he spied the dead man half in the water.

"Beat!" he called over his shoulder to his unseen partner, then rushed out and bent over the body.

Like picking cans off a wall, Speaks thought, and smiled as he watched the second man jerk and fall beside his comrade.

Two down. One to go. He prayed Clytie didn't miss. A minute passed. Then two. He strained to see, then began creeping down the steep bank, heedless of the fact that he was now a perfect target. The shotgun roared.

Reaching the creek, he waded across, paying no attention to the water that came to his knees, stopping to check the two bodies. Both were dead, but he took no chances, pitching their rifles into the brush, taking the pistols they had stuck in their belts. Quite a collection—one worth keeping in a place like this one was turning out to be.

At a sound behind him he whirled, his own pistol cocked.

"It's me!" Her hat was gone. She had a scratch on one cheek and her hair had come loose, but her eyes glowed, pieces of topaz, the creek with the sun in it.

"Don't you ever come sneaking up on me like that again." Fright turned his voice hoarse. He'd nearly killed her himself.

"That's a fine thank-you." She shifted the shotgun and stood there, legs planted, oddly appealing in her man's clothing.

"Why'd you come?" He had to know.

She frowned, then shook her shoulders as if ridding herself of an unwanted, invisible weight.

"It was like I knew there was trouble. When I got so I couldn't wait it out, I came. Guess I was right." Her grin was cocked and suddenly lopsided. "The other one's back there. I killed him. I never killed anyone before."

Now that she had time to think, all she could see was the last man, his head blown apart. Her doing. She swallowed hard.

"It's done." Speaks put his arms around her.

She went on as if she hadn't heard.

"I didn't think how it would be. All I thought about was living instead of dying. Of them, those rotten crooks, and how nobody was going to take anything else away from me. They had no right, them and their stinking still, lining their pockets on other folks' grief. Except I never figured his brains would fly all over. I never thought about that part at all."

She buried her face in his shoulder, and he could feel her heart pounding like a drum. He remembered how he'd felt after stabbing the Comanche—as if he'd puke out his guts, as if he were somebody else who belonged nowhere, had no name or purpose.

Vindication brought its own curse that was often harder to bear than revenge. She'd be seeing the dead man in her dreams for a long time, and he'd be seeing the determination on her face as she stalked into the woods, shotgun in hand, a woman defending her own.

"Why'd you come?" he asked again, softly, into her ear.

She pushed away and looked at him, struggling to find the words to explain, not only to him but to herself. It was hard saying what was simply there, what she had no name for.

Finally she said, "If you'd never come back, I couldn't have stood it. There's only so much waiting a woman can do. You said how a man and a woman should go on together, in bad times and good, and I figured this was one of those bad times. I reckon I was right."

"Reckon you were at that," he said. "Does this mean the month is over?"

Again he watched as she seemed to retreat into some inner world only she could reach, and he guessed it would always be this way, her with secret places denied him. But wasn't that true of everyone, himself included?

Still, as he'd told her, he wasn't a patient man. He tightened his hold on her and saw the beginning of a smile, the crinkling of the fine lines at the corners of her eyes.

"Well?"

The smile shivered across her face. "Life's too short as it is," she said. "A month is a plain waste of time."

"Amen to that."

And, after all, how simple it was when you'd taken the right way, made the correct choice.

"All I've got to offer is a shack," he said. "For right now."

"I've been worse places." She looked around, then took his hand. "Let's go home," she said.

Montana, 1901

"Mrs. Speaks is an impressive woman," Fellows said as he finished writing his last line.

"She is that," November said.

Fellows set aside his notebook and looked at November across the fire.

"May I ask you a question?"

"Why not?"

"It appears to me that you don't like Mrs. Speaks much," Fellows said, first looking behind him to make sure Speaks was asleep.

"Don't know what you been lookin' at, boy," November said. "I like Clytie fine."

"But—"

November put his hand up and said, "Now, hold on. You asked me a question, I'm gonna answer it. There's a lot to admire about Clytie, and I'd defend her to my last drop of blood, but I just don't like what she's done to Lyle."

"Which is?"

"Well, he says she's made him a better man," November said.

"And you think she's made him old?"

"Old before his time," November said. "You've seen him these past few days on the trail. It's like he's reborn, he's the old Lyle again, the one I rode with for—well, for nigh on fifty years."

"What do you think will happen when you get back?" Fellows asked.

"Youngster," November said, "first we got to see *if* we get back."

"But—"

"Get some sleep," November said. "Big day ahead of us tomorrow."

Chapter Thirty-two

The next day November decided to tell Fellows a story on the trail.

When Speaks asked him why he would do this November said, "We're gettin' closer to meetin' up with those murderin' rustlers, and the lad is gettin' nervous about it."

Speaks said, "Ah, we just won't let him get involved, is all. Let him stand back and write about it."

"And what does he do," November asked, "if we're the ones who get killed and not the other way around?"

Speaks grinned and said, "Now who's talkin' like an old man?"

"I ain't talkin' about old, Lyle," November said seriously, "I'm talkin' about the string runnin' out. We've had us some awful powerful good luck over the years. It's got to run out sometime."

"And here I thought we lasted all these years because we was good," Speaks said.

"Well," November said, "that too."

Speaks wondered—just for a moment—if his old partner might not be a bit nervous about engaging these murderers. After all, it had been a few years since they saw this kind of action.

"Go ahead, then," Speaks said. "Tell him whatever story you like."

He had to admit he was starting to feel a little of it, himself.

"Cedar Rapids," November said. "Do you mind?"

"Mind?" Speaks asked. "Why should I mind. I'll just ride up ahead of you fellas so I don't hear you tellin' him about the first time I ever really experienced fear."

"I can only tell it to him, Lyle, the way you told it to me."

Speaks had looked at his friend and said, "That'll do."

So, on the trail, November told Aubrey P. Fellows the story of Cedar Rapids, and the rats . . .

Cedar Rapids, Iowa, 1893

Speaks should have known better. Hell, he was dealing with Harry Creed, and Harry Creed was one crazy son of a bitch.

"Where the hell you takin' me, Harry?" Speaks said.

"Oh, you'll see, you'll see," Harry Creed said, sounding like a kid teasing his younger brother. But at a hard-lived sixty-three, Speaks sure didn't look like any kind of kid.

The date was September 2, 1893. The place was Cedar Rapids, Iowa.

"We almost there?" Speaks said after they'd walked four more long blocks.

"Almost, almost." Harry Creed laughed.

These days Harry was dressing like a pirate. He wore a bandanna over his head, a golden ring on his right lobe, and he had a wee bit of a knife scar on his right cheek. Speaks wondered cynically if Harry had given himself that scar.

For all his bitching, Speaks was enjoying the day. This was one of those golden, lazy autumn days when the flat autumnal light of the sun seemed to penetrate to your core and warm your very soul. The air smelled of burning leaves, and there was no headier perfume than that, and the trees were so colorful they almost hurt the eye. He wanted to be a raggedy-ass kid again.

And just then, Harry Creed steered them around a corner and down a dusty alley.

Speaks was hot now, in his black suit coat and gray trousers, sweating. When they got where they were going he'd take the coat off. He was wearing a ruffled white shirt. He'd been doing a little gambling this year, and had decided to dress appropriately. His Navy Colt was back in his hotel room. Cedar Rapid had a full force of police. They'd throw your ass in the jug if they saw you sporting a handgun. The old days were long gone. Long gone.

The first thing he saw was the big red barn that said BLACKSMITH over the double doors. The first thing he heard was the shouts and curses of men who'd already been doing some drinking at ten o'clock on this fine fall morning. He could also smell blood, but he wasn't sure if it was human or animal. The scent of fresh blood tainted the air. He'd been around enough of it to recognize it instantly.

"You bring me to a cockfight?" Speaks said.

"Hell, no, man." Harry Creed grinned. "Somethin' a lot better than that."

And he just beamed his ass off right then. Speaks half expected him to start skipping at any moment. Skipping. A grown man.

The barn smelled of the smithy's fire and new-mown hay and horse shit. The smithy, a wiry little bald guy with a toothless grin and a wary eye, nodded them toward the back of the barn. His wary eye was fixed on Harry Creed's pirate getup. "You wouldn't happen to be Captain Kidd, would you?" he said, and winked at Speaks.

"Asshole," Harry Creed muttered as they walked to the back where maybe a dozen men stood in a circle, their hands filled with greenbacks just pleading to be bet. This was Saturday, and Friday, at least in most places, had been payday.

"You get the old Master in here, and I'll bet he gets through three of them little peckers in under a minute." The man speaking wore a cheap drummer's outfit and puffed on an even cheaper cigar. "And I got three dollars here to say I'm right."

Another man, a youth really, dressed in a blue work shirt and gray work trousers, said, "I'll see that three and make it four."

The other men laughed.

"This ain't poker, kid," one of them said.

Speaks still couldn't figure out what Harry Creed had gotten him into.

The barking dog got everybody's attention. It was a boxer, and a damned good-size one, and when it moved you could see its muscles move in waves down its back. Tear your damned leg off, this one would.

The men made loud cheering noises, as if a favorite politician had just walked into the barn.

"Master's gonna do it, aren't ya, boy?" said the young guy. "You're gonna make me a rich man, ain't ya, Master ol' boy?"

A couple of the men separated then and Speaks got his first look at the ring. It ran maybe three feet high, was metal, and was maybe four feet across. This was the kind of ring cockfighters used.

"Next batch!" a pudgy guy shouted as he came through the back door carrying a round, lidded metal can.

"God, I hate them things," one of the men in the circle said, and shuddered for everybody to see.

"What the hell's in the metal can?" Speaks asked Harry Creed.

But all Harry did was smile that stupid pirate smile of his. "Ain't you gonna be surprised?" he said.

As the man with the can reached the ring and started to pull the lid off, all the men, without exception, moved back. It was clear they wanted no part of whatever was in the can.

Master was in the ring now, crouched low, his eyes mesmerized by the can in the man's hands. Master's jowls flickered and snapped. Master knew what was in that can, all right.

The men got excited too. Their eyes gleamed. Some of them made eager, lurid noises in their throats. In many respects, they were even more animal-like than the rats. Killing had never been something Speaks cared to see, even if the victim was an animal. In Houston once, admittedly carrying more than a few drinks around in his belly, he'd broken the nose of a hobo who was trying to set a cat on fire for the amusement of his pals.

The man was swift and sure. In a single motion he jerked the lid away and upended the can.

At least eight or nine fat, angry, filthy, tail-twitching rats fell to the floor of the ring. When they hit the floor they went crazy, running around in frantic circles, bumping into each other, trying to cower when there was no place to hide or cower at all.

Master was jubilant with blood lust.

He didn't need any encouragement.

He leapt upon the first rat, seizing the thing between his teeth, catching it just right so that when teeth met belly, blood spurted and sprayed all over Master's otherwise tan face. The way a burst balloon would spurt and spray.

Speaks had enough already.

This little wagering sport was called ratting. You bet on how many rats a dog could catch and kill in a sixty-second period. Ratting was even more popular in the East than out here. Easterners just didn't talk about it much. They always made you think that they were very civilized people and that you, a westerner, were somehow heathen. But Speaks had been to New York a couple of times and he knew that civilization was not a dream shared by everybody. He'd seen a man cut out the eye of his opponent with a Bowie knife.

While Speaks was not partial to rats in any way, he still couldn't see torturing them this way. He didn't like cockfighting, either, far as that went.

"Hey, where ya goin'?" Harry Creed said. "Master here just got goin'."

But Speaks just wanted out. Who the hell wanted to watch a dog get himself all bloody by killing rats when it was such a beautiful day outside? Life versus death; and at this point in Lyle Speaks's years, he always chose the way of life and not the way of death.

He was just turning around when he felt something press against the lower part of his back.

"You just walk out of here real nice and easy, Mr. Speaks," a voice whispered in his ear, "and everything's gonna be just fine. Just fine. You understand me?"

Speaks was wondering who it was. You lived a life like Speaks's, it could be almost anybody, anybody from anywhere for almost any reason at all.

"You understand me, Mr. Speaks?" the voice asked again.

Speaks nodded.

If there was one thing he understood without any difficulty at all, it was having somebody hold a gun on him when he was unarmed. He understood it very, very well.

The gun nudged him around until Speaks was facing the double front doors of the barn. Then the gun nudged him right on out of the barn.

Chapter Thirty-three

He didn't really get a good look at the guy until they were almost out of the alley, and the only glimpse he got then was by looking over his shoulder.

He was a kid. By Speaks's standards, anyway. Twenty-two, twenty-three at most. One of those freckled frontier faces with the pug nose and the quick grin that made them look like altar boys until you noticed the pugnacious blue eyes. Speaks had seen kids like this all over the West. Not knowing what they were looking for but somehow all finding the same thing: trouble. There used to be a lot more of this kind in the West, self-styled gunsels who strutted and peacocked all over the place, just trying to prove how tough they were. But that was the old West, when there were a lot of bona fide gunfighters roaming around, and when kids like this one always got themselves killed in saloons for saying the wrong thing to the wrong man. This kid was out of place and out of time, a decade too late to live out his dime-novel dreams.

A couple of times Speaks thought of trying a move or two on the kid, but he decided against it. These old bones weren't what they used to be, and his glimpse of the kid told him that he was dealing with a very serious pistolero, or whatever the dime novelists were calling punks this year.

"I'm going to make it easy for you," Speaks said.

"Just keep walkin'."

"I don't have much money, and I don't know where I can lay my hands on any, either."

"I don't give a damn about money."

"You will when you get to be my age, kid."

"Just shut up and keep walkin'."

Now they were on the sidewalk. In one of the newspapers that he'd read last night, an editorial had boasted that Cedar Rapids possessed seven hundred telephones, fifteen blocks of electric streetlamps, and more than a mile of paved streets. A lot of the sidewalks were still board, though. Like this one.

"They're onto you."

"Who's onto me?" the kid said.

"The people. They can see you got a gun on me."

"Bullshit."

"Look at their faces, kid. These aren't dumb people. One of them's gonna get a cop."

The kid went for it, not right away maybe, but after a minute or so. He started watching the faces of the passersby, the women in big picture hats, the men in·fancy Edwardian-style duds, the farmers with their sun-red faces and hat-white foreheads. Speaks could sense the kid's step falter as he started to watch passing faces closely. Falter, and make him vulnerable.

Speaks wheeled around. The kid was right-handed, so Speaks came in left, fast, under the arc of the kid swinging his gun around.

He got the kid in the ribs with his elbow and in the groin with his fist. The kid folded in half, and Speaks ripped the gun out of his hand.

Speaks knocked off the kid's fancy-ass cow-boy hat, grabbed him by the hair, and dragged him all the way back to the alley.

"My hat!" the kid kept saying, as if Speaks had taken his magical talisman away. He didn't seem to notice that in the meantime Speaks was tearing out a good handful of his hair.

Speaks found a wall and threw the kid up against it and then, to send him a clear and un-mistakable message, started slamming the kid's head against the wall, never once letting go of the greasy hair.

Three, four, five times the kid's head came into slamming contact with the wall until finally his eyes rolled back, and the kid started sliding to the dusty alley, whereupon Speaks kicked him in the chest for good measure. Holding a gun on an unarmed Speaks was not the way to curry favor with the big man.

"Who the hell's this?" said the pirate.

Speaks looked over at Harry Creed and sighed. "What's the matter, they run out of rats?"

Speaks wished his traveling buddy Sam November was here. He'd be able to shoo Harry Creed away. But Sam was up visiting a sick relative in the Decorah area, which was why they'd traveled up the Mississippi from New Orleans in the first place. So now Speaks was stuck with a punk who meant him harm, and the antics of Harry Creed. He'd come here to see an old friend, Keegan, but now he wondered if he should've come here at all. Harry Creed was not somebody he wanted to spend any time with. And the punk just made things worse.

"Them rats really bothered you, huh?" Harry Creed giggled. "You shoulda seen yer face, Lyle-boy. You was whiter than a frozen tit."

The kid was just coming around.

"Who's this?" Harry Creed said.

"Don't know yet," Speaks said. "But I sure aim to find out."

In Cedar Rapids, the courthouse was on an island in the middle of town. The original inhabitant of the island, back in the Indian days, had been a horse thief whose luck ran out years later in Missouri, where he was hanged. Local folks never tired of telling this tale. When asked if it was really true or not, this unlikely tale, the residents of the town would point you to the public library and tell you to go look it up. And by God, if it wasn't true, as the books verified, a horse thief had been the first resident of what later became the town. How was that for a rough beginning?

A number of taverns lined the streets two blocks north, giving a good view of the island and, farther down, the ice works.

Harry Creed went and got them beers while Speaks shoved the kid into a booth at the back of the place. It was a choice seat. Hot wind carried the smell of the outhouse through the screen door. The men playing pinochle didn't seem to notice Speaks, or the smell.

"Who the hell are you?" Speaks asked.

"None of your business."

"Kid, I don't need much of an excuse to kick your ass, so you'd better start talkin'."

The kid sighed. "My name's Pecos."

Speaks laughed. "Pecos, huh?"

"Yeah, what's wrong with that?"

"Kid you got farm all over your face, and your twang puts you in Nebraska. So how the hell do you get 'Pecos' out of that?"

But before Pecos could answer, Harry Creed sat the beers down and they proceeded to drink.

"Guess what his name is?" Speaks said to Harry Creed.

"His name?"

"Yeah."

"Now, how the hell would I know what his name is?"

"Take a guess."

Harry Creed shrugged. "Jim?"

"Nope."

"Bob?"

"Uh-uh."

"Arnell?"

"Pecos."

"Oh, bullshit," Harry Creed said.

"Ask him."

Harry Creed took another sip of brew. "What's your name, kid?"

"Go fuck yourself."

"I'd be watchin' my mouth if I was you," Harry Creed said. Then he grinned. "With all due respect, I mean, Mr. Pecos."

"You assholes think this is funny, huh?" Pecos didn't wait for an answer. "Well, it won't be so funny when your friend Chris Keegan gets here and I get him in a gunfight."

"Aw hell," Speaks said. "That's what this's all about."

"What's it all about?" Harry Creed said.

"His name and wearin' his holster slung low like it is," Speaks said. "This dumb kid thinks he's a gunfighter."

"Not thinks," Pecos said, "am."

Speaks made a sour face and shook his head. "Kid, there haven't been any gunfighters since they shut down the trail towns ten years ago. And most of what you hear about gunfighters is bullshit anyway."

"Not about Wild Bill," Pecos said.

"Especially about Wild Bill," Speaks said. "And the only reason Chris Keegan ever got into any gunfights was defendin' himself against kids like you who forced him into it."

"He killed twenty-two men."

Harry Creed snorted. "More like four or five, kid, and Lyle's right, he didn't want to get into any of them. Kid came up to him one night in Abilene and called him out. He woulda killed Chris, but he was so drunk he tripped over his own feet and Chris killed him."

"Yeah," Speaks said, "and another time Chris was standin' at the bar and he saw this kid comin' through the batwings and he saw this kid start to draw and that gave him plenty of warning, so he ducked down and turned around and shot the kid before the kid could clear leather. Didn't take a whole lot of brainpower to do that."

"Plus which," Speaks said, "Chris Keegan is a year older'n me, which'd put him right about sixty-seven. Even if he used to be a gunfighter, he sure isn't anymore."

"I could still be the man who beat Chris Keegan," the kid said.

"You're a crazy bastard," Harry Creed said.

But a dangerous one, Speaks thought. He said, "That why you put a gun in my back? So I'd be sure to tell Chris about you when we meet his train tonight?"

The kid nodded. "That way he'd know I was serious. Real serious."

Speaks threw his beer in the kid's face.

Even the pinochle players glanced over to watch this one.

"Hey, Lyle," Harry Creed said. "What the hell you do that for?"

"Because I'm sick of this little prick."

The bartender came over. "You got trouble, take it outside."

"No trouble," Speaks said. "I'm just leavin', is all."

He stood up and did just what he said.

"You son of a bitch," the kid said as Speaks walked out the front door. "You son of a bitch."

Chapter Thirty-four

The train was eight cars long, all passenger cars except for the caboose. Behind the windows easterners sat staring imperiously at the small train depot. Not until they reached San Francisco would they be able to inhale civilized air again.

Chris Keegan looked fifteen years younger and ten years better than Speaks. They were almost the same age.

Keegan had always been something of a dude, and he was a dude still, what with the black silk gambler's vest, the flat-crowned Stetson, and black Wellington boots shined to blinding perfection.

Amy Keegan was a perfect match for her husband, blond, poised, beautiful in a slightly wan way. Her dark blue traveling dress clung to curves that time had not ruined as yet. There was just a hint of arrogance in her eyes as she beheld Lyle Speaks. Clearly, she considered both her husband and herself his superior. Once again, Speaks wondered why this woman had ever taken up with Harry Creed.

Thinking about Harry Creed reminded him that Keegan was now married to a woman he'd stolen away from Creed. Why hadn't Harry erupted at the simple mention of Keegan? *Strange*, he thought. *Man stole a woman from me, I'd curse every time I heard his name. I surely would.*

"How about a drink?" Speaks said.

"I'd really like to freshen up," Amy said.

Keegan said, "Why don't we freshen up a little first and meet you down in the hotel bar? I assume they have one."

"Yeah," Speaks said, "a nice one."

Speaks walked them back to the hotel. The lamplighters were at work, pushing back the night. Player piano music from the saloons. Violins from the Hungarian restaurant down the street. The steady clop clop clop of horses pulling fancy carriages toward the opera house. The dusk sky was vermillion and gold and filled Speaks with a sadness he couldn't articulate, not even to himself. Rainy days and dusk skies always did that to Speaks.

When they reached the hotel entrance, passing couples strolling the sidewalks beneath the round red harvest moon, Keegan said, "Oh, hell, honey, why don't I have a drink with Lyle here and then I'll come up to the room."

Speaks expected her to say no, but she surprised him.

"That's a good idea. Then maybe your dear old friend Speaks here can explain what Harry Creed was doing at the depot."

"Harry Creed?" Keegan said.

"He was standing at the west end of the platform," she said. "Watching us."

"Is Harry Creed in town?" Keegan said to Speaks.

"I'm afraid he is. Sam November ran into him up in Dubuque and told him we'd all be down here today."

"He's not exactly Amy's favorite person," Keegan said.

"I don't want to be in the same town with the man," Amy said. "In fact, I think I'll change our plans, Chris. I think we should leave first thing tomorrow."

For the very first time since he'd met her ten years earlier, Speaks felt sorry for Amy Keegan. Tears shone in her eyes, and she looked genuinely frightened. Speaks wondered just what the hell Harry Creed had done to her, anyway.

Then, as if she sensed that this was one of the few times Speaks liked her, she said in a very soft voice, "Oh, why don't you two have your drink. I'll just go on up to the room." Then to Speaks, smiling sadly: "People will think I lead him around by the nose all the time."

"Oh, honey," Keegan said.

She really was crying now, gently.

"See you in a little bit," Keegan said, and kissed her good-bye on the cheek.

The tears had softened her face; and as he looked at her now, Speaks was almost rocked by her beauty.

"The last night the bastard raped her," Keegan said. "Then he broke her arm."

For all of Harry Creed's antics, for all of his prairie-boy affability, he was a treacherous and ruthless son of a bitch, part of a lower order of men who had drifted through the frontier scavenger-like, mostly as con artists who unburdened the dumb and the greedy of their money. But they had more sinister sides, too. They were arsonists and stickup men and hired assassins, too. Whatever was needed in a particular time and place, they would be.

"That's why she's the way she is," Keegan said. "Never lets me out of her sight, because she's scared he's going to show up sometime."

"What I can't figure out is how the hell she ever got with a man like Creed, anyway."

They were in the taproom of the hotel. Men in Edwardian suits and women in bustled dresses filled the room. The waiters wore starched white shirts with celluloid collars.

Keegan said, "Her father was a missionary to the Indians. Lutheran. She got some of that from him. She's always trying to save people. When we lived in Kansas City, she spent half her time working at the Salvation Army." He shook his head. "Well, you know Harry. Back when she was living over in Peoria, he met her at a temperance meeting and her husband had just died of influenza and she was very lonely

339

and . . . well, she ended up marrying him. Didn't last long. Four months, I guess." He made a face. "He made her do all kinds of filthy things I'd rather not talk about. And he beat her up all the time, too." He made a fist. "Nearly every night."

"You never went after him?"

"She won't let me. She's afraid he'll kill me. I mean, a fair fight, guns or fists . . ." He shrugged. "But you know our Harry. It wouldn't be a fair fight. He'd be up to something."

Just then Speaks looked up and saw Amy coming toward them.

"I decided I'd rather be down here with you two," she explained as she sat down. "I got a little scared upstairs all alone. Knowing Harry's in town."

Keegan hadn't been exaggerating her fear. She looked agitated, all right.

Then she said gently, touching Keegan's hand, "I'd really like to leave tomorrow morning."

He nodded. "That's what we'll do, then." To Speaks: "Sorry, Lyle."

"I understand." Speaks looked at Amy. "I would've run him out of town if I'd have known what he did to you, Amy."

"He's always lurking someplace," she said.

"This has happened before?"

"Oh, sure," she said. "He's shown up several places over the past five or six years, hasn't he?"

"Yeah," Keegan said, "and he always leaves little reminders of himself. A note. A photograph of the two of them. Only time I ever called him on it, he denied it, of course. You know Harry."

"Yeah," Speaks said, "unfortunately, I do."

They drank through two hours of conversation, good conversation, fond memories of a good friendship, once they found out about Harry Creed, anyway. Keegan asked after Speaks's wife of five years, Clytie, and Speaks told him they were still very happy together in Montana. Ranching, he said, was agreeing with him.

Amy contributed too. The booze took away her slight air of superiority. She was just a good woman then, and Speaks could see how they loved each other and took care of each other, and he was happy for Keegan. Keegan was one of the good ones. Despite his years as a reluctant gunfighter, he was a peaceful, fair-minded, and decent man, and he deserved good things. There was no meanness in him.

Keegan had just ordered another round when Harry Creed came into the taproom.

Harry's pirate getup was gone. He wore a tweed coat, white shirt, dark trousers. His hair was slicked back in the fashion of the day. He actually looked handsome, and for the first time Speaks could imagine Harry and Amy walking down streets together. He came straight over to the table, as if they'd been expecting him.

Amy bowed her head, wouldn't look up at him.

But Keegan looked up, all right. "You got sixty seconds to get out of here, Harry."

Harry Creed smirked.

"You try to do an old friend a favor and look what you get."

Speaks wasn't sure which old friend Harry was talking about, Amy or Keegan.

"Sixty seconds, Harry," Keegan repeated.

Amy still wouldn't look up.

"There's a kid, Noonan's his real handle—Lyle here met him this afternoon—and anyway, he wants to shoot it out with you, Keegan." Says you're the last gunfighter and he wants the honor of puttin' you away. I'm tryin' hard to talk him out of it."

Now it was Keegan's turn to smirk.

"I'll bet you're tryin' real hard, Harry. I'm sure you wouldn't want anything terrible to happen to me, us bein' such good friends and all."

"I'm doin' everything I can," Harry Creed said. "I just thought I'd let you know. I'd be very careful where you go tonight."

Then he looked at Amy.

"You're lookin' lovely tonight, Amy."

Her head remained bowed, eyes closed. She was trying to will him out of existence.

The waiter appeared.

"Will you be staying?" he asked Harry Creed.

"No, he won't be," Keegan said harshly.

The waiter set down their beers and left quickly.

"I'm gonna try'n talk him out of it, Keegan," Harry Creed said.

"You do that," Keegan said. "Now get the hell out of here."

"You sure do look pretty tonight, Amy," Harry Creed said. Then he laughed. "Not quite as pretty as when she was with me, of course, but she was a lot younger then." He glanced at Speaks. "By the way, the kid likes ratting a lot better than you do. I can hardly drag him away from the barn." He patted his stomach. "Guess he's a little younger than you are, Speaks."

That was Harry, always getting in the last line.

They sat in silence for nearly two minutes. Amy brought her head up and reached over and touched her husband's hand again.

"Someday you won't be able to stop me, Amy," Keegan said softly. "Someday I'm going to kill him."

"Then they'd hang you," she said. "And he's the one who should hang."

Speaks said, "I'm going to take care of the kid for you. You two just go ahead and have yourselves a good meal."

"Don't get into trouble," Amy said.

Speaks shrugged.

"I've been in trouble a few times before." He smiled. "And I probably will be again before they plant me."

Keegan frowned.

"I wish there was a train out of here tonight. I want to get out of this town."

"Just relax and enjoy yourselves," Speaks said. He took out some greenbacks and laid them down on the table. "The next round's on me."

"Amy's right," Keegan said. "I don't want you to get into any trouble."

"I'll be fine," Speaks said, then shuddered inwardly. He'd be fine except for seeing the rats in the ratting cage. Kinda funny, the way you could feel sorry for something you hated. Speaks hated rats, and yet now he felt sorry as hell for them. He wasn't at all surprised that a punk like Noonan would enjoy ratting. He wasn't surprised at all.

He said good-bye and set off for the blacksmith's barn.

Chapter Thirty-five

Two blocks away Speaks started hearing the dogs barking as they went after the rats. This was something he'd have to keep to himself, feeling sorry for the rats and all. People would think he was one strange cowpoke for taking the side of the rats.

The next thing he heard, this a block away, was the men. This time of night they were drunk, words slurred. But you could hear the blood lust in the timbre of their voices. They didn't much care whose blood it was as long as somebody excited them by bleeding.

Speaks went inside the barn and moved to the far doors where the crowd gathered.

Harry Creed and Pecos stood together, watching as more rats were dumped into the

345

ring. They were at the back of the crowd, which made things easy for Speaks.

Pecos's face glowed with glee. This was something to see, all right. He even giggled like a little girl.

Speaks moved up carefully behind him, and then returned the favor Pecos had done for him that afternoon.

Speaks shoved his Colt hard against Pecos's back.

"We're going to turn around and walk outside."

Pecos looked over at Harry Creed. Creed saw what was going on. He nodded to Pecos.

The three of them went outside.

Pecos obviously figured he was going to get it first, but Speaks surprised him by turning around and kicking Harry Creed right square in the balls, then slashing the barrel of the gun down on the side of Harry Creed's head. Harry dropped to his knees.

"That's for what you did to Amy," Speaks said. "And this is so you don't get ideas about Pecos here doin' your killing for you." And with that he brought the toe of his Texas-style boot straight into Harry Creed's jaw. Harry had the good sense to scream.

Pecos he just pistol-whipped a little. Nothing special, nothing for Speaks to brag about or Pecos to bitch about, not for long, anyway, just enough so that Pecos had a couple of good-size welts on his face, and one very sore skull. There was a little blood, but again not enough to warrant bringing a reporter in.

Inside, the dogs went crazy. So did the crowd.

Harry Creed picked himself up. He was pretty wobbly. He started to say something, but then gave up. Very difficult to talk with a mouthful of blood.

"There's a train," Speaks said, "and it leaves in twenty minutes. I want you on it." This train was heading in the direction from which Keegan and Amy had just come.

"A train to where?" Pecos asked, trying to stand up.

"It doesn't matter where," Speaks said, "as long as you're on it."

Harry Creed, having apparently swallowed a mouthful of blood, said, "Amy gonna give you some of that nice sweet ass of hers, is she, Lyle?"

One punch was all it took, a straight hard shot to the solar plexus, and Harry Creed was sitting on his butt again.

"Maybe I should break your arm the way you broke hers, Harry."

"It was an accident."

"Sure it was, Harry."

"The bitch didn't appreciate nothin' I did for her."

"The train," Speaks said. "Be on it. Both of you."

"You son of a bitch," Pecos said as Speaks walked away. "You son of a bitch!"

Speaks went back to the hotel. Amy and Keegan were gone. Probably up in bed already. He had three brews, and then he was upstairs, himself.

He stripped to his long johns, the smell of his boots sour, meaning he'd have to powder them down inside again, and then he lay on his bed in the darkness, the front window and its shade silhouetted on the wall behind him.

He thought briefly of Clytie, waiting for him to return to their ranch in Montana. He wished Sam November would finish up his visit to his relatives so they could head back.

That was the last thing he thought before he fell asleep.

Somebody was pounding on his door so hard, all he could think of—now that he was starting to think clearly—was that there must be a fire.

"Hey! You in there!" a man's voice shouted.

Speaks was off the bed and at the door in seconds.

The man was familiar-looking somehow—then Speaks remembered. A man at the bar downstairs earlier that night.

"You know that friend of yours, the one with the pretty wife?" the man said. He had gray hair and muttonchop sideburns and a belly bursting the vest of his dark three-piece suit.

"What about him?"

"He's got trouble downstairs, mister. There's some punk kid tryin' to get him into a gunfight downstairs in the street." The man shook his head. "Hell, mister, we don't have no gunfights here. This is Cedar Rapids. We've got over seven hundred telephones."

"Son of a bitch," Speaks said. Then: "Thanks."

He got dressed in seconds and hurried down-stairs.

Pecos had read way too many dime novels.

He stood spread-legged in the middle of the street, his right hand hovering just above the pearly handle of his Peacemaker.

He'd gotten a crowd surly enough, too. His kind always wanted crowds around. In the electric light of the new lamps, Pecos looked like a raw kid wearing his older brother's duds.

"I'm givin' you ten more seconds to draw, Keegan," Pecos said to Keegan's back.

He was slurring his words. He was drunk.

Speaks looked over at Harry Creed and scowled. No mystery here. Harry Creed had decided to let the kid do his killing. He got the kid drunk and pushed him out on stage.

Amy Keegan grabbed Speaks's arm when he reached the sidewalk.

"You hear me, Keegan?" Pecos said.

"He's callin' you out," Harry Creed said, "fair and square."

"My Lord," said the man who'd roused Speaks from sleep. "This is Cedar Rapids." He didn't mention the seven hundred telephones this time.

"He doesn't want to kill the kid," Amy whispered to Speaks.

Speaks nodded and then looked over at Keegan. He was standing with his back to his tormentor. You could see the anger and humiliation on Keegan's face. Obviously, a part of him wanted to empty his gun into the kid. But the civilized part of him—the part that had changed for the better under Amy's guidance—declined the pleasure.

Without turning around Keegan said, "Kid, I'm going to walk up these stairs and go into the hotel. And if you want to shoot me, you'll just have to shoot me in the back."

"You think I won't?" Pecos snapped.

Keegan couldn't resist.

"Even a punk like you wouldn't shoot a man in the back."

And with that Keegan started up the stairs.

"You think I won't?" the drunken kid called out again. "You think I won't?"

Keegan took another slow, careful step up the stairs to the front porch of the hotel.

"Draw, you bastard!" Pecos shouted, weaving a bit as he did so, the alcohol slurring his words even more now.

"Shoot him, kid!" Harry creed said. "You gave him a chance! Now shoot him!"

Even boozed up the way he was, the kid was passing fair with a handgun.

His gun cleared leather before Speaks even noticed. The kid brought the gun up and sighted in a quick, easy movement and—

Speaks shot the gun out of his hand.

The kid cried out, dropping the gun and looking around, as if some dark demon had delivered the shot and not some mere mortal.

Speaks walked directly over to Harry Creed. Harry turned and started to move away quickly, but not quickly enough. Speaks grabbed him by the hair, got his arm around Harry Creed's throat, and then proceeded to choke him long enough to make him puke.

A few moments later Harry Creed was on his hands and knees like a dog, vomiting up chunks of the evening's repast.

For good measure and because sometimes he was—he had to admit—a mean son of a bitch, Speaks then kicked Harry Creed in the ribs twice.

Harry did a little more throwing up.

Speaks went back to Amy and Keegan and said, "C'mon."

Keegan said, "God, friend, I really owe you one."

Speaks took Amy by the arm and helped her up the stairs. "I want to get you two into your own room and then I'm going to stand guard all night."

"All night," Amy said. "Are you kidding?"

"No," Speaks said, knowing that Harry Creed would try something else later on. "No, I'm not kidding at all."

Speaks found a straight-backed chair and hauled it down in front of Keegan's door. He sat down and put his weapon in his lap and rolled himself another one of his sloppy, lumpen cigarettes.

He was just enjoying the first couple of drags when he heard footsteps coming up the hall stairs. Moments later, a cop appeared.

Out west they were wearing those kepi hats, the kind favored by Foreign Legionnaires and other types of fancy-uniform complements. But Cedar Rapids would apparently brook no such foolishness. This hefty Irishman wore a blue coat and a blue cap and a dramatic star pinned on the chest of his coat. He carried a nightstick and wore a squeaking holster filled with a shiny Navy colt.

"You the man in the gunfight?" he asked Speaks.

"There wasn't any gunfight."

"There almost was."

Speaks shook his head.

"Some punk named the Pecos Kid stepped out of line."

The big Mick grinned.

"The Pecos Kid, huh? In Cedar Rapids?"

"That's what he calls himself."

"So it's all over?"

"All over."

"You a Pinkerton man or something?" the Mick asked.

"No, why?"

"You're guarding the door."

"Oh. No, I just want to see that my friends get a good night's sleep."

"You think the punk'll be back?"

Speaks shrugged.

"I just don't want to take any chances."

The Mick said, "Pecos, huh?"

Speaks smiled.

"Pecos."

"Wait till I tell the boys."

In the silence again Speaks listened to the various sounds of humanity up and down the hall. A few doors away a couple was having enviably noisy sex. Then there was the man with the tobacco hack. And then there was the nightmare-screamer. And then there was the snorer. The guy was sawing logs so loudly Speaks half expected to hear the door ripped off its hinges.

Every time he got dozy, Speaks rolled another cigarette. By the fourth one, three hours after he'd applied the seat of his pants to the seat of the chair, he was really starting to get the hang of rolling smokes. Imagine, after all these years, he was finally learning to do it right.

He heard the noise then, and he knew instantly that Harry Creed had outfoxed him.

Creed knew Speaks was sitting in the hall. So Harry decided to shinny up the side of the hotel and go in the window.

The bastard.

Speaks burst through the door into darkness. He glimpsed shifting figures in the gloom, but that was all because just then somebody hit him very hard from behind with a gun.

Pain. Anger. Then a rushing coldness. And then—darkness. Speaks was out, sprawled on the floor.

Chapter Thirty-six

Pain.

He wondered what time it was.

The hotel room was empty.

More pain. Then anger again as he remembered how Harry Creed had come up the side of the hotel.

Muzzy streetlight filled the window frame.

The town of Cedar Rapids was quiet.

Speaks pushed himself to his feet. He'd been out long enough for the blood on the back of his head to dry and scab over a bit.

He poured warm but clean water from the metal pitcher into the washing pan. He splashed water across his face and the back of his head.

Not until now had he seen the small white

piece of paper on top of the bureau. He picked
it up.

BARN

    The one word.
    Nothing more.
    He wondered what the hell Harry Creed was
up to now.

    Moonlight lent the old buildings lining the
alley a shabby dignity. A couple of cats sat atop
a garbage can, imperiously noting Speaks's
passing.
    Only one of the smithy's doors was open now.
The interior was completely dark.
    A kind of metallic chittering sound reached
Speaks's ears.
    At first he couldn't fathom what could make
such a noise.
    But as he pushed into the barn, his gun lead-
ing the way, he had a terrible premonition of
what he was about to see.
    And of what was making that noise.
    One of the rear barn doors was ajar just
enough for Speaks to see the shape of the ring.
    Keegan was in the ring. Or what was left of
him, anyway. The rats had eaten most of his
face. One of his eyeballs was already gone.
They'd probably fought each other for the sake
of eating it. Keegan's forehead glistened. Harry
Creed had borrowed an old trick from the Indians. Cover a man in honey and let the rats at

him. The rats had also eaten out Keegan's throat. They were working on his stomach and groin now. The air stank of fresh blood and feces.

He was about to fire at the rats, drive them away, when he felt a rifle barrel prod the back of his head, the wound inflicted earlier. He winced.

"Kind of makes you hungry, don't it?" Harry Creed laughed from the darkness behind Speaks.

"Where's Amy?" Speaks snapped.

"Ain't that sweet?" Harry Creed said. "He's worried about Amy. I knew he was interested in that sweet ass of hers. I just knew it."

He stepped out of the shadows. He was wearing his pirate getup again. He plucked Speaks's gun from him. "Pecos went and got hisself killed."

"I'm really sorry to hear that."

"Forced Keegan into a gunfight. Guess you were right, Lyle. Keegan killed Pecos right off."

"Then you tied Keegan to the ring."

Harry Creed shook his head.

"I love that woman, Lyle. I purely do. And she was my wife before she was his. I had to teach him a lesson, didn't I?" Then Creed smiled. "He didn't scream for very long. They killed him right off. I mean, there wasn't all that much pain for him, if that's what you're worried about."

"Where's Amy?"

"I guess that's for me to know," Harry Creed laughed, "and for you to find out. Now it's gonna be your turn, Lyle. You always did think you was a little better'n me. Now you're gonna find out otherwise."

Harry Creed nudged Speaks toward the pit.

"You get in there and sit down."

Speaks hesitated a moment. Not until a few minutes before had he realized how crazy Harry Creed really was. Speaks had no doubt that Creed would shoot him right now if he disobeyed.

Speaks looked in the pit at the rats swarming all over poor Keegan. Poor Keegan was going to be poor Speaks in just a few more seconds.

"Climb in," Harry Creed said.

Speaks raised his leg, climbed into the pit. The rats were too busy feasting on Keegan to pay much attention to Speaks.

Speaks saw the honey pot then, stashed over in the shadows near the right side of the pit. It was about the size of a coffeepot.

"Start daubin' that stuff on your face and hands," Harry Creed said.

Speaks thought of refusing, but why die sooner rather than later? But it'd be better to be shot than to have rats rend you. It'd be much better.

The honey pot was a lidded ceramic bowl. Speaks took the lid off and plunged his hand deep inside.

Sticky honey oozed around his hand, sucking it ever deeper into the bowl.

"Now start rubbin' it on your face, Speaks."

For the first time a few of the scrambling rats looked over in his direction. The sweet smell of the honey pot was what did it. There was a whole new feast over here. Their eyes glowed red in the oppressive darkness.

Harry Creed came right over to the edge of the ring now.

"Start rubbin' it on your face, Speaks. You heard me."

Speaks had no choice. His hand dripping honey, he began to wipe the thick stuff on the angles of his face.

Already a few of the rats had drifted over and were starting to climb his legs. At this point, he could still kick them away. But not for much longer.

"Now sit down."

"No."

Harry Creed aimed the rifle right at Speaks's face.

"I said sit down."

Speaks had one chance, and if he muffed it he was going to be eaten alive the way his friend Keegan had been.

Speaks slowly sat down on his haunches.

More and more rats swarmed around him.

"All the way down," Harry Creed said.

Speaks reluctantly sat all the way down.

Now the rats were all over him, on his back and arms and legs. All he could think of was the illustrations he'd seen of *Gulliver's Travels*, a book Clytie had given him to read, all the tiny people walking up and down the giant.

A rat scrambling over his shoulder lashed out at Speaks's honey-painted face.

Speaks jumped half an inch off the pit floor

and made a wild wailing sound in his throat.

"Scary little buggers, aren't they?" Harry Creed said. "Now lay down."

"What?"

"You heard me, Lyle. Lay down. Flat. On the floor."

"No way."

The bullet passed so close to his ear, he could smell the metal of it. A few of the rats scattered. Most continued to cling to Speaks. There were maybe two dozen of the things on him now.

"Lay down, you son of a bitch."

So Speaks lay down. The pit was so small that he had to prop his legs up on the edge of the ring.

Then he screamed.

The rats seemed to suddenly triple in number, and they were all over him, especially his head and hands.

The small honey pot was four inches from his right hand. He would have to be quick. And then he would have to roll away from where Harry Creed was likely to fire.

"My, these fellas sure have big appetites," Harry Creed said. "You and Keegan in one night. My, my."

A rat sank teeth into Speaks's left hand. Speaks sobbed with pain and terror and reached for the honey pot.

He caught Harry Creed right in the center of the forehead.

Then he rolled quickly to the right. Harry Creed staggered, then pumped three bullets into the exact spot Speaks had occupied only moments earlier.

Speaks jumped to his feet, rats hanging off of him as he did so, and lunged at Harry Creed.

He tore the rifle from Creed's hand and drove a punch deep into Harry's stomach. Harry doubled over. Speaks took the rifle and started clubbing Harry Creed on the side of the head until the man slumped forward into unconsciousness.

Once he had slapped and shaken the rats off of him the first thing he did was take the rope off Keegan's wrists and ankles and carry the ripped and bloody body out of the pit. Bleeding from his own bite wounds, he found a horse blanket and covered him with it.

His final act was to pick up the honey pot and empty it lavishly over the length of Harry Creed's face and body, back and forth, back and forth, until Harry was saturated with honey.

A few minutes later, Speaks found Amy up in the haymow. She'd been bound and gagged.

She was sobbing when she got to her feet.

"I'll never forget the screaming," she said, leaning on Speaks for support. "He died so slowly."

He let her cling to him, let him be her strength for a long moment. He kept seeing how Keegan's face had looked after the rats had finished with it. He wanted to slice a knife blade into his brain and cut out the memory forever.

"Where's Harry?" she said finally.

"Don't worry about Harry."

"You're going to turn him over to the law, aren't you?"

Grimly, with no hint of humor, he said, "Let's just say I've taken care of Harry in my own way."

They went down the ladder to the ground floor and then out the door. He steered her away from the ring so she couldn't see. Being a good Christian woman, she might try to talk Speaks out of what he was doing.

"We'll go to my hotel room and wash up," Speaks said.

"But Harry. Where's Harry?" Amy said. "Shouldn't we turn him over to the law?"

Harry Creed regained consciousness just then. Two, three, even four blocks away they could still hear him screaming.

"Oh, my God," she said. "You put the rats on him, didn't you?"

Speaks said nothing.

Just took her arm a little tighter and escorted her out of the alley.

After a block or so you couldn't hear Harry scream hardly at all.

Part Six

Chapter Thirty-seven

It was midday when they crossed the Powder River. November had just finished his Cedar Rapids story, and Fellows was shivering even as he wrote the last words in his notebook. Rats! He didn't know how Speaks had done what he did with so many of the creatures hanging from him. Even though he admitted having been afraid, Speaks had been unbelievably courageous.

"Lyle don't see it that way," November said, looking ahead of them at his friend's back.

Fellows put away his notebook, confident he'd be able to read the scribbling he'd managed in a shaky hand while on horseback.

"How does he see it?"

November shrugged.

"He done what he had to do to survive," he

365

said. "And he's always blamed himself for Keegan's death."

"Why?"

"Because he had enough chances to kill Creed, and he didn't."

"Why not?"

November looked over at the younger man and lowered his voice.

"He was married then," he explained, "about five years, and Clytie was startin' to change him."

"So you think the old Speaks would have killed Creed, and Keegan would still be alive?"

"Who knows?" November said with a shrug. "Remember, Keegan lived by the gun, he might have died by it."

"Well," Fellows said, "that would have been preferable than being killed by . . . rats."

They rode across the river, suspending conversation until they reached the other side. Speaks had managed to find a place to cross where the water wasn't very high. Their feet got wet, but that was the worst of it.

"What about that business of calling Keegan 'the last of the gunfighters'?" Fellows asked. "To be honest, I never heard of Chris Keegan."

"That's because he died before you was born." It wasn't true, because Fellows wasn't *that* young, but the writer got the idea. "Do your research," November went on. "Anybody'll tell you he'd be as big a legend today as Earp or Masterson if he'd lived longer."

"As big as Lyle Speaks?"

"Maybe."

"Can I ask you something, Mr. November?" Fellows said. "Something that's been bothering me for a while?"

November looked over at Fellows, studied him for a few moments, then asked, "You gonna write down what I say?"

"Not if you don't want me to, but what about your own legend?"

November snorted.

"I ain't got a legend."

"But that's not true," Fellows argued. "You have one, it's just . . . hitched to Mr. Speaks's."

"What are you jabberin' about, boy?"

"I guess my question is, how do you feel about being in Mr. Speaks's shadow?"

November didn't answer at first, and for a moment Fellows thought he might have gone too far.

"Let me tell you somethin' about that man up there," November said, inclining his head toward Speaks, who was still ahead of them. "There wouldn't be any kind of legend for you to write about if it wasn't for him. His, mine, ours. None! I'd be dead ten times over if it wasn't for that man, and he'd be dead half a dozen times if not for me. I begrudge him nothing!"

"But . . . you didn't want him to get married," Fellows pointed out.

"That doesn't mean I don't want him to be happy," November said. "I just never thought men like us should get married."

"Are you . . . envious?"

"Of what?"

"His life, his wife, his ranch, which was supposed to be partly yours."

"We were supposed to start a ranch together before he got married," November said. "Once he did get hitched, he had to make a home for himself and his wife, not for him and me. I could have gone on and made my own way, but he and Clytie both convinced me they wanted me to stay. They said it was my home as much as theirs."

"But then . . . you became their employee."

"*I* was the one who came up with the idea of being foreman." November was becoming exasperated with Fellows. "Boy, maybe I should take a look at what you been writing in that book of yours."

"Honestly, Mr. November," Fellows said, "I've been recording what you and Mr. Speaks have been telling me . . . plus things I've observed, and learned, while riding with you."

"Then why all these questions? Am I envious? Am I jealous? You tryin' to figure out if I'm mad at Lyle Speaks? Well, the answer is no. I ain't mad. The man is like a brother to me."

"But . . . he has a brother," Fellows said, "which brings up another question—"

"Hold on to it," November said, cutting him off. "Lyle sees somethin'."

November gave his horse a little kick in the ribs and left Fellows behind. The young writer was wondering why everybody changed the subject whenever the subject of Speaks's younger brother came up.

* * *

November rode up alongside of Speaks and said, "What is it?"

"This looks familiar, Sam," Speaks said, "doesn't it?"

November surveyed the terrain, studying the distant peaks as well as the closer ones.

"We've been this way before," November said.

"Separately," Speaks said. "I came ahead and you drove the herd."

"With Artax," November said.

They had hired Clay Artax and some boys temporarily just to drive their stock up to Montana. It wasn't until a couple of years later that they were able to hire him back permanently.

"That pass," Speaks said. "We were through there."

"Yeah," November said, "fifteen years ago. A good rock slide could have closed it off by now."

Fellows came riding up at that point.

"Is something wrong?"

"No," Speaks said, "we just realized we know where we are. Another couple of hours we'll be in that pass."

"I have a question," Fellows said.

"What's that?" November asked.

"What happens if while we're riding in one end of the pass, they're riding in the other?"

"Can't happen," Speaks said.

"Why not?"

"Because one of us will scout out first," November said. "We'll be able to tell if anyone has gone through recently."

"We'll know if we've beaten them there," Speaks finished.

Fellows couldn't help but notice—after traveling with the two men for a few days—that they had a habit of finishing each other's thoughts. He wondered if Speaks and Clytie did that, but then, they hadn't been together as long as Speaks and November had.

"How will we know if they're not coming at all?" the writer asked. "If they changed direction, even after all the figuring."

"That's easy," Speaks said.

Fellows waited for an answer, but the man rode away from him and—not surprisingly—it came from November.

"They won't show up," he said with a shrug.

"Hold up!" Speaks said, raising his hand.

"Thank God," Fellows said. "My behind feels like it's on fire."

"Takes a while for your butt to get used to this kind of ridin'," November said.

"Sam," Speaks said, "I'll go up ahead and scout out the pass. If I remember correctly it should be right around this here bend. You and young Shakespeare, here, can dismount and rest a bit."

"Sure you don't want me to go?" November asked.

"Naw," Speaks said. "I ain't ready to get down from the saddle yet."

November dismounted as Speaks rode away, and so did Fellows—painfully.

"Well," Fellows said, "if that pass is so close maybe it won't be much longer."

"Don't forget," November said, taking out a

piece of beef jerky and offering it to Fellows, "we still got to ride back when this is all over."

"Oh, yeah, I didn't—"

"If we ain't dead."

Fellows frowned, and November grinned as he chewed the meat the writer had refused.

Chapter Thirty-eight

Fellows and November were sitting on rocks when Speaks reappeared half an hour later. November told the writer there'd be no more stories now until they got back to the ranch.

"If we get back to the ranch, you mean," Fellows replied mournfully. "Why have I been taking all these notes if we're going to die?"

"I was just funnin' with you, boy," November said. "We're not gonna die. Lyle and I will take care of these yahoos."

"I won't have to do anything?"

"Well," November said, "maybe just pull the trigger and make some noise so it sounds like there's more of us than there are. If Lyle and I can get up in the rocks on either side of the pass we can pick them off with our rifles when they come through."

"You mean . . . ambush them?" Fellows asked.

"I mean use whatever advantage we can get," November replied. "Remember, they killed Clay Artax and two other men."

"Still, they deserve a trial. Isn't that what your whole life, your whole legend has been about? Upholding the law?"

"Partly it's been about justice," November said, "at least the time when we wore badges. Other times it's been about makin' money."

"But . . . don't you intend to take them back to the proper authorities?"

"We'll take our advantage where we find it," November said, "and then see what happens. If any of 'em survive, sure, we'll take 'em back."

Fellows wasn't sure he could follow the logic here.

"Why ain't you writin' any of this down?"

"I'm . . . not at all sure this fits in with the legend I'm writing about."

November fixed the writer with a hard stare.

"Didn't you tell Lyle you'd write the truth?"

"Yes, but . . . bushwhacking these men—"

"Murders," November said, "and rustlers."

"But—"

"And they'd put a bullet in you just as soon as look at you, writer. You better hope we get an advantage, but you might have to do a lot more than make noise with that cannon I gave you."

Suddenly, Fellows didn't have much to say. He was examining his eastern footwear when Speaks returned. It was not suffering the terrain very well, and one of the heels had come loose.

November stood as Speaks rode up.

"It's the pass we remember, all right, Sam," Speaks said.

"Can we get up on either side?"

"A little climbing's involved," Speaks said, a bit uncomfortably. Truthfully, if they were only ten years younger he'd have thought nothing of it.

He noticed the glum look on Fellows's face and asked, "What's wrong with him?"

"He's havin' an attack of conscience."

"About what?"

"About ambushin' these rustlers."

Speaks looked at Fellows from astride his horse.

"Young fella, you'd like to write that Sam and me faced these jaspers fair and square and did away with them, wouldn't you?"

Fellows banged his left foot on the ground in an attempt to secure the heel and then looked up at Speaks.

"I suppose that's what I thought," he admitted, "but Mr. November has shown me how foolish I was being."

"You're in this with us now, you know," Speaks said. "You can't go back, and you can't just wait for it to be over without doin' somethin' to make sure it's us you'll have to deal with when it's finished, and not them."

"I realize that."

"Well, get on your horse, then," Speaks said. "Let's get set up in that pass before they show up."

"How long do we have?" Fellows asked.

"Not long," Speaks said. "I seen some dust in the distance, could only have been kicked up by a small herd."

"So then they are coming this way." Fellows sounded disappointed.

"Oh, yeah," Speaks said, "they're comin', all right. They're comin'."

When they reached the pass November remembered it immediately.

"It's not as wide," he said.

"You were right about rock slides," Speaks said. "Over the years there have been a few, and they've narrowed the pass down. Still, it's wide enough for five men and fifty horses."

"Only just," November said. "Which is good."

He looked up at the rocky walls on both sides. He could see what Speaks meant about some climbing, but there were plenty of hand-and footholds. It was just a matter of stamina.

November looked around and saw that Fellows wasn't in earshot.

"There's somethin' you should know, Lyle," he said. "I been keepin' it from you."

"What's that?"

"My hip."

"Which one?"

"The one I got shot in back in '88," November said. That was a story they had not yet told Fellows. "It's been actin' up."

"Can you make this climb?" Speaks asked.

November looked at both sides of the pass again.

"Partway, I think. There," he said, pointing,

"is a good vantage point, and it's not too far up."

"I know," Speaks said. "You'd be pretty close there, Sam."

"I know it."

Speaks took a turn now, looking at the other side.

"If you take that side, I got to go up a little higher on this one," he said.

"Can you make it?"

"If I can't," Speaks said, "and you can't, young Fellows is gonna have himself a helluva story to write."

"If he survives."

"There is that." Speaks stood in his saddle and tried to see out the mouth of the pass. "We better get into position . . . somewhere!"

"Where do we put the boy writer?"

"He's young," Speaks said. "He can climb almost to the top."

"He'll never hit nothin' from up there."

"Good," Speaks said, "then he won't shoot one of us by mistake. You better get started. We can leave the horses just around the bend. If they get past us and run 'em off, it won't matter. We won't be needin' 'em anyway."

They rode back to where Fellows was sitting his horse, still looking glum, holding the big Walker Colt in both hands nervously.

"Put that thing away before you shoot yourself," Speaks snapped.

"Yes, sir."

He tucked it into his belt.

"Get down from your horse," November said. "It's time to climb."

Speaks and November both dismounted, taking their rifles with them.

"How come I don't get a rifle?"

"Can you shoot a rifle any better than you can shoot a handgun?" November asked.

"Well, no . . ."

"That's why."

Fellows stepped down and November took all three horses to the face of one wall, grounded the reins, and then pinned them with a large rock.

"That'll hold 'em unless the rustlers get past us."

"Won't the horses get past us?" Fellows asked.

"Not if we execute our plan right," November said.

"What plan?" Fellows asked. "I didn't know we had a plan."

"We don't," Speaks said, "but we been thinkin' on it."

"How do you know you've been thinking the same thing?" Fellows asked.

"There's only one way to do this," November said, looking at Speaks.

"Turn the herd," Speaks said, and November nodded.

"How do we do that?" Fellows asked.

"We time our shots right," November said, "we can turn the herd into the rustlers. While they're busy trying not to get trampled we can pick them off."

"And what do I do?"

Speaks took the boy aside and started walking with him to one of the walls.

"You're gonna climb up this wall as far as you can go and find a place to sit."

"And then what?"

"And then when *we* start shootin', so do you."

"At what?"

"Just into the pass," Speaks said.

"At the men? And horses?"

"If you don't want to do that then just fire into the air, but make noise."

"What do I do when the gun is empty?"

"Reload, and start shootin' again."

"And when do I stop?"

"You'll know when to stop."

Fellows looked up the face of the wall, which had once been sheer but had since been graded by rock slides.

"This doesn't look too hard," he said.

"I'll be below you, boy," November said. "Just make sure you don't shoot in my direction."

"Okay, Mr. November."

"Kid," November said, "just call me Sam, okay?"

"Okay . . . Sam."

"Good luck . . . Aubrey," Speaks said, sticking out his hand.

"Good luck . . . Lyle," Fellows said, shaking it. It surprised him, because it was a much firmer handshake than he had gotten back at the ranch when they first met.

Now this, he thought, was the handshake of Lyle Speaks.

Chapter Thirty-nine

They all began climbing into position.

November's hip began to flare up as soon as he started. Riding never bothered the hip as much as walking did, and this was worse than walking. He'd kept his pain from Speaks for years, because he thought it was a sign of getting old. Not being able to chew steak the way he used to, or pee as easily as he used to, those he could live with. Getting shot in '88 had been his own fault, and now he was paying for it.

He decided to ignore it as best he could. Once he got into position on the rock's face he might never be coming down, anyway.

For the moment, he'd forgotten that Chilito was supposed to be coming up behind the rustlers.

Speaks started to get winded halfway up the slope. Riding had come back to him easily, and after the first day he felt as if he'd never left the saddle. But this climbing, he didn't even know if he could have done it when he was younger. He remembered the climb he'd made in that cave where Devereaux and his men were hiding out. That had been difficult, and he'd been no spring chicken then, either.

Wouldn't it be a hoot if he and November both died of heart attacks before the rustlers even got there?

Fellows made the climb fairly easily, then watched as Speaks and November made theirs. Neither looked like he was having an easy time of it. November seemed to be favoring a leg or a hip, and Speaks was climbing higher than his partner.

Fellows took the gun from his waistband and held it tightly in both hands. Could he even hit anything from up here with it? Was it right to leave all the shooting to Speaks and November? True, they'd done it before, but it had been a lot of years, and wasn't three to five better odds than two to five? In that moment—like November—he'd forgotten about Chilito.

He decided to keep his eyes open when the shooting started—yes, he'd thought about closing them when the time came—to see how Speaks and November were handling things. If it looked like he could help, he was going to climb down, get a little closer—and hope he wasn't too scared to even move.

*   *   *

They heard the horses approaching before they saw anything. As Speaks had figured, the first thing they saw were the front horses in the herd. The riders were driving the horses into the pass from behind.

Speaks and November had placed themselves and Fellows far enough into the pass that the fifty-horse herd would be able to enter, along with the riders coming behind. They all had to be in view before any shooting started.

Speaks and November had their rifles ready. It took about an hour of waiting before they could hear the horses. By then November's hip was screaming, and Speaks's knees were cramped. Fellows was feeling fine physically, but the longer it took the more frightened he became, and the more he perspired. The sun baked the rocks around them, and all three men felt as if they were in a stone oven.

Speaks was concerned that he was too high up to see well enough. He dismissed the thought, however, by convincing himself he wasn't going to be trying for any head shots. Just the way he had taught many men to shoot, he was going to go for the largest part of the man, the torso. If he had to, he'd shoot the horses out from beneath them.

When he heard the horses he waved at November, who waved back. He then looked up at Fellows and waved. The younger man either didn't see him, or was too scared to move.

The horses came into the pass and filled it. They were about five or six abreast. Speaks waited, hoping—knowing—that November would wait too. They may not have done this in a long time, but they'd done it often enough to rely on the same internal clock.

The horses moved along in the pass and then the men appeared behind them. Speaks counted five figures on horseback, although from where he was he could not recognize any of them. It didn't matter, though. These were his horses. Who else could the riders be but the rustlers who had killed Clay Artax?

But just for a moment he hesitated. What if this wasn't the men? His eyes were not good enough to identify his brand on the animals from his vantage point. What if—

That's when November fired, and all hell broke loose.

Fellows heard the gunshots. His first instinct was to close his eyes, but he forced himself to keep them open and focus down into the pass. He had to watch and memorize everything that happened, for when he would write it down.

When he finally did, it would read something like this:

Speaks and November began firing in front of the horses, and as they had predicted, the animals turned. They began to run back towards the rustlers, who became confused by the turn of events.

I watched from my vantage point, saving

my bullets in case I was needed to help—
but these two legends were magnificent.
They stood and fired, heedless of any injury
that might befall them.

Down in the pass the rustlers were trying
to get the horses to go back, and at the same
time see where the shots were coming
from. One man was suddenly yanked by
some unseen force from his saddle, and he
fell among the thundering hooves of the
herd. If he was not dead from a bullet
wound, he soon would be trampled to
death. I did not know who had fired that
fatal shot, Speaks or November, but it did
not matter.

First blood had been drawn!

Neither Speaks nor November had taken that
man from his saddle. Instead, it was Chilito.
Coming up from behind the rustlers, he had
found himself a vantage point on one side of the
pass and now the rustlers were caught in a
stampede, and a cross fire.

Speaks fired as quickly as he could lever the
rounds into position, then reloaded just as fast
as he could. It was more the sound of the shots
fired by Speaks and November that spooked the
horses, rather than bullets striking the ground
in front of them. The horses were confused
now, and circling. This worked to their favor,
because the animals continued to jostle the rustlers among them.

Speaks had seen the first man fall, and assumed the shot had been fired by November. He also knew that he was going to end up with some dead horses out of this, but that could not be avoided. Of course, if he and November had the eyesight they had twenty years ago—or even ten—they could pick these yahoos off their horses without injury to any of the animals.

It made Speaks mad thinking he might be killing his own animals, and he decided to get closer.

He started down the rock face, firing as he did so, putting himself in plain sight.

Damn fool! November thought when he saw Speaks moving down the cliff. What the hell did he think he was doing?

November had been closer to the action to begin with, but he still thought the first telling shot had been fired by Speaks. He wasn't hitting anything from where he crouched, he hated to admit, except maybe some of their own horses.

Speaks had the right idea, he thought. Get closer.

He stood up, began firing, took a step, and then his hip gave out on him.

He fell.

Fellows would later recount:

I could not tell from my vantage point if November had been hit or not, but I knew that he was down. The time had come for me to show my mettle, to be a force or remain helpless.

I stood up and started down the face of the wall, finally thumbing back the hammer on my gun and firing into the pass. I didn't know if I was hitting anything, and if I was it might have been a horse rather than a man, but at least I was doing something. I was in there firing side by side, as it were, with Lyle Speaks and Sam November. I was coming to the aide of my *compadres*, as the Mexicans would say . . . and that was when I was shot by one of the blackguards!

The writer was out of the play, and November was down on the ground. Speaks could see this, and still he continued to fire. He became aware that they had help, and suddenly remembered Chilito. The Mexican was undoubtedly making each of his shots count. He could see perfectly, damn him!

November was on the floor of the pass, and if the rustlers succeeded in turning the horses he'd be trampled. Speaks stopped and fired. He knew he had taken one of the rustlers from his saddle. There were three more to be reckoned with, but the horses were still a danger.

He didn't know how badly the writer was hurt. He only saw him stumble and go down. He wasn't sure about November, either, until his friend staggered to his feet, hat off, bleeding from a scalp wound and, back braced against the wall, began firing again.

Two of the rustlers had worked their way through the herd and were now riding toward

November. As Speaks reached the floor of the pass, he and November both shouldered their rifles and fired at the approaching riders, who were firing handguns.

The sound of a bullet striking flesh is something a man never forgets. Speaks heard it several times over the next few seconds and knew that one of those bullets had smacked wetly through him.

Sweat was running down into his eyes, but suddenly he could see the rustlers' horses, riderless, galloping on by. Two figures were lying on the ground. He looked across the pass and saw that November was down on one knee. He rushed to his friend's side.

"Are you hit?" he asked breathlessly.

"I . . . don't know," November gasped. "Damn hip!" November looked at Speaks. "Lyle, you're hit!"

Speaks looked down at himself and saw blood on his shirt, on his side, just above the hip.

"That's funny," he said. "I don't feel nothin'."

"Shock . . ." November said, but words failed him after that.

Speaks examined his friend. The scalp wound seemed to have come from the fall. Otherwise he was unhurt.

"How many did we get?" Speaks asked, and he suddenly became aware that the shooting had stopped.

November used the wall to once again get to his feet.

"What the hell—" he said.

The pass was empty. Apparently, the horses had succeeded in getting out the other side. Lying on the ground were four men. A fifth was sitting his horse in the center of the pass. Behind him Chilito was standing, holding his rifle on him.

"Forgot about the Mex," November said.

"Me too."

Suddenly, they both remembered Fellows and looked up. Rocks came rolling down the grade, and November had to move away to avoid being hit. When Fellows appeared it was clear that he'd been shot.

"Sam . . . Lyle . . . I . . . don't know . . . what happened . . ." The young man was gasping out his words.

November went to the man and gave him a shoulder for support.

"Easy, youngster," he said. "You been hit."

"What?"

"Set down," November said. "Dammit, I can't hold you! Set!"

Suddenly, Fellows's legs went out from under him and he fell on his ass.

"How bad is he hit?" Speaks asked.

"I'm checkin' . . ." November said.

Speaks turned and saw the last rustler riding toward him, Chilito walking behind. There was something familiar about the man, the way he sat his horse, but Speaks couldn't place him.

"Get off your horse!" he shouted as they got closer.

The rustler dismounted and Chilito walked him closer.

"You okay?" Speaks asked Chilito, who nodded and waved.

"Good work," Speaks said.

"I don't believe it," the rustler said. "It's actually you, isn't it?" There was a southern twang to the man's voice, Mississippi or Tennessee.

"You know who I am, then?" Speaks asked.

"Oh," the man said, "I've known all along whose horses I was stealing . . . Uncle."

Speaks hesitated, then squinted. "What?"

The man was close enough now that he could make out his features, familiar features . . .

"Do I know you?"

"I hardly think so, since you've never seen me before," the man said.

"But you look familiar," Speaks said. "And what did you call me?"

"Uncle," the man said again. "Uncle Lyle. I look familiar because my name is the same as yours—Lyle Speaks. You see, dear Uncle, I'm your brother Jeffrey's son."

Chapter Forty

Five weeks later . . .

That announcement had staggered Lyle Speaks
more than any bullet ever had. Sitting on his
porch, the wound in his side all but healed, he
still replayed the words in his head, over and
over: . . . *I'm your brother Jeffrey's son.*

Even November had stared at the man,
dumbfounded.

And Jeffrey had named him after Speaks.
That was the worst part.

He started to replay the scene in his head beyond those words, but was interrupted.

"Lyle?"

He opened his eyes and watched Clytie approach him.

"Don't do that."

"What?"

"Play it over and over in your head," she said. "I know you."

She put her hand on his shoulder, and he covered it with his.

"I know you do."

"It wasn't your fault," she said. "Any of it. Tennessee, it just wasn't in your life."

"I should have *made* it part of my life," Speaks said. "I should have gone there to see Jeffrey, but . . . I was too busy tryin' to burn the hate out of me. I didn't want him to see it, even after he was grown, even after he got married. . . . The time just never seemed right."

"You wrote him," she said. "He wrote you. I know. I saw the letters."

"Letters," Speaks said, "badly written by me, polite from him . . . What the boy said—"

"That boy was a thirty-year-old man who rustled your horses and killed three of your men, including your friend Clay."

"I know, I know . . . ," Speaks said, shaking his head, "but he was my brother's son."

"You only had his word for that," she reminded him. "What if he was lying?"

"Not just his word," Speaks said. "I had him in front of me. He looked like—"

"You can't say he looked just like Jeffrey," Clytie said, interrupting him. "You never did see Jeffrey as an adult."

"That's my shame," Speaks said, "but it wasn't Jeffrey I saw. It was Pa, it was *me*! There was no denying him, Clytie. He was family!"

"But you needn't have given any credence to his words, Lyle."

"Why not?"

"From what you tell me he was very bitter."

"Bitter, yes," Speaks said, "but right, Clytie, so right. When Jeffrey died five years ago and they wrote me—why didn't he ever tell me he named his son after me?"

Clytie didn't have an answer for that.

"When they wrote me he was dead I never went to Tennessee."

"He was buried," Clytie said, "and you were busy—"

He laughed bitterly.

"Always busy! Too busy for Jeffrey. Why did I save him, all those years ago, just to ignore him the rest of his life?"

"You didn't do it on purpose," she said, putting her arms around him from behind. "Things happen. People have separate lives."

They both heard the bootstep on the porch. They looked up and saw Sam November limping toward them. Even while Speaks's wound healed, November's hip got worse.

"Hope I'm not interruptin' . . ." he said.

"Not at all, Sam," Clytie said. "I was just going to put dinner on. Can I get you something?"

"No, thanks, Clytie," November said. "I'll sit a spell with Lyle, if I can."

"Of course you can," she said, and went inside.

She had made a fuss over all of them when they returned: Speaks, November, even the writer, Fellows. November and Chilito, the two who weren't wounded, had to bring back Speaks and Fellows, who were. Clytie treated them until they were able to bring a proper doctor out to the ranch. The doctor said she likely saved their lives. She pooh-poohed it and said if they were going to die they would have done it on the trail. After that Chilito took some men out to gather the horses back up.

"How're you doin'?" November asked Speaks.

"Fine," Speaks said. "Where have you been keepin' your scrawny ass? Ain't seen you in weeks an' you just come limpin' back. Maybe Clytie accepts you back without a word, but I want to know where in hell you been!"

"Here and there," November said. "Camped out, thinkin'."

"About what?"

"About you, me, Jeffrey . . ."

"One of us feelin' bad about Jeffrey is enough, Sam."

"What that boy, your nephew, said, Lyle. It had a ring of truth."

"That I treated you more like a brother than I treated Jeffrey?"

November nodded.

"Hell, it was true," Speaks said. "You were always more of a brother to me than he was. That's 'cause we was around each other all the time."

"Shouldn'ta been that way, Lyle."

"I know that now, Sam," Speaks said. "It's too late."

"I know," November said. "That boy's got

your name, Lyle, and he's full of hate the way you were—"

"But it's me he hates," Speaks finished, and November nodded.

"Still don't think we just shoulda let him go."

"He was my brother's son, Sam."

"He killed Clay Artax and two other men."

"Who's to say who pulled the trigger?" Speaks asked.

"You know it don't matter."

"Don't argue this with me, Sam. We let him go and that's that."

"He'll be back."

"Maybe."

"You know what it's like to carry that much hate."

"I do, yes," Speaks said. "He probably will be back."

They both looked up as Aubrey P. Fellows came limping out of the house, leaning on a cane.

"Mrs. Speaks said you were back, Sam. Welcome. Are you all right?"

"I'm fine," November said. "I just needed to get away some."

"I'm glad you're both here," Fellows said. "No, keep your seats. I want to be on my feet."

Speaks and November, both about to rise, sat back.

"I have a problem."

"What problem is that, Fellows?" Speaks asked. He'd called the younger man "Aubrey" only that one time, when they shook hands in the pass.

"Well, recovering here I've had a lot of time to write everything down," Fellows said. "I mean, everything you told me, and everything that . . . happened."

"So?" Speaks asked.

"There's one thing I'm having trouble with."

"What's that?" Speaks asked, even though he thought he knew.

"Well, that . . . nephew of yours. I mean, that your own nephew was rustling horses hereabouts, with you as his ultimate goal . . . you know, catching him, letting him go . . ."

"What's the problem?" November asked.

"Well, quite frankly . . . I don't know what to write about it."

There was a time he simply would have written what happened and considered it a coup. Now that he had ridden with Speaks and November, gotten to know them, he was loath to write something that would reflect badly on either of them, his publisher be damned.

"That's a problem," November agreed.

"I mean, here I'm writing your legend, Mr. Speaks, and . . . how can I write this down? I mean, the things he said about you, and your brother . . ."

"Not exactly the stuff legends are built on, eh, youngster?" Speaks asked.

"Well . . . no, sir. Tell me, what do I do? What do I write? I'll write anything you tell me." Fellows sounded genuinely confused.

"I told you the day we met what to write, and you said you would. Remember that?"

394

"Yes, sir," Fellows said. "You asked me to write the truth, and I said I would."

"Well, then," Lyle Speaks said, "you go ahead and do that, and the consequences be damned. Understand?"

"Yes, sir."

The three men were silent for a few moments, and then Sam November said, "Of course, you could leave out the part about shooting yourself in the hip with that cannon when you fell. . . ."

DON'T MISS OTHER CLASSIC LEISURE WESTERNS!

High Prairie by Hiram King. Cole Granger doesn't have much in this world. A small spread is just about all he can call his own. That and his honor. So when he gives his word that he'll deliver some prize horses to a neighbor, he'll be damned before he'll let those horses escape. And anything that gets between Cole and the horses will regret it.

___4324-6 $3.99 US/$4.99 CAN

Stillwater Smith by Frank Roderus. There are two kinds of men on the frontier. There's the kind who is tough with a gun in his hand, who preys on anyone weaker than himself. Then there is Stillwater Smith, who doesn't take easily to killing, but who is always ready to fight for what he believes in. And there's only so far you can push him.

___4306-8 $3.99 US/$4.99 CAN

Dorchester Publishing Co., Inc.
P.O. Box 6640
Wayne, PA 19087-8640

Please add $1.75 for shipping and handling for the first book and $.50 for each book thereafter. NY, NYC, and PA residents, please add appropriate sales tax. No cash, stamps, or C.O.D.s. All orders shipped within 6 weeks via postal service book rate. Canadian orders require $2.00 extra postage and must be paid in U.S. dollars through a U.S. banking facility.

Name_____

Address_____

City_____State_____Zip_____

I have enclosed $_____ in payment for the checked book(s).

Payment <u>must</u> accompany all orders. ❏ Please send a free catalog.

WILL HENRY
SAN JUAN HILL

Bestselling Author of *Death of a Legend*

The year is 1898 and Fate Baylen of Arizona's Bell Rock Ranch joins the cavalry to fight the Spanish. But it looks as if the conflict is turning into a haven for graft grabbers, a heyday for incompetent officers, and a holiday for Fates and other boys from the West. Then the fighting starts, and men sweat, curse, turn cowardly, become heroes—and even die. Under the command of the valiant Teddy Roosevelt, Fate musters all the courage he can. Yet as he and the Rough Riders head into battle after battle, Fate can only wonder how many of them will survive to share in the victorious drive to the top of San Juan Hill.

_4045-X $4.99 US/$6.99 CAN

Dorchester Publishing Co., Inc.
P.O. Box 6640
Wayne, PA 19087-8640

Please add $1.75 for shipping and handling for the first book and $.50 for each book thereafter. NY, NYC, and PA residents, please add appropriate sales tax. No cash, stamps, or C.O.D.s. All orders shipped within 6 weeks via postal service book rate. Canadian orders require $2.00 extra postage and must be paid in U.S. dollars through a U.S. banking facility.

Name_____
Address_____
City_____State_____Zip_____
I have enclosed $_____ in payment for the checked book(s).
Payment <u>must</u> accompany all orders. ❑ Please send a free catalog.

WILL HENRY

JESSE JAMES
DEATH OF A LEGEND

Beneath the bandanna, underneath the legend, Jesse James was a wild and wicked man: a sinister and brutal outlaw who blazed a trail of crime and violence through the lawless West. Ripping the mask off the mysterious Jesse James, Will Henry's *Death Of A Legend* is a novel as tough and savage as the man himself. Only a great Western writer like Henry could tell the real story of the infamous bandit Jesse James.

_3990-7 $4.99 US/$6.99 CAN

TROUBLE MAN

ED GORMAN

Ray Coyle used to be a gunfighter. And when he gets word his boy has been killed in a gunfight in Coopersville, he has to go there—to bring the body home. But when the old gunfighter steps off the train, he brings his gun with him, along with something else . . . trouble.

___4440-4 $4.99 US/$5.99 CAN

Dorchester Publishing Co., Inc.
P.O. Box 6640
Wayne, PA 19087-8640

Please add $1.75 for shipping and handling for the first book and $.50 for each book thereafter. NY, NYC, and PA residents, please add appropriate sales tax. No cash, stamps, or C.O.D.s. All orders shipped within 6 weeks via postal service book rate. Canadian orders require $2.00 extra postage and must be paid in U.S. dollars through a U.S. banking facility.

Name_____

Address_____

City_____State_____Zip_____

I have enclosed $_____ in payment for the checked book(s).

Payment <u>must</u> accompany all orders. ❏ Please send a free catalog.
CHECK OUT OUR WEBSITE! www.dorchesterpub.com